WHISPERS AT THE BLUEBELL INN

(HOPE COVE BOOK 4)

HANNAH ELLIS

For my favourite person in the world,
You know who you are

Chapter 1

"Are you going to wear a suit?" Emily asked.

Jack was fresh from the shower and his wet hair looked unusually dark. "No. There is no way in the world I'm wearing a suit."

"It's a funeral," Emily said, perching on the edge of his bed.

"It's definitely not a funeral. They're scattering the ashes, that's all. I'm not wearing a suit." He pulled on a pair of clean jeans and rummaged in the drawer for a T-shirt.

"You're wearing jeans?" The words came without a lot of thought, but the look he gave her made her regret it immediately. She didn't want to be the kind of girlfriend who told him what to wear. They'd only been together a couple of months and she was still navigating the role of girlfriend. It would be easier if he could figure out for himself that it would be appropriate to dress smartly. Emily was worried enough about how the day would go. But she supposed what Jack was wearing probably shouldn't be high on her list of concerns.

"Who's going to be there?" he asked, ignoring her clothing comments.

"I don't know. I guess there won't be many people. Just Josie and Sam. Maybe Lizzie and Max. Some of Josie's friends from the village. I'm really not sure. What does it matter?"

"I don't understand why we're going."

"To support Josie," she said adamantly. "You already agreed to this. Why are you being awkward? Just get dressed. If you don't hurry we'll be late."

He pulled his T-shirt on and turned to her. "I really don't want to go."

"I already said we would."

"Josie won't mind if we're not there. And there's no way her family will expect me to turn up. I never went to this sort of thing when we were together. Why should I go now?"

"Because Josie is my best friend. I'd like to go and support her. And I want you to come too. Also, I feel a bit guilty that we didn't make it to the engagement party."

"She gave us a day's notice. I'm fairly sure she didn't actually expect us to go. It was only drinks in the local pub."

The engagement had come as a surprise. Josie and Sam hadn't been together long and Emily had no clue a proposal was on the cards – although things had been strained between her and Josie, so perhaps that was why she hadn't seen it coming. They were planning the wedding for that summer, which seemed a bit of a rush job to Emily. It was typical of Josie to do things impulsively.

"I don't want to keep saying no when Josie invites us to things. She's making an effort, and I think we should do the same."

"It's going to be awkward with Josie's family. They don't like me."

"It's only Lizzie and Max."

"They *really* don't like me. And I'm not that keen on them either."

"They're lovely. Stop being so negative."

"I feel like it might be better if you go alone."

A cold rush of panic swept through her. He wasn't going to back out at the last minute, was he? What would she say if she turned up alone? She remembered how Josie used to complain that Jack would start arguments before family events to get out of going. Emily had always thought it was Josie who caused the issues, but maybe it really was Jack.

"I told Josie we'd both go," she said, trying not to get worked up. She was a calm, rational person. No need to freak out. "I'm excited to see the farm and the village and everything. I haven't been to visit yet." She hoped her level-headed approach would work. Otherwise she'd have to start shouting at him. "And after everything that happened between us and Josie, I feel like we need to make the effort." She stood and crossed the room to him. "Please will you come?"

"I'll come," he said hesitantly. "But I'm not wearing a suit. All they're doing is scattering the ashes and then going to the pub. I'll look ridiculous in the village pub in my suit. Why are you wearing black? It's not like you're in mourning."

"What's wrong with what I'm wearing?" Emily looked down at her black jersey dress and thick tights. She was relieved he'd agreed to come but felt suddenly self-conscious. Was she over-dressed?

"Nothing." Jack snaked his arms around her waist. "You look hot."

"I'm not supposed to look hot," she said. "It's a

sad occasion."

"We have a problem then – if you're not supposed to look hot."

When she gave him a playful shove, his arms tightened around her and he leaned down to kiss her.

"Come on," she said. "It's a long drive. We need to leave." She picked up her jacket and her overnight bag. "I know Josie is upset and everything, but I'm looking forward to a night away. I bet an evening in the local pub is really good fun..."

Chapter 2

"This is Averton," Jack announced, slowing the car as they entered the pretty little village. There was a village green bordered by neat flower beds bursting with colour. It gave the place a truly quaint feel.

"There's the pub," he said, pointing.

Emily craned her neck to read the sign. "The Bluebell Inn. Oh, it's so cute. I love this place."

"You've only seen the pub," Jack said. "Although, to be honest, I'm not sure there's much else to see."

"There's a little corner shop beside the pub," Emily said, before turning to look at the road ahead.

Houses were set back from the main road and a few smaller streets branched off from it. The view became blocked by high hedges on her side. "I bet that's where the fancy houses are – hidden behind the hedges." At the other side of the road was a wooded area. "I feel like I know the place already," Emily said. "This is the way Josie walks home from the pub. She told me how creepy it is in winter when it's pitch black. You know, that's how her and Sam got together. He used to walk her home from the pub."

"Hmm." A muscle in Jack's cheek twitched.

"What?" Emily said, amused by his sudden bashfulness.

"Fairly sure she was still seeing me at that point."

"Aww." She gave a mocking pout and slid her hand onto his thigh. "Are you going to get all upset about it now, a year later? I was under the impression you'd moved on . . ."

He flashed his boyish grin. "What gave you that idea?"

"I heard you're moving in with your new girlfriend in a few weeks." Emily had insisted they wait three months before they moved in together – not wanting to rush things – but she was excited by the prospect. They'd been together for two months and it had been such an amazing time. She'd spent most of it feeling like she was floating on air.

"That's just a vicious rumour," Jack said jokily.

She squeezed his thigh until he swatted her away, complaining about dangerous driving. "Here we are," he said, slowing the car again.

Emily leaned on the dashboard for a better view. There was a big wooden sign by the open gate engraved with: *Oakbrook Farm – Boarding Home for Dogs*.

As they crawled slowly along the driveway, Emily turned in her seat to look back. "The gate shuts automatically! That's so creepy. It all looks so quaint and old-fashioned, but the gate closes itself." Jack chuckled at her enthusiasm and she resumed gazing around, trying to take it all in.

The property was bordered by a wooden fence, and big old trees were dotted around the place. They passed a barn before reaching the house in the far corner of the property. It was a gorgeous old stone farmhouse with a lovely little patio surrounded by colourful flower beds.

A couple of cars were parked beside the house, and Jack pulled up alongside them. Emily inhaled deeply as she stepped outside. The air was wonderfully fresh. Everything was so green, and rolling hills stretched gloriously in every direction. It was stunning.

"Hello," a warbly voice said.

Emily turned her attention to the house and the grey-haired woman standing in the doorway. A golden retriever stood obediently by her side.

"You must be Annette," Emily said. "It's so lovely to finally meet you." After all she'd heard about Annette, she felt she knew her already and moved to give her a hug.

"I'm so glad you're finally visiting." Annette put both her hands to Emily's face and squeezed. Emily couldn't help but laugh.

Annette turned to Jack then. They'd met once before, when Josie had first started working for Annette – almost a year ago. "Come here, you." She pinched his cheek, making him grimace.

"Hi, Annette!"

"Sorry," she said. "I'm old. You laugh at me now, but before you know it you'll have the overwhelming desire to squeeze people's cheeks too!"

"You hardly look a day over twenty-one," Jack said. Annette was actually in her eighties, but from what Emily had heard she was very fit and active. She certainly didn't look like a frail old lady.

Annette rolled her eyes in Emily's direction.

"He's a charmer that one. Come on in. I'll put the kettle on."

They followed her into the homely kitchen and Jack bent to the dog.

"You met Charlie last time you were here, didn't you?" Annette asked.

"Yeah. We met. Hello!" He gave the friendly dog a good pat down.

"He's gorgeous," Emily said, moving to stroke his head. "It makes me want a dog. Look at his lovely big eyes."

Jack raised an eyebrow. "Don't get any ideas."

"Tea or coffee?" Annette asked.

"Whatever's easiest," Emily said, answering for them both.

"I'll make a pot of tea."

"We *were* supposed to come here, weren't we?" Emily asked. "Josie said to meet here but we're a bit later than we thought. Traffic was bad."

"Oh, don't worry. They've just taken the babies for a walk. Sam wanted to show Max and Lizzie some work he's been doing to the house so they all wandered down that way. They'll no doubt be back soon. I've made a few sandwiches for dinner." There was an array of plates on the kitchen table, all covered in foil. It looked like a feast – definitely not just a few sandwiches.

"Jack!" Emily hissed as he eased the foil off a plate and stole a mini sausage roll. He stopped chewing and smiled innocently when Annette turned.

"I saw that." She grinned and passed them each a cup of tea. "Let's sit in the other room. I've got the fire going. It gets draughty in this big old house."

They followed her out of the kitchen and into the charming living room. It was old-fashioned with a worn couch and mismatched armchairs. There were pictures and trinkets all around.

Emily stopped at a framed photo on the dresser. "Is this you?" It was a grainy old photo of two young women beaming into the camera. There was a sign for the kennels in the background.

"Yes. Me and my Wendy. We hadn't been here long when that was taken. It was the day we opened the kennels. That sign cost us a small fortune." She smiled contentedly. "It's lasted well, though."

"It's the same sign?"

"Yes." Annette's voice was full of pride. "Sam did a bit of restoration work on it a while back. But it's the same sign."

"Wow. How long have you lived here?"

"Just over sixty years. It's a lot different now than when we got the place. Wendy would have such a giggle if she could see that fancy gate that you can control from the house." She gave a bemused smile. "Another of Josie's brilliant ideas."

"Have you got photos of how it used to look?" Emily asked eagerly.

"I have," Annette said. "But if Josie comes and finds I've got the old albums out she'll accuse me of trying to bore you to death."

"I find it fascinating."

"She really does like that sort of thing." Jack settled himself on the floor with his legs stretched out. Charlie lay beside him, sprawled in front of the fire, offering his belly for Jack to rub. "But I should warn you, Emily writes romance novels, and if you tell her about you and Wendy and this place, she's likely to take notes."

Emily sat beside Jack and stroked the contented dog. She was desperate to see the old photo albums and looked hopefully at Annette. "I promise not to write about you."

"I wouldn't mind if you did," Annette said. "I'd be honoured."

"Please don't give her ideas," Jack said. "She's got three books on the go as it is."

"Josie told me," Annette said. "The ones set in Oxford Castle and prison. I can't wait to read them. I loved your other books." She pointed to the bookshelf. "Make sure you sign them for me before you leave."

"I will. If you show me the old photos!"

"Okay. Hang on a minute." Annette walked out of the living room, chuckling to herself.

"It's so lovely here," Emily said, leaning to kiss Jack.

"Do you think we missed scattering the ashes?" Jack said quietly.

"I don't know. Maybe."

"Can you imagine if I'd worn a suit?"

She spluttered a laugh. "Okay. A suit might have been a bit much. Sorry. I think I was panicking about all this."

Emily was definitely a little apprehensive about spending time with Josie. They'd had a meal with her and Sam in Oxford when she and Jack had first got together. It had been a really enjoyable evening, but spending a weekend with them – and on Josie's turf – felt different. "I just want the weekend to go well," she added.

"It will." He gave her a gentle kiss on the lips, and she felt reassured immediately.

"Found them," Annette said as she walked back in with a couple of hefty albums in her arms.

"I was really sorry to hear about your other dog," Emily said, moving to sit on the couch with Annette.

"My poor little Macy. It's strange without her around the place." She sighed, putting one album aside and passing one to Emily. "We scattered the ashes earlier so you've avoided that drama."

"How was it?" Emily asked.

Annette's lip curled and she gave a slight shake of the head. "You'd think it was the end of the world the way Josie carried on. She sobbed and sobbed. I wouldn't mind, but she seems to forget Macy was *my* dog."

"Oh." Emily was surprised at Annette being so forthcoming. "She did seem very upset on the phone."

"Don't get me wrong," Annette said. "Of course it's upsetting. I was devastated, and they are like Josie's dogs too. But sometimes Josie seems to lose all perspective about things. She's been in a funny mood these last few weeks. Sam panders to her, of course, and I'm not sure that helps. Anyway, ignore me rambling on and have a flick through those . . ." She tapped the album in Emily's lap.

The first page held black and white photos of the outside of the farmhouse. Annette gave a running commentary as Emily slowly turned the pages. It was fascinating to hear stories of her younger days, and Emily was slightly perturbed when they were interrupted half an hour later.

"You're here!" Josie said as she came rushing into the living room.

Emily put the album aside and stood to hug her best friend. "Sorry we were late. How are you?"

Josie didn't reply but hugged her tightly and for just a few seconds too long. Then she moved to Jack and buried her head in his neck as she embraced him.

"Are you okay?" he asked when Josie finally pulled away.

She cast her head down, reaching to stroke Charlie as she discreetly wiped tears from her cheeks. "Just feeling a bit emotional after we scattered the ashes. I'm fine." She beamed at Emily. "I'm so happy you're finally here."

"Let me see your ring." Emily reached for Josie's hand. She'd seen a photo of it but wanted to see it up close. It made her a bit emotional looking at it. "It's gorgeous. Congratulations!"

"Thanks." Josie hugged her again. "I can't believe I'm getting married."

"And so soon!" Emily said. That was a stupid thing to say. Emily had a habit of blurting things out without thinking.

"You know me," Josie said. "Always impatient. Come on." She gestured for them to follow her with a nod of the head. "Max and Lizzie are here with the twins. You missed my friends Tara and Amber. They had to head off but they said they'd meet us for a drink later."

"That'll be nice," Emily said.

In the kitchen, Lizzie was walking in from outside and greeted Emily and Jack warmly.

"Where are the babies?" Emily asked.

"Outside. Asleep in the pram. Hopefully they'll stay that way for a while. It would be nice to eat in peace."

"I'll uncover the food," Annette said. "Then you can all tuck in."

"We can eat out on the patio," Josie suggested. The dog trailed at her side. "It's lovely in the sunshine."

Sam came inside to greet them then, and Max waved through the open doorway as he rocked the pram.

"Phoebe will wake up if the pram's not moving," Lizzie explained.

Sam opened the fridge. "Who wants a beer?"

Jack took one eagerly.

"I can open wine if anyone wants . . ." Sam added.

"I'm not drinking," Lizzie said.

Emily looked to Josie.

"I'm not bothered," Josie said. "But you have one."

Jack automatically put a hand to Josie's forehead. "What's wrong with you?"

"I'm trying to be healthy," she said, swatting him away. "I want to get in shape for the wedding." She pulled a face at Jack. "Anyway, what's wrong with *you*? You've not cleared the buffet yet?"

"Give me a minute!" He turned and took the plate Annette offered him and began loading it up. It was strange for Emily to see Jack and Josie interact so naturally. Emily had spent so long with them as a couple that she had to remind herself everything had changed. The old jealousy was void now.

"Emily?" Sam was still standing by the fridge, looking at her questioningly. "Wine?"

She snapped out of her trance. "No thanks. Maybe later."

They drifted out to the patio with plates loaded with sandwiches, sausage rolls and quiche. It was a beautiful spot, and Emily marvelled at the surroundings as they ate. She mentioned the old photos she'd been looking at, and Annette joked about Emily writing her memoirs.

Lizzie thought it was a great idea. "I had another idea for you too," she added. "Did you know Hope Cove has a history of smuggling? Now that you've moved to writing historical romance, I thought that could be something for you to write: *Smugglers at Hope Cove*."

"Oh, that's catchy," Josie agreed. "You should do it!"

"I'm snowed under as it is with the books about the castle. I'll keep it in mind for my next project though." Emily paused. "And I would definitely love to visit Hope Cove after hearing so much about the place."

"You should." Lizzie popped the last of her sandwich in her mouth.

"It's gorgeous," Josie said. "You definitely have to visit. We won't have time this weekend, though, if you're only staying one night."

"We'll come back again," Emily said. Jack was

happily tucking into his sandwiches beside her and kept out of the conversation.

"Why don't you come for the girls' christening?" Lizzie said. "Come for a long weekend and have a little holiday. It's the end of next month. May's a lovely time to visit."

Emily was a little taken aback by the offer. "Isn't it just a family thing?"

"You practically are family," Josie put in.

Lizzie wiped a crumb from the side of her mouth. "You'd be very welcome to come."

"Thanks." Emily was touched by the invitation. "That would be lovely, wouldn't it, Jack?"

His eyes widened, and as Emily glanced back at Lizzie she caught the slight tightening of her lips as her smile became forced. Emily felt utterly stupid; the invite clearly wasn't meant to be extended that far.

"I'm not sure I'd be able to get the time off," Jack said lightly. "But you should go."

"It's the bank holiday weekend," Josie said quickly. "You don't work bank holidays, do you?" She didn't wait for a reply but turned to Lizzie. "What's happening with the new house? Could Emily and Jack stay there for the weekend?"

Lizzie seemed flustered as she glanced around for Max. He wandered out of the kitchen with a plate full of food.

"It'd be okay for Emily and Jack to use the Lavender Lane house for the christening weekend, wouldn't it?"

"I guess so," Max said vaguely. "I told Conor he could stay but there are three bedrooms . . ."

"It'll be so much fun," Josie said. "Maybe Sam and I can come and stay for a night or two as well."

Emily smiled benignly. What house were they talking about? And who was Conor?

"We bought a house," Lizzie explained, clearly sensing Emily's confusion. "We'll rent it out eventually, but it needs some work doing to it so it's just sitting empty at the moment."

"Oh, lovely," Emily said. "Are you sure it's okay for us to stay?"

Lizzie nodded. "As long as you don't mind sharing with Max's nephew."

"Conor's great," Josie said. "He's always good for a laugh. How old is he? Like twenty-one or something?"

Max looked thoughtful. "Yeah. About that. Twenty-two maybe."

"I can't wait," Josie said. "We need something to look forward to."

Emily found it a strange remark for someone who had a wedding on the horizon.

Chapter 3

The Bluebell Inn had a number of guest rooms above the pub. Emily had found it when she searched online for a place to stay. She'd told Josie it looked so cute that she was dying to stay there. In reality, she just thought it might be awkward to stay at Josie's place given the history between Jack and Josie. Sam would surely have been uncomfortable with it.

After a pleasant day at Annette's place, they went ahead to the pub to get settled. They were going to meet Josie and Sam for a drink later.

Jack was standing by the window of the basic but cosy room, looking out over the darkening village. "I'm not going to the christening, by the way."

Emily walked out of the bathroom with only a towel wrapped around her. Water dripped from her hair down her shoulders.

"It'll be lovely," she said. "I'm dying to go to Hope Cove. And a holiday would be nice. I've been working so hard on the books. A bit of time away would be wonderful."

"I'm not even invited. Did you see the look on Lizzie's face when you mentioned me coming?"

"Of course you're invited," she said quickly. To be honest, he was probably right, but if Emily was going she wanted Jack to go too. It would be fun to have a little getaway. Their first holiday together.

"You look good, by the way." He let the conversation drop and crossed the room to her. She grinned as his hand slipped inside the towel to graze over her stomach and land gently at her hip. He pulled her eagerly to him as he kissed her.

"Get off," she said, laughing. "We're meeting Josie and Sam down in the bar. Hurry up and shower if you're going to."

"We've got loads of time."

"No. We were supposed to meet them five minutes ago. Josie wants us to meet her friends."

"At least Max and Lizzie won't be there." He blew out a breath. "Maybe it won't be too bad."

"What's wrong with you?" She moved to the dressing table and unzipped her make-up bag. "You're such a misery today."

"You'd be moody too if you were forced to spend your weekend with people who don't like you . . ."

She glared at him until he laughed. He sounded petulant and he knew it.

"It's only Lizzie and Max who don't like you," she said sweetly, making him laugh some more.

***

It was surprisingly busy when they walked into the bar. Emily had expected to find a few men drinking pints and playing dominoes, but there was quite a mix of people. They were waiting to order drinks when Emily noticed a familiar red-headed woman at the bar beside her. She was fairly sure she was one of Josie's friends who they were meeting that evening – she'd seen photos on Facebook. The woman with her had beautiful long dark hair and was also very familiar.

Emily was dithering over whether or not to say something when the barman came over and took their order. He was a friendly guy called Andy. They'd met earlier when he'd shown them up to their room.

They ordered drinks and then Emily leaned into Jack. "I think they're Josie's friends," she whispered, tilting her head in their direction. "I should say something . . ." She turned and opened her mouth, but the dark-haired woman started talking so Emily retreated slightly, not wanting to interrupt. She was then stuck listening in to their conversation and felt increasingly awkward.

"I'm never having kids," the dark-haired woman said firmly.

"I think we've had this conversation before," the redhead said. Amber, that was her name – Amber and Tara. Emily had heard all about them from Josie.

"I know I say it a lot, but seeing Max and Lizzie today confirmed my decision."

Emily widened her eyes at Jack. She really should interrupt them.

"Those babies are gorgeous," Amber said.

"Gorgeous little relationship wreckers. That's what they are."

"What are you talking about?" Amber asked, amused.

"Didn't you see the way Max and Lizzie look at

each other? It's pure hatred."

Amber clicked her tongue. "Don't be daft. They're just tired."

"Miserable, more like. You know, I used to have a bit of a thing for Max. I thought kids were supposed to make men more attractive, but it's like they're sucking the life out of him. He barely said two words all morning." She paused and took a sip of her drink. "And then Lizzie's doing that thing where she's trying hard to be cheerful but it's so obviously fake. She's trying to keep up appearances – make out they're a happy family. I don't buy it for a minute. They'll be divorced before we know it."

"That's a terrible thing to say. They'll be fine. Babies are hard work. And twins! I can't even imagine."

"A tenner says they're divorced within a year."

"I told you – we're not making bets on our friends' lives."

"You're very boring." She lowered her voice and Emily had to strain to hear. "If you change your mind, I'm now willing to increase my bet on Josie being pregnant to twenty quid."

"I really don't think she is pregnant," Amber whispered.

"Oh, come on. She's my pro drinking buddy, and all of a sudden she's stopped drinking alcohol with some flimsy excuse about dieting before the wedding. I don't buy it. And she's obviously a big mess of hormones. You only have to look at her the wrong way and she bursts into tears."

"She's upset about the dog."

"She's an emotional wreck. Not that I blame

her. I would be too if I couldn't drink for nine months."

Andy appeared with the drinks for Jack and Emily. "Sorry. I had to change the barrel."

They smiled and paid for the drinks.

"What are you two gossiping about?" Andy said to Amber and Tara.

"We're not gossiping," Tara replied with a grin. "Gossiping is beneath me!"

"Good." He nodded in Emily's direction. "Josie's friends have come all the way from Oxford. We don't want them thinking this is your stereotypical village pub where all anyone talks about is each other's business." He grinned with no idea of the accuracy of his comment.

As he wandered away, Emily turned and smiled at Amber and Tara. They wore identical tight-lipped smiles and both had a look of panic in their eyes.

"Sorry, I'm late!" Josie had perfect timing. "Oh, great – you already met."

"Almost," Amber said, slipping off her stool and taking charge of the awkward situation. "I'm Amber and this is Tara. You've probably heard all about Tara – she's the loudmouth."

Josie laughed. "That's not how I described her. Is it, Emily?"

Still reeling from the overheard conversation, Emily struggled to find her voice.

"It's all true," Sam said from behind Josie.

Tara looked as though she hoped the ground would open up and swallow her. Emily almost felt sorry for her.

When Andy wandered over, Sam ordered a pint

and then looked to Josie.

"I'll just have an orange juice, please."

Silence descended and Emily didn't know where to look. Her head was spinning, trying to process what Tara had said. Was Josie pregnant? She couldn't quite get her head around the idea. It *was* very strange for Josie not to have a drink. And the quick wedding. And being so emotional . . .

"Shall we sit down?" Jack glanced at the empty table on the back wall, then put one hand on the small of Emily's back as they moved in that direction.

"Oh my God!" she hissed under her breath. She was desperate to talk to him but knew it would probably be a good couple of hours before she got him alone.

At the table, she turned to see Tara whispering something to Amber with a pained expression. They quickly fell silent. Tara seemed as though she was about to say something, but Josie arrived and they shuffled around the table.

"What do you think of Averton?" Amber asked. Thankfully, Josie hadn't seemed to register the awkward atmosphere.

"It's lovely." Emily glanced at Josie. "It's very strange being here after I've heard so much about it."

"Is it how you imagined?" Josie asked.

"I'm not sure. I think so."

"I can't believe you're staying at the pub. I didn't even know you *could* stay at the pub."

Amber chuckled. "It does say above the door, Josie."

"I've noticed that now!"

"Fancy a game of pool?" Sam asked Jack. They set off across the pub to the pool tables.

"It's nice how they get on," Josie remarked, watching as they casually chatted and racked up the pool balls at the other side of the pub. She turned to Emily. "I'm sorry Max and Lizzie were a bit off with him. It's always been awkward between them. Max is in a weird mood at the moment too. I don't think they sleep very much."

"It was fine," Emily murmured.

"You're very quiet, Tara. You've been dying to meet Jack." Josie glanced at Emily with a cheeky grin. "Tara thinks it's a very weird situation – you being with Jack now." She turned back to Tara. "I thought you'd have loads to say. You don't need to be shy around Emily."

Tara twirled the stem of her wine glass. "He seems lovely. I wasn't sure what to expect, that's all." She swallowed hard and her gaze drifted across the pub. "He's younger than I imagined."

"He's twenty-seven?" Josie looked to Emily, who nodded confirmation. "I went from a younger man to an older man," Josie continued with a cheeky smile. "I can't believe Sam's getting on for forty!"

"He's still got a few years," Amber said. "Don't start saying Sam's old."

"Because that would make *you* old?" Tara said.

Amber raised an eyebrow. "I'm not old! Can we please change the subject?"

They chuckled and the atmosphere was instantly more relaxed.

"Tara, tell Emily your idea about the book,"

Josie said excitedly. "Tara works in a bookshop. She read your books and they stock them in the shop."

"Wow." Emily was really touched. "Thanks."

"I love your writing style," Tara said. "I can't wait for the new books. Josie's told me all about the series you're working on."

"Thanks. The first in the series comes out in a couple of weeks. I'm not with a publisher for this one so I'm having to wrap my head around all the marketing and promotion."

Her first two books were contemporary women's fiction and had been published through NewBridge Publishing, a small publishing house. Sadly, they didn't publish historical romance so rejected her pitch for the Oxford Castle series. Full of determination, she'd decided to self-publish and read everything she could on the subject. She'd had some online chats with authors doing well for themselves. It spurred her on and she'd even become excited by the idea. But as release day approached, it all felt a bit daunting.

"Tara wants you to come and do a book signing at the shop," Josie said.

"It was just a silly idea." Tara shifted uncomfortably in her seat. "I think I'd had too much to drink. You must get people asking you to do stuff all the time . . ."

"Not really," Emily said.

Josie grinned. "We were thinking of making it an evening event. A little meet and greet with the author, and we'd have drinks and nibbles."

"It sounds fun," Emily said half-heartedly. She always hated the idea of being the centre of attention. "It's not like I'm famous, though. I don't know how much interest you'd get."

"People would definitely be interested," Tara said. "We've done a couple of author events before and it always draws a crowd."

"I'll be honest, I hate the thought of it. Having everyone looking at me makes me nervous."

"I understand," Tara said. "No pressure."

"What?" Josie said. "You usually bully people into doing whatever you want. Why does Emily get special treatment? Are you star-struck or something? You're very subdued this evening."

"If she doesn't want to do it . . ."

"Emily's just shy. All she needs is a nudge and some reassurance that it will be fine."

Emily shrugged. It was true.

"Tara would look after you," Josie insisted. "She'd make it completely stress-free. It would be a relaxed evening with people interested in your book. It's great publicity."

"I could do with the publicity," Emily said. "It's nerve-wracking, not having the publishing company behind me this time. I don't even know how to go about getting it into physical stores without the traditional publisher."

"We can definitely stock it," Tara said kindly.

"That would be amazing," Emily said. "But you haven't even read it. You might hate it."

"I doubt it. I loved your other books. Any chance you could get me an advance copy?"

"Yes, of course."

"You should definitely do the book signing," Josie said. "I need you to come back one weekend anyway so we can go wedding dress shopping. We can organise it all for the same weekend."

The conversation moved to weddings. Josie filled Emily in on all her ideas and plans. It seemed like it would be a fairly small affair. The ceremony would take place in a nearby town hall and then the reception in a marquee on the lawn at Annette's place. It seemed fitting, but Emily had expected Josie to go for something more elaborate.

"Have we come back at the wrong time?" Sam said, resting a hand affectionately on Josie's shoulder.

"No, it's fine." She smiled up at him. "I'm trying to convince Emily to come for a weekend so we can go dress shopping, and she can do a book signing at the same time."

"Tara works at a bookshop," Emily told Jack as he slipped into the seat beside her.

"Perfect," he said. "Can you set it up soon, so it coincides with when the book releases?"

"Yes!" Josie said. "It can be a book launch party."

"We might not have time to set it up for the release," Emily said.

"I can start organising it first thing on Monday," Tara said. "I just need to get my boss to agree to it, but he's pretty good about stuff like that."

Emily nodded vaguely.

They got another round of drinks and chatted easily. Oddly, as everyone else loosened up with alcohol, Josie faded into the background, hardly joining the conversation at all.

Amber was in the middle of an anecdote about

her little boy getting hold of a pair of scissors and trying them out on the living room curtains when Sam leaned into Josie and quietly asked if she was okay. Emily had been wondering the same. It seemed as though Josie was lost in a daydream. She wasn't even bothering to pretend to follow the conversation.

She smiled weakly. "I'm fine."

"Do you want to go?"

The nod was almost imperceptible.

"I think we're going to head home," Sam said.

Amber looked a little taken aback by the interruption, but Sam hardly seemed to notice she'd been speaking.

"Sorry," Josie said. "I've got a bit of a headache." She turned to Emily as she pulled on her coat. "Sorry. You came all this way and I'm going home early."

"Don't worry about it," Emily said. "I feel like heading to bed soon anyway. We'll see you tomorrow, though?"

"Yes. Definitely. I need to show you our place. And I've not shown you the kennels. Annette's cooking lunch for us too."

"A roast?" Tara asked.

A smile played on Josie's lips. "Of course."

"They'd starve if it wasn't for Annette," Tara told Emily and Jack. "She cooks for them every day."

"That's not true." Sam stood and put a protective hand on Josie's back. "On Saturdays we usually do our own thing."

"Annette's all on her own," Josie said with a

shrug. "We like to keep her company."

Tara laughed loudly. "You're so generous!"

That at least brought a chuckle from Josie. "Well, who has the energy to cook after working all day?" She raised her eyebrows at Tara. "And I'm not sure you should comment. How often do you stop at Annette's on the way home from work with some flimsy excuse for a visit?"

"She's a good cook," Tara said, grinning broadly.

Emily stood to hug Josie goodbye. "I hope you feel better tomorrow."

"I'll be fine," Josie insisted. "I just need some sleep."

They said their goodbyes and left, leaving an awkward silence in their wake.

"You heard me at the bar before, didn't you?" Tara said with a sigh.

Emily nodded and grimaced.

"I'm so sorry." Tara's cheeks were flushed. "I can't believe you heard all that. I was talking rubbish. My mouth gets carried away sometimes, doesn't it, Amber?"

"Quite often," Amber agreed.

"You must think I'm awful. I don't even know what to say. I wouldn't talk like that to anyone other than Amber. It's only because I know she doesn't take me seriously."

"Don't worry," Emily said. She glanced beside her at Jack, but he only took a sip of his pint and leaned back in his seat.

"I'm so sorry," Tara said. "What a terrible first impression."

"Really, it's okay," Emily said. "Let's forget about it. Shall we have another drink?" It was the last thing Emily wanted, but she thought it would look rude if they left as soon as Josie had gone. Like they were annoyed with Tara. She obviously felt bad enough as it was.

"I should probably go," Amber said. "Kieron's going through a phase of getting up at five o'clock, so I should probably be in bed already."

"I'll walk back with you," Tara said. "I'll get a taxi from your place." She turned to Emily. "I'm sorry, it's not been the most exciting of evenings."

"It was really lovely to meet you," Emily said earnestly. It was good to put faces to the names.

"You too," Amber and Tara said at once.

Tara paused by the table. "I know you probably think I'm a horrible person, but I really would be happy to help with the book. I could definitely put a launch party together if you wanted." She rooted in her handbag and handed a business card to Emily. "My details are on there."

"Thank you." Emily smiled. Tara might not have made the best first impression, but when it came to her books, Emily needed all the help she could get. "I'll be in touch. And I'll send you over the review copy. Can I send a digital copy to this email?"

"Yes." Tara seemed to relax. "Perfect."

Chapter 4

Emily sat on the edge of the bath in her pyjamas. Jack was looking at her like he had absolutely no idea what she was saying. He spat toothpaste into the sink and rinsed his toothbrush. "You realise that about once a week you try and have a conversation with me while you're brushing your teeth and every time you're surprised when I can't understand a word."

She nudged him out of the way to spit out the foamy toothpaste. "I think it was obvious. I said I felt a bit sorry for her."

"Tara? She was slagging Josie off. Why would you feel sorry for her?"

"Because she was so embarrassed. And she wasn't slagging Josie off." She put her toothbrush by the sink and followed Jack into the bedroom.

"She's supposed to be Josie's friend and she was just idly gossiping about her behind her back."

"She didn't think anyone was going to hear. And she was talking to Amber, who's also friends with Josie. It's like us talking about Josie."

"They were in the local pub. If you're going to talk like that about your friend, at least do it somewhere private."

"To be fair, she *was* whispering."

"Hardly. I'm not sure why you're defending

her." He pulled back the covers and climbed into bed. Emily did the same at the opposite side.

"Because I think they're generally good friends to Josie, and it's unfair to judge her based on one encounter."

Jack sighed heavily and frown lines appeared around his eyes. Why was he so bothered by Tara? It wasn't that bad.

"Do you think Josie *is* pregnant?" she asked.

"I don't know." His frown deepened.

"It is odd that she's given up alcohol. And she has been acting strangely. And why are they getting married so quickly?"

"Why don't you ask her instead of discussing it with me? She is your best friend, after all."

"It's not the sort of thing you can ask. She might not want to tell anyone yet."

"Obviously. And she probably doesn't want everyone speculating about it behind her back either."

"You're in a weird mood."

He stared at the ceiling and didn't comment.

"Does it bother you?" She regretted the question almost as soon as she asked it.

"What?"

"Seeing Josie with Sam. Planning their wedding and everything."

"Are you serious?"

She definitely shouldn't have said anything. It was a stupid question. There was only one way for him to answer – at least one way that wouldn't lead to the demise of their relationship.

"I just don't know why you're in such a bad

mood," she said. "And being so defensive of Josie."

"Because she's my friend." There was a hint of irritation to his voice. "Maybe *you* should be defensive of her too."

"Okay," she said weakly.

"Do you honestly think I have a problem with Josie getting married?"

"No." She lay on her back and avoided looking at him. "I only wondered why you're so grumpy."

"Probably because you insisted I come here, and it's all a bit awkward."

"No, it's not," she said.

"Do you know what Tara and Amber were probably whispering about before we got there . . .? Me! They were probably discussing how weird it is that I was with Josie and now I'm with you. I'm sure they all have something to say about it, and it's probably why Lizzie and Max have a brand-new level of dislike for me."

"They do not. You're being dramatic. Why are you making issues out of nothing?"

He reached to switch the lamp off. "Because you asked me why I was in a bad mood . . ."

She scooted over and nestled into his chest. "At least you get on with Sam."

"Yeah. He's a good guy." There was a hint of amusement in his voice.

"What's funny?"

"Nothing."

"Tell me what you were going to say."

"No. You'll hit me."

"I'll hit you anyway."

"I was going to say Josie's got good taste in

men."

She jabbed him in the ribs and he laughed.

"You know what I was wondering?" Emily said, changing the subject. "What Tara said about Max and Lizzie. Do you think they will end up divorced?"

"You really shouldn't pay so much attention to the village gossip. How on earth I know what's going on with them? How would Tara know?"

"I hope everything's okay between them . . ."

"Are you ever going to stop gossiping and let me sleep?"

"No," she said flatly. "I'm going to lie here all night gossiping."

She blurted out a laugh when he rolled over and pinned her under his weight. "In that case, I'm going to have to keep kissing you so you can't talk. Okay?"

She beamed and pulled his face down to hers. It was more than okay with her.

Chapter 5

Lizzie was exhausted by the time they left Annette's place. She should probably do what the girls did and sleep the whole way home. It was about a forty-minute drive back to Hope Cove – plenty of time to nap. Unfortunately, her mind was whirring too much to sleep. Every muscle in her body felt tense. Glancing into the back of the car, she smiled at her peaceful babies. It was incredible how much her life had changed – and how quickly.

Her mind drifted to the day she'd found out she was pregnant. She'd felt oddly nauseous one lunchtime. Her first thought was how much wine she'd drunk the night before – but it had only been one glass, certainly not enough to make her feel unwell. She'd hoped she wasn't coming down with something and was glad when she felt better after some lunch. It niggled at her, though, and by mid-afternoon she was driving to an unfamiliar chemist to buy a pregnancy test.

Children had definitely been in their plans. They'd talked about it seriously only a few weeks before and agreed it was what they both wanted. Lizzie had stopped taking the pill on the assumption that it would take her body a while to get back to a regular rhythm. But obviously not.

She'd stared at the little white stick as though it

was some great mystery. It said *pregnant* quite clearly. You didn't really need to be a code-breaker. She was stunned and half expected the word *pregnant* might fade and *just kidding* would appear on the display instead.

Back at her desk in the corner of the living room, she tried to get on with her work. Of course that wasn't going to happen. All she could do was stare at the pregnancy test. When Max came home from work, she was still transfixed.

It was a year since he'd moved to Hope Cove to be with her. He'd proposed the previous spring and the wedding was only a couple of weeks away. And she was pregnant. Her head spun at the thought.

"How was your day?" Max asked happily. Lizzie worked from home as a freelance fiction editor, and Max had found a job locally as a property manager, looking after many of the rental properties in the area.

"I had a bit of a weird day, actually."

He hung his jacket in the hallway, then came and kissed her cheek and gave her shoulders a rub. "What happened?"

She craned her neck to look at him and swallowed hard.

"What's wrong?" His features were etched with concern.

"I'm pregnant," she said flatly.

"What?"

Nodding, she reached for the test and held it up to him.

He squinted at it and then raised his eyebrows. "We're going to have a baby?"

"It seems like it." She stood and held his hands, nervous at his silence. "It is good, isn't it? It's what we want?"

"Yes!" Finally, his face broke into a smile, and he laughed as he hugged her.

She hugged him back, then looked at him seriously. "You're happy?"

"So happy." He grinned. "I'm a bit shocked. I didn't think it would happen so quickly."

"Me neither!"

"It's amazing." His arms tightened around her as he kissed her. He was laughing when he pulled away. "We're going to have a baby!"

Of course, that was only the half of it – Lizzie had barely got used to the idea of one baby when they found out they were having twins. She'd been terrified and excited all at once. It was daunting, but at the same time everything had seemed so perfect and romantic. When she'd imagined how tired she would be with two babies, she'd envisioned her and Max happily cuddled up on the couch in the evening, laughing about how exhausted they were.

Which was absolutely not how things turned out.

The girls were six months now and there was no laughing and no cuddling up on the couch. Lizzie could barely even remember the last time they had hugged.

The atmosphere between them was tense as they drove home from Annette's place. Although that was nothing unusual.

"You could have made a bit more effort," Lizzie said tersely. "You barely spoke to anyone all day."

"I don't know why you insisted we go over there. I barely slept last night."

Lovely, now he was going to make her feel guilty for sleeping in the spare room. She'd only managed about five hours' sleep herself. Apparently her body had forgotten how to sleep for long periods, and her slumber was annoyingly disturbed even though she didn't get up with the girls.

"It's nice to see everyone. And Josie really wanted us to go over."

Max snorted. "I'm sorry but your sister's a bloody drama queen. I know she was fond of the dog but come on . . . It was embarrassing how much she cried."

"You're really heartless sometimes, you know."

"It was a farce." He paused. "And why were Emily and Jack there? It was all very strange."

"Why was it strange? Emily is Josie's best friend. They came to visit for a weekend."

"Jack is her ex-boyfriend. Is it only me who thinks it's odd that he's now with Emily?"

"It's not really any of our business so what does it matter what you think? Josie is fine with it and Emily seems happy."

"I can't believe you invited them to the christening." He shook his head as though she'd done something terrible. Admittedly she hadn't thought it through when she'd blurted out the invitation, but it wasn't so bad.

"I thought you couldn't stand Jack," he continued. "Now you're inviting him to stay."

"I'll admit I'm not overly fond of Jack." There had been so much drama when he and Josie were together, and naturally Lizzie had always taken Josie's side. She'd definitely never really taken to him. And yes, it was weird that he was now with Emily, but Lizzie was reluctant to agree with Max about anything at that moment.

"And why shouldn't I invite them? It will be nice to see more of Emily, and I doubt Jack will come anyway. He didn't join our family events much even when he and Josie were together. Plus we're only having a christening to keep your mother happy. I don't think you can really complain about who I invite."

That had been another issue. As an atheist, Lizzie had no interest in having the girls christened, but Max had insisted it was easier just to do it than suffer his mother's disapproval.

"We'll have to sort out the Lavender Lane house a bit now," he said wearily.

"It needs sorting out anyway so it's good motivation. I'm really not sure why you thought you had time to renovate a house yourself. Why don't you hire someone to do it?"

"I told you. Because the quotes I got were crazy."

"Hmm." That's because he'd underestimated the amount of work the house needed. The previous owner had been a little old lady who kept to herself. None of the locals knew much about her. When she died, the house had been inherited by her grandson, who only seemed to be interested in a quick sale. Max had negotiated a good deal with the agreement that they'd buy it as it was and organise the house clearance themselves.

Then Max had decided he could save more money by clearing it out himself. It was a couple of months after the sale had been finalised, and he'd barely done anything.

"Sam and I are going to renovate it. It's a sound investment."

"Hmm." Actually, it seemed like the house was just something else for them to argue about. Although it made a change from the usual arguments about who slept the least, or who changed the last nappy, or who forgot to buy baby wipes.

"It would be a good investment if you paid someone to get it in shape so we can rent it out."

"I'm not sure why you're worrying about it so much. It's not a problem if it's empty for a while. At least it wouldn't be if you didn't invite people to stay in it."

"You already told Conor he could stay," she reminded him angrily.

"Conor doesn't care about the state of the place."

"Neither will Emily," Lizzie said, less confidently.

They fell into silence for the rest of the journey. That was the soundtrack to their lives – heated arguments and tense silences. Lizzie turned in the seat to look back at the girls again. They were both fast sleep. She wondered if their arguments had any effect on them. She hoped not.

Her gaze landed on Max for a moment when she turned back in her seat. They hardly seemed to look at each other any more. The muscles along his jaw were tight and he looked tired.

She remembered the days when she used to get butterflies in her stomach every time she looked at him. It wasn't that long ago, really.

It just felt like a lifetime.

Chapter 6

After full English breakfasts in the back room of the pub, Emily and Jack set off to Josie and Sam's house.

It was a nice little walk through the village. They passed Annette's place, then kept walking for a few minutes until they reached the lovely little house set back from the road.

Sam greeted them cheerfully, holding the door and ushering them into the living room. "Josie's still out with the dogs but she should be back any minute. How was breakfast at the pub?"

"Really good," Jack said. They were both stuffed.

"Coffee?" Sam asked.

They nodded in unison.

"Make yourselves at home." He left them in the living room and wandered through to the kitchen at the back of the house.

The living room was cosy and Emily settled on the couch beside Jack. She stood up again almost immediately when a framed photo on the mantel caught her eye. It was Josie, Emily and Jack sitting outside the Boathouse in Oxford. They were all beaming as Josie took the selfie. They'd spent so many wonderful afternoons at the cafe together.

"I love this photo." She put it back in its place,

then turned at a noise in the kitchen. Automatically, she moved to peek through the doorway between the living room and kitchen. Josie burst through the back door.

"I lost the bloody dog again," she said to Sam. Her voice was ragged and her cheeks were damp with tears. "Stupid Pixie slipped through my legs and jumped the fence. I can't find her anywhere."

Sam looked at her sympathetically and wrapped her in a hug. "We'll find her."

"But I feel so crap." She was crying hard and Emily felt awfully intrusive, watching them. If she tried to move away they'd see her and think she was spying. "I feel horrible and I'm chasing dogs around the countryside."

"I told you I'd walk the dogs. Why didn't you let me go?"

"Because it's *my* job," she said firmly. "You can't work all week and do my job too. I need to get on with it. I'm not ill. I could do without runaway dogs, that's all."

Emily moved further into the doorway to make her presence known.

"Hi!" Josie said, surprised. "I didn't realise you were here already."

"Are you okay?" Emily stepped into the kitchen.

"Yes." Josie forced a smile and wiped tears from her cheeks. "I lost the neighbour's dog. And I didn't sleep well. And I really want to hang out with you but I have to go and find this annoying dog."

"I can go and look for her," Sam said. "You stay and catch up with Emily and Jack."

"I won't be able to relax. I need to go and find her. Do you mind?" She looked sadly at Emily.

"Of course not. We can help if you want?"

"It's fine. You stay here and relax." When she headed to the back door, Sam followed her.

"Can you take over with coffee?" he said. "Milk's in the fridge. Help yourselves."

Josie paused by the back door. "Hi, Jack," she shouted.

"Morning!" he called back.

He joined Emily in the kitchen after they'd left.

"Did you hear all that?" Emily handed him a coffee and he leaned against the sideboard.

"Yep."

"I'm worried about her."

"Me too."

"I'll try and get her alone later and see if I can find out what's going on with her."

"Good idea," he said vaguely as his gaze roamed the kitchen.

"It's a gorgeous house," Emily remarked.

"Sam fitted the kitchen himself."

"Quite handy having a builder around."

"I think he made most of the furniture too. Definitely the table and chairs."

"He restores furniture in his spare time I think." Emily recalled Josie telling her about it and moved to run a hand over the sturdy dining table.

"He was telling me about it last night." Jack gazed out of the kitchen window. "He uses the garage as a workshop."

"We'll have to get him to show us. I hope they find the dog quickly. Josie looked exhausted."

They sat at the kitchen table with their coffees and it wasn't long before Josie and Sam arrived back.

"Found her," Josie said. She looked much cheerier, but Emily had the feeling it was an act. There was still something off about her. She didn't seem herself. "Come on," she said. "I'll give you a tour of the house."

"Great," Emily said. "Then we want to see Sam's workshop."

"That was next on the itinerary." Josie grinned as Sam nodded his agreement. "Then we'll go out for a walk. I want to show you my favourite spots where I take the dogs."

"Don't feel like you have to entertain us," Emily said. "If you're not feeling well, we're happy to hang out here. Or we can take ourselves off exploring."

"No, I'm fine," Josie insisted. "I want to show you."

***

It was a beautiful sunny morning and they spent a good couple of hours wandering over the rugged countryside. The view from up on the hills was fantastic. You could see for miles. Peaceful rolling hills stretched out all around like a giant patchwork blanket.

Emily was exhilarated from the exercise and fresh air when they reached Annette's place. She was even starting to feel a bit hungry, which was surprising after the huge breakfast.

"There you are!" Annette said cheerfully.

"Lunch will be about half an hour."

"It smells delicious," Jack said. It really did. Emily inhaled deeply to savour the aroma.

In the living room, Charlie was sprawled in front of the fire. He stood slowly and went to nuzzle at Josie's leg, then settled himself by her feet when she sat in the armchair.

"Did you enjoy the pub last night?" Annette asked.

"It was good fun." Emily sat close to Jack on the couch.

Annette slowly lowered herself into the second armchair. "And you met Tara and Amber?"

"Yes. They're lovely."

"Did Tara persuade you to do the book signing? She's been excited about meeting you."

"We talked about it, but there's nothing definite planned."

"You should do it," Josie said, stroking Charlie's head. "It'd be fun."

"I sent her over a copy of the book this morning," Emily said. "I'll have to see what she thinks of it first."

"She'll love it," Josie said confidently.

Emily smiled at her positivity. It was always nerve-wracking waiting to get feedback for her books. The book signing idea was also starting to make her uncomfortable. It felt like she wasn't going to have much choice since everyone else was so keen for her to do it.

The conversation moved on and Emily pushed thoughts of book launches from her mind. Lunch tasted every bit as good as it smelled, and the atmosphere was wonderfully relaxed.

"I can't move," Emily complained as Sam and Jack began to clear the table. "I'm so full."

"Hello!" Tara appeared at the door.

"You're too late," Josie said jokily. "We've eaten everything."

"There are some leftovers." Annette stood to help the men tidy up.

"I already ate." Tara's gaze shifted to Emily. "Any chance I can steal you away to talk shop for a few minutes?"

"Yes." Emily smiled at Josie before following Tara out into the bright sunshine. Charlie trailed after them and sniffed at the flower beds before lying down in the sun.

They walked a little way from the house before Tara finally spoke. "I really wanted to apologise again about last night. I feel terrible."

"Oh, it's okay."

"It's not okay." Tara looked at her in earnest. "I had a weird day yesterday and I was rambling away."

"I understand," Emily said politely.

"I'm not sure you do." Tara shook her head and looked genuinely remorseful. "I love Josie to bits. I can't believe I was talking about her like that. I'm honestly not usually such a bad friend."

"I definitely don't think you're a bad friend."

"You must. If I heard someone gossiping about Josie, I'd flatten them."

Emily couldn't help but laugh.

"I could hardly sleep because I was worrying about what you must think of me." They'd wandered all the way down the drive and stopped by the gate. "Jack must think I'm awful too."

Emily didn't like to tell her the truth: that Jack was far more annoyed than she was. "Jack's worried everyone's gossiping about *him*," she said, avoiding the question. "He thinks everyone must be talking about him because of his history with Josie."

"I don't think so." Tara leaned against the gate. "I was a little intrigued but that's only because I've heard so much about Jack – and I'm a bit nosey. Josie's never had a bad word to say about him. She only ever said that they weren't right for each other. She's obviously very fond of him."

Emily smiled, ignoring the slight increase in her heart rate.

"If Josie isn't bothered by you and Jack being together, I don't know why anyone else would be." Tara stood up straighter and they began to amble back in the direction of the house. "She always seemed happy for you."

Emily let out a short snort of laughter. "She really wasn't okay with it for a while."

"She didn't mention that to us. Although, she has a habit of keeping things to herself. She's been the same recently. I'm sure there's something going on with her but she won't talk to us . . ." She stopped and looked squarely at Emily. "Oh God. I'm gossiping again. I came over to try and redeem myself and I'm digging my hole deeper."

"I think it's more like sharing concerns. I'm worried about her too. Do you really think she might be pregnant? Sorry," she added quickly. "Now I'm gossiping."

"Sharing concerns," Tara corrected her with a smirk. "I don't know what's going on. I'm sure she'll tell us when she's ready. And Sam's great. He'll take care of her."

Jack and Josie walked out of the house as they approached.

"Have you got the big launch party all figured out?" Josie asked.

"Erm . . ." Emily looked to Tara.

"Yep!" Tara said.

"We're doing it," Emily chimed in, trying hard not to laugh.

"I knew Tara would persuade you. I can't wait. Come on, I want to show you the kennels."

Chapter 7

They started back down the drive toward the barn and Jack slipped his hand into Emily's. "Everything okay?"

She smiled up at him and nodded.

"Annette and Wendy converted the barn into kennels when they bought the place," Josie said, swinging back round to them. "She showed you the photos, didn't she?"

"Yes. It's fascinating."

"I've been doing it up since I got here," Josie said.

"It's a luxury stay for the dogs," Tara said.

The barking began as soon as Josie pulled the barn door open but soon died out as she moved inside, chatting to the dogs to calm them down.

"It was originally stables," she said. "It still has some of the original features."

Emily turned her nose up at the smell inside the barn. It was a pungent mixture of wet dog and tinned dog food. She leaned over a stable door and said hello to an excited springer spaniel.

"I've been on a mission to get furniture for each kennel," Josie said. "But I have to find stuff free or cheap . . ."

"Every couch tells a story," Tara said, laughing.

"It's been fun finding it all." Josie launched into

several anecdotes about saving old couches from skips and bartering for armchairs at car boot sales.

As they reached the far end of the barn, Jack slipped into the last stall to play with a lovely chocolate Labrador with gorgeous big brown eyes.

"Where did Sam propose?" Emily asked, leaning on the red brick wall of the stall. She'd already heard about the proposal over the phone, but it was nice to see where it took place.

"Right in the middle there." Josie pointed back through the barn and beamed at the memory. "It was so sweet."

"Proposing in a barn." Tara rolled her eyes dramatically. "And they say romance is dead!"

"It *was* romantic." Josie's features were full of amusement. "And it was all Emily's fault."

"How was it my fault?" Emily asked.

"Because Sam was going to propose on Valentine's Day, but you called and shouted at me and I was so upset that I cancelled the dinner plans. I didn't know he was planning to ask me to marry him."

Emily's hand shot to her mouth as she inhaled a sharp breath. "Really?"

"Yes." Josie didn't look the least bit annoyed.

"I'd had a glass of wine." Emily remembered the phone call well. "It was Valentine's Day and I was missing Jack and I was in a horrible mood. I was really mean, wasn't I?"

Josie nodded. "You said you didn't want to be friends with me any more!"

Looking back, it was hard to feel bad about it. That conversation had been the catalyst for her and

Jack finally getting together. If Emily hadn't shouted at Josie, she still might not be with Jack.

"Sorry," she said through a laugh. "Poor Sam!"

"He kept trying to find the perfect time and place to propose and then in the end he gave up and came running in here to ask me. It was really cute. And the timing was perfect . . ." The smile which lit up Josie's face faltered and she turned away.

Each of the kennels had a little chalkboard hanging outside with the name of the dog, and Josie busied herself straightening the one nearest her.

"Why was it perfect timing?" Tara asked.

"Oh, you know." She swallowed hard. "I'd been thinking about it, wondering if he might propose. So it felt like great timing . . ." She went over to Jack, telling him to pass her the dog bowl so she could fill it with water. "When are we having the launch party?" she called behind her with false cheer.

"Don't know," Tara said. "We hadn't got that far in the organising!" She eyed Emily questioningly as though trying to gauge whether she was really okay with it.

It was hard to say no at that point. "It would be great if we can make it as close to release day as possible," Emily said.

"Perfect! I'll work on some promotional material this week and send it over for you to look at."

"Are you sure your boss will go for it?"

Josie handed the full water bowl back to Jack. "Her boss is in love with her. He'll agree to anything."

"Not true," Tara said with a sigh. She seemed

used to this topic of conversation. "He will be fine with it, though. Why wouldn't he?"

"You've not even read the book yet," Emily pointed out.

"I've read the first half," she said with a twinkle in her eye.

"Really?"

"I started reading as soon as you sent it this morning. I love it." She glanced at her watch. "In fact, I think I might go so I can finish it this afternoon."

"I told you she'd love it," Josie said. She wandered round the barn, checking on dogs and straightening things out. It was fun to see her in her place of work after hearing so much about it. It seemed to suit her perfectly.

"I'm going to say bye to Annette," Tara called to Josie, who nodded in acknowledgement.

Emily set off up to the house with Tara, chatting about the book and what they would do for the launch party.

Annette was sitting on the patio with Sam. There was a pot of tea and dainty china cups and saucers set out on the patio table. Smoke billowed from the chimney above and fluffy white clouds hung in the bright blue sky. The daffodils and colourful crocuses in the flower beds were stunning. It was picture perfect.

"We've gone a bit posh." Sam raised his cup and saucer. "You're like royalty."

"I love it," Emily said, pouring herself a cup as she sat with them.

"I presume there's cake somewhere around

here?" Tara said. "I've got to go but I don't want to miss out on anything yummy."

"It's on the kitchen table," Annette said. "Bring it out and you can have a slice to take with you."

"You're the best," Tara said as she went inside.

Emily took a sip of tea, enjoying the feel of the delicate china cup. She was gazing across the fields when movement by the barn drew her attention. Josie and Jack walked out and wandered slowly back up to the house, chatting animatedly. When Josie leaned into him, Jack casually slung an arm around her shoulder and rubbed her arm.

Automatically, Emily looked to Sam. He didn't react, just turned his face to the sun and closed his eyes. It must be awkward for him, seeing Josie so affectionate with her ex-boyfriend.

"Don't forget to bring plates out too," Annette called to Tara. "Make yourself useful at least."

Emily couldn't drag her attention from Josie and Jack. They were laughing loudly and Josie playfully pushed Jack away from her. When they reached the house they were still chuckling, though they didn't share the joke.

Jack stood behind Emily and massaged her shoulders. "You're supposed to be on holiday," he said. "Why are you so tense?"

"I think I need a longer break than just a night away."

Her little massage ended abruptly when Jack caught sight of the sticky chocolate cake. Emily took the plate that Tara held out to her. Really, she was still stuffed from lunch. She felt like she'd done nothing but eat all day, but the chocolate cake was too tempting.

"I'm going to love you and leave you." Tara held her thick slab of cake on a napkin. "I'll be in touch with you in the next few days," she said to Emily and then said goodbye to the group at large before setting off down the drive.

"We'll have to get off soon too." Jack checked his watch as he sat beside Emily. "I don't want to get back too late."

It had only been a short visit, but Emily was glad they'd made the effort. It was good to see Josie and her new life in the country. After all the issues between the three of them, Emily wanted them to find a new kind of normal.

It felt like they were on the right track.

Chapter 8

"Did you manage to get anything out of Josie?" Emily asked Jack in the car. They weren't even out of the village. "I didn't get a minute alone with her. I'm sure there's something going on with her."

"She didn't say anything to me." He kept his eyes on the road. "Although if she were pregnant it would be weird for her to tell me before anyone else." He sounded irritated again.

Emily wondered what they'd been chatting about when they walked up from the barn. It didn't look like a deep conversation, but they were obviously having a good natter about something.

Finally, curiosity got the better of her. "What were you guys talking about?" She tried her best to sound casual, but she suspected she may have missed the mark.

"When?"

"When you were walking back from the barn."

"I don't know." He shrugged. "Dogs."

"She was just talking to you about the dogs?"

"Think so."

"You think so? It was only an hour ago – how can you not remember what you were talking about?"

He switched the radio on, turning the volume down when it came on too loud. "I didn't realise I should take notes on the conversation."

"Why are you in such a bad mood?" She shook her head in frustration. He clearly knew what they'd been talking about; he just didn't want to tell her. "I only asked what you were talking about. I don't know why you're being so cagey about it."

"I can't remember what we were talking about. Why is it such a big deal?"

"It's not."

"Can I point out that I didn't want to go this weekend? I went because you wanted me to. Now you're annoyed with me for talking to Josie . . ."

"I'm not annoyed with you for talking to Josie." Her voice came out strangely high-pitched. "I'm worried about her. I thought she might have said something to you, that's all. Forget it."

Emily reached into her bag and pulled her Kindle out. There was no way she could concentrate enough to read, but the screen seemed like a good place to direct her attention.

They fell into a stony silence and the three-hour journey seemed never-ending. They stopped once for diesel and a quick break, then carried on driving in an uncomfortable silence. The snippets of conversations they managed were forced and awkward.

They'd already pulled up outside Jack's place when he asked if she was staying at his.

She sighed heavily. "Would you prefer it if I didn't?"

"No. But you won't move in with me so I wondered where you were planning on sleeping tonight."

"I am moving in with you. In a few weeks. I just didn't want to rush into it, and you said you were fine with that."

"I am fine with it."

"So what's the problem?"

"I think the problem is you don't like me for talking to Josie. But I'm not really sure. I obviously did something wrong."

"You're being ridiculous. Why would I have a problem with you talking to Josie?" She shook her head. "Just drive me home, please."

For a brief moment, she thought he was going to say more, but he started the engine again and pulled away down the road. Neither of them spoke, and when they arrived outside Emily's mum's house, she turned to say goodbye, expecting that they'd probably get into an argument. This was the closest to an argument they'd ever got, and she didn't like it one bit.

She was surprised when Jack switched the engine off and got out of the car. When he opened her door, she stepped out beside him.

"Will you please move in with me?" He stood close, gently taking her hands in his.

"I already said I will."

"I mean today. Move in today. I only asked if you were staying at my place because I never know where you're staying. I don't want to have to ask, and I don't want to listen to you telling me you're going home. I want your home to be with me."

She stepped forward, wrapping her arms around his waist and resting her cheek against his. He'd caught her off guard. She was sure they were going to end up arguing and instead he was asking her to move in with him. "I thought you were annoyed with me."

"I am," he whispered, chuckling lightly. "But I still want to live with you."

"Okay."

"Okay, we can go in and pack?"

"You're very keen," she said lightly. She should just say yes. Why couldn't she say yes? Just jump in feet first and see how it went. Why did she always have to over-think things?

"I *am* very keen," he told her seriously. "I would've thought that was obvious by now."

"It is." She smiled nervously.

"It's also becoming quite obvious you're not so keen."

As he loosened his arms around her, she tightened her grip on him. "It's not that I'm not keen. But I told my mum I was moving next month. That's what we planned and I just feel like . . ."

"Like I'm pressuring you to do something you don't want to?"

"No." She shook her head and wished she was better at explaining. It would probably be easier if she understood it herself. "I'm not used to being in a relationship," she said honestly. "And I've never lived with a boyfriend before. It's not that I don't want to. I just don't want to rush into it. And I don't want to move in with you spontaneously because we had an argument."

"It was hardly an argument!"

"You know what I mean, though."

"Okay." He opened the back door of the car and

64

got her bag out. She was surprised when he slung it on his shoulder and took her hand.

"Are you coming inside?"

He narrowed his eyes. "Yeah. I was planning on it."

"Why?" she blurted out, pulling on his arm. It was very confusing. Surely he should be storming away in annoyance?

"I was going to say hello to your mum." He tilted his head to one side. "It's a bit rude to just drop you off and run. Shouldn't I come in?"

"Oh. Yeah. It's fine. I just thought . . ."

"You thought I'd run away in a bad mood?" He rolled his eyes. "It's you who's annoying me, not your mum!"

Emily couldn't help but laugh. It was lovely how well Jack got on with her mum. She bumped her shoulder against Jack's as they walked to the house. He was really very sweet.

Chapter 9

On Monday, Emily got the bus into the centre of Oxford and then walked the few minutes to the castle. The manager, Doug, was in the office, and he chatted with her as she checked the rota for tour guides hanging on the noticeboard.

"You've only got me down for three tours in the next two weeks," she said, interrupting Doug. She'd only been half listening to him.

"Yes. You said you wanted to do less so you've got time for the writing and organising the book release. Bernie and Mel both need more hours so I thought it worked out nicely. It's not a problem, is it?"

"No." She winced. It was completely her fault. It had seemed like a good idea at the time to ask for fewer hours at the castle. It was only now occurring to her that she hadn't factored in money. "It's fine," she said to Doug. He was looking at her expectantly.

"You did say you wanted to cut down?"

"Yes, I did. I guess. Maybe I shouldn't have said that. Anyway, it's not your fault."

"Should I talk to Bernie and Mel? They'd probably give you a couple of theirs."

"No, don't do that." It seemed unfair when they were sensible enough to think about how to feed and clothe themselves. "It's fine. Maybe next time you do the rota you could give me a few more hours."

"Okay. I can also let you know if there are any shifts in the cafe or the shop?"

"Hmm." She screwed her face up as she pondered the suggestion. The problem was, she really wanted to get on with the writing so she could get the whole series out as quickly as possible. That was her plan, though she was starting to think she hadn't thought it through very well. "Yeah. Maybe. Let me know if you're stuck, anyway."

The urge to get home and do some calculations consumed her. She had a feeling she ought to be paying more attention to money than she had been. Her time living in London had burned through most of her savings, and since she'd moved back she hadn't managed to build them up again. She'd been too focused on turning her writing into a career to notice that she hardly had any money left at all.

The part-time job at the castle – along with the small royalties from her first two books – had sustained her. Her lifestyle was fairly frugal and the rent was cheap with her mum so it had been enough. But publishing her book entailed some extra costs, which she hadn't considered when she asked Doug to reduce her hours.

After noting which days she was rostered to take tours, she said a quick goodbye to Doug and went on her way. The sinking feeling lasted all the way home, and only got worse when she started jotting down numbers, making lists of how much she was spending versus her income.

By the time her mum came home that afternoon she felt like she was on the verge of a nervous breakdown.

"What's wrong?" her mum asked, joining her in the living room.

"I went into work to see when I'm scheduled to take tours and Doug only has me down to take three tours in the next two weeks."

"That's good, isn't it? You said you need more time for writing."

"But I forgot to think about money." She always used to be so sensible about money, but the last year had been chaotic to say the least.

"Oh," her mum said flatly. "Can't you ask Doug for more hours?"

"Yeah." She sighed, leaning back on the couch. "I just had this plan for getting these books out quickly. But I won't get them finished if I'm working at the castle."

"It's not the end of the world if it takes a little longer, is it?"

"No." But she knew that by her tone anyone would think it *was* the end of the world.

"As soon as the first book is released you'll start making money from that and everything will be fine."

"It seems fairly optimistic, Mum. What if it doesn't sell? I'll have wasted a load of time and money."

Her mum patted her knee affectionately. "It will sell."

"I hope so. I've just ordered a box of paperbacks for the launch party."

"Did you speak to Tara?"

"Yes. We've been emailing today. The party's

all set for the Friday after it releases."

"Perfect." Her mum seemed far more excited than her. "It's good of her to set all that up for you. I'm supposed to be up in York that weekend catching up with the old uni crowd, but I'll cancel and come to your launch party instead."

"No." Emily felt a slight pang of disappointment. It would've been nice to have her mum at the launch, but she didn't want her to give up her annual reunion. She knew how much she looked forward to it. "Go for your weekend. The launch party isn't a big deal. It's only a small do."

Her mum frowned. "I feel like I should come. It's the first book that you're publishing yourself."

"I'll be busy shopping for Josie's wedding dress for the rest of the weekend anyway. You go to York."

"If you're sure." She gave Emily a brief squeeze. "I'm so proud of you."

"I know." Emily smiled, then a thought occurred to her. She slapped her hand to her forehead. "That also means I can't borrow your car, I suppose?"

Her mum grimaced. "Sorry."

It felt like her day couldn't get worse. Why was nothing going right?

"Can you get a train?" her mum asked.

"Yeah. I guess." She pulled out her laptop to see what her options were. "I'd have to get the train to Exeter and see if Josie can pick me up from there. How am I going to manage all the books on the train, though?"

"Why not ask Jack if you can borrow his car?"

She turned her nose up, not liking the idea. "I think he's probably a bit precious about his car. Besides, he uses it to get to work."

"I'm sure he wouldn't mind getting the bus for a weekend . . ."

"I'd rather not ask," she said after considering it for a moment. "He'll feel like he can't say no and it'll be awkward. I'll manage on the train. It's not that many books."

"Whatever you think," her mum said.

"I also have a favour to ask," Emily said sheepishly. She hated asking her mum for financial help, but she was a bit stuck. "After paying for the editing and cover designer and some advertising, I'm a bit stuck for money."

"Do you need me to lend you some?"

Emily always knew her mum would help her, but she didn't like to ask. "No, but I can't really afford to pay you any rent at the moment." She wasn't paying much anyway but felt guilty nonetheless.

"I'll manage," her mum said with a smile. "I suppose I should get used to not having the extra money. I only hope Jack's as understanding as I am!"

"Oh no." Emily put a hand over her mouth. "I didn't even think about that."

"I was joking." Her mum gave her leg a gentle slap. "You worry too much. Jack won't mind."

"But I can't move in with him and not pay rent!" It occurred to her that Josie had never paid Jack any rent, and Emily had been horrified when she found out. And now she was thinking about the fact that Josie used to live with Jack. The day was nosediving quickly.

"What am I going to do?" She looked to her mum for answers as panic washed over her. "I said I'd move in next month. He's already being impatient about it."

"Talk to him," her mum said as though it was obvious. "I'm sure he'll be fine."

"I know he'll be fine about it," Emily said. "But I'm not."

Her mum looked thoughtful for a moment. "Your book releases at the end of next week so you'll have an income from that. And you can ask Doug for more hours at the castle. It'll be fine."

"But even if the book sells really well, I don't get the money immediately. It takes a couple of months to get the royalty payments." She flopped back onto the couch. "This is a nightmare. Why didn't I think it through? When did I get so irresponsible?"

Her mum spluttered out a laugh. "I don't think you're quite irresponsible yet. I promise you everything will work out."

"I hate it when you say that." She couldn't help the childish pout. "It makes me feel like I'm being trivial. I don't think it's trivial that I can't afford to pay rent."

"You're just going to have to be a bit careful with money for a couple of months. You'll survive. Are you going to Jack's tonight?"

"No. It's Monday. He'll be working late." Emily smiled sweetly. "You get the pleasure of my company."

"Good." Her mum stood and walked out of the living room. "I'll see what I can find for dinner."

Chapter 10

Emily actually enjoyed the arrangement of splitting her time between her mum's place and Jack's. She got on well with her mum, and it was nice to have a bit of time to miss Jack. She saw him the following night and then he was working some extra hours so she wouldn't see him again until Friday.

His job driving non-emergency ambulances suited him well. He was good with people and enjoyed the chatter as he drove patients to and from appointments. Often, he'd come home with stories of the regulars, who he'd become quite attached to.

Emily had a key to his place and went over there mid-afternoon on Friday. It was good to have a change of scene to get some writing done, and she'd bought some food so she could cook for them when Jack got home.

As she got comfy on his couch with her laptop on her knees, her mobile rang with a call from Josie. Emily had been trying to get hold of her all week to chat through arrangements for the launch party weekend.

"Finally!" Emily said jokily as she answered the call. "I kept trying to call you. You never answer."

"Hey! I called you last night and you didn't answer either!"

"That's true."

"Right," Josie said. "Tara has the launch party set up for Friday evening. You've been talking to her about that?"

"Yep."

"Good. That's all sorted then. I've booked a couple of appointments at wedding dress shops for Saturday. Amber and Tara are going to come too. Lizzie also might, who knows!"

"You don't sound overly excited about it," Emily remarked.

"You know I'm not a fan of shopping."

"It's your wedding dress! It'll be fun."

"Maybe," Josie said with a sigh. "I presume you're staying at our place this time?"

"Yes, please." Emily had the impression Josie had a checklist of things to discuss.

"Great. What time will you arrive on Friday?"

"That's what I wanted to talk to you about. I'll need to get the train. Can you pick me up from Exeter?"

"I suppose. Can't you borrow your mum's car."

"She's away for the weekend."

"Why don't you come in Jack's car? It's a pain getting the train down."

"I'm not worried about getting the train. It's a bit annoying because I'll have books to carry, as well as my weekend bag, but I'll manage. I only feel bad relying on you to pick me up."

"It's not a problem. I just need to check the schedule, I think we've got a couple of dogs arriving that morning." She paused for a moment. "Why don't you ask Jack? I used to borrow his car all the time. He won't mind."

Emily put her laptop aside and sat up straighter. "Why did you borrow his car? You've got your own."

"If mine didn't have diesel in or something . . ."

Probably quite often then, Emily thought bitterly. "I don't want to ask Jack." She shook her head, trying not to dwell on Josie's history with Jack. It actually made her more determined not to ask him to borrow his car. She'd always been independent and didn't want being in a relationship to change that. "I'm fine on the train. If you can't pick me up, I can get a taxi."

"Don't be daft, it'd cost a fortune. I'll pick you up. Message me the train times and I'll let you know which is best."

"Thanks."

"No problem. I've got to go, I've got about a million things to do this afternoon."

When they ended the call, Emily was left with an underlying feeling of annoyance. She couldn't put her finger on why. It was weird hearing Josie talking about Jack. Emily still wasn't used to it.

Thankfully, she managed to focus her mind and get some writing done. By the time she moved to the kitchen to start cooking, she was feeling relaxed again. With the radio on, it was enjoyable cooking up the bolognese sauce. She wasn't the best cook, but when she'd worked at the Italian restaurant, the chef had given her tips now and again, and she had a couple of signature dishes which usually turned out well.

Jack's face lit up when he came home to find her there. Although it could have been the food that he was excited by.

"It smells amazing!" He hugged her so hard he lifted her off the ground.

"It's only spaghetti bolognese," she said.

"I love it when you cook for me."

So it *was* the food! To be fair, she didn't cook very often. She could probably make more effort.

"Have I got time for a shower?" He leaned over the stove and inhaled the aroma from the bubbling pan.

"Yep. I'll put the pasta in now."

He kissed her nose. "You're the best."

Emily was just plating up the food when he came back into the kitchen ten minutes later. They sat at the kitchen table to eat, deciding to be civilised instead of eating in front of the TV as they often did.

"I could get used to this," he said with a boyish smile. "It's nice coming home to find dinner on the table."

"I wouldn't expect it to be a regular occurrence. You know I can only cook three things."

"I just like coming home to you." He stretched his legs out under the table, nestling them against hers.

"Me too." She felt a wave of happiness as she looked at him. Not long ago she'd been convinced that she could never be with him. Now she sometimes had to pinch herself because it all felt like a wonderful dream. It was hard to believe that soon she'd be living with him.

That thought burst her bubble somewhat. She needed to postpone moving in with Jack. And she had no idea how she'd break that news to him.

"I told Clive I'd open the Boathouse tomorrow," he said. "But I'll try and finish early. I said I can't work Sunday – I thought we could do something, seeing as you're away next weekend."

"That'll be nice," she said. "I'm taking a tour group round the castle tomorrow afternoon but that's it."

He nodded and there was a pause in the conversation while they ate.

"Is everything set up for your launch party?" he asked when his plate was empty. He'd talked about coming, but it was difficult for him to get the time off, and Emily thought it would be easier without him around for the weekend. She'd have to ditch him all day on Saturday when they were dress shopping.

"I think so," she said. "I talked to Josie today. I just need to check the train times."

"You're going on the train?"

"Mum's away for the weekend, otherwise I'd have taken her car."

"Take my car," he said casually.

"No, it's okay. You'll need it."

"I can manage without it for a few days. It'll be annoying for you to go on the train. Won't you have loads to carry?"

"Some books and stuff. I don't want to leave you stuck without a car, though."

He picked up the plates and took them to the dishwasher. "I don't mind," he said. "Take it."

"Are you sure?" She really thought he might be reluctant, but he seemed completely happy with the idea. It was slightly annoying now how much she'd grappled with the idea of asking him. Although she felt much better that he'd offered without her having to ask.

"Of course." He planted a kiss on the side of her head.

Later, as she moved into the living room, Emily messaged Josie to tell her she wouldn't need to pick her up from the station after all. The reply consisted only of a smiley face.

Emily lay curled into Jack on the couch as he flicked through the TV channels. His eyes were drooping, and she was certain he'd be asleep before long.

"Why are you staring at me?" He chuckled as she propped her chin on his chest and gazed at him instead of the TV.

"Because I love you so much."

"I love you too," he said with a happy sigh.

Laying her head on his chest, she listened to the sound of his heartbeat and felt wonderfully content. Somehow, she'd ended up with everything she always wanted.

It was a little while later when Jack's phone vibrated on the coffee table. Jack was fast asleep. Leaning over to look at the phone was instinctive for Emily. It was set to show messages on the locked screen and displayed a message from Josie which merely said 'thank you', followed by a row of smiley faces blowing kisses.

Emily's heart rate increased and she looked at Jack and then back at the phone in time to see the screen go dark again. Every muscle in her body tensed.

Jack stirred and looked up at her. "You okay?"

"Yeah." She forced a smile. "Bedtime?"

He nodded, blinking as he sat up.

"I think your phone buzzed earlier." Emily tried to sound casual as she moved to the bedroom. She turned in time to see him looking at the message.

He read it and returned the phone to the table without a word. Emily was desperate to ask who it was. What would he say? Tell her the truth or feed her a lie? And why was Josie messaging him? Thank you for what? That's when it dawned on her. Jack offering her his car after she'd discussed it with Josie perhaps wasn't purely coincidental.

Avoiding eye contact, she went into the bedroom to get changed. When Jack crawled into bed beside her, he wrapped his arms around her. Her mind was whirring, trying to process the fact that Josie and Jack had been messaging each other. They were friends, so it shouldn't be a big deal that they were in touch. And Josie was obviously trying to do her a favour.

"Are you okay?" Jack asked again.

"Fine," she said. "Just got a lot on my mind with the book launch and everything."

"Okay," he mumbled, pulling her closer and nuzzling her neck.

She turned away from him. "I'm tired," she whispered.

Except she wasn't tired. Jack was asleep again in a few minutes and she lay awake for a long time, churning everything over in her head.

Jack and Josie being in touch was completely innocent. That's what she tried to tell herself. Except she remembered how relaxed they had been together at the farm and how Jack had refused to tell Emily what they'd been talking about.

No matter how hard she tried to tell herself everything was fine, there was a knot in her stomach that wouldn't go away.

Chapter 11

"So basically he's messaging his ex-girlfriend behind my back. And lying about it."

Emily paced the kitchen. She'd filled her mum in on what had happened; now she was just ranting.

"Did he lie?" Her mum sat at the table, squinting at her.

"Well, no." Emily paused from her pacing. "But I'm fairly sure he would've done if I'd asked who the message was from."

"I feel like you're not being very rational," her mum said calmly.

"I didn't sleep much," she admitted. After tossing and turning all night, she'd woken feeling terrible. Her thoughts were one big mess. Jack had got up and gone to work early so Emily had gone back to her mum's hoping that she'd feel better after talking it through. "It's not really okay, though, is it? Him messaging his ex."

"It's not that simple. It's Josie. And I'm sure she thought she was doing you a favour – nudging Jack to get him to offer you the car. And to be fair, if you'd told him earlier you were going on the train, he'd have offered you his car anyway."

"So it's all my fault?"

"Possibly." Her mum grinned.

"But what if that wasn't even what she was

messaging about? What if they message each other all the time?"

Her mum raised her eyebrows as though she couldn't even be bothered to dignify that comment with an answer.

"I don't know, though, do I?" Emily insisted. "There might have been loads of messages that I don't know about." Deep down, she didn't believe that was the case, but the sliver of doubt twisted itself around every rational thought she had.

"Have you stopped to consider the fact that Jack adores you? And that Josie is marrying Sam? Then there's the fact that neither of them would do anything to hurt you . . ."

"What am I going to do?" Emily said, leaning heavily against the sink.

"I think stopping reading Jack's messages should probably be high on your list."

"It was on the table! And he shouldn't have anything to hide."

Her mum rubbed the side of her head as though the conversation was exhausting.

"And why did she send all the kissy faces?" Emily said, frowning.

"Because it's Josie," her mum said emphatically. "She can't write anything without a string of smileys and hearts attached. Have you seen her Twitter posts?"

She had a good point.

"I'm going to wrap this conversation up before it drives me insane." Her mum flashed a sweet smile as she spoke quickly. "Here's the plan: don't mention any of this to Josie or Jack; borrow his car next week; visit Josie, have a lovely time, then come back and move in with Jack." She paused for breath. "And live happily ever after. It's pretty simple."

"You think you're very wise, don't you?" Emily said with a hint of a smirk.

"Yes! I used to think you'd inherited it, but apparently love has made you crazy and neurotic."

Emily couldn't quite bring herself to deny it.

Chapter 12

Lizzie felt terrible as she realised she hadn't been in touch with her sister since they had gone over to scatter the dog's ashes. Almost two weeks had passed, and Lizzie had thought about calling her every day. She'd picked her phone up several times but was always side-tracked by the babies' demands.

Josie had seemed out of sorts that weekend, and she'd wanted to check in with her. In the end, it was Josie who got in touch with her. It was a Thursday and Josie had called and asked if she could come over for a visit. That was weird in itself. She usually turned up without warning.

Lizzie had said yes immediately, keen for a catch up and always excited by the prospect of adult company. Although she'd been at her neighbour's house that morning too so it was turning out to be a busy day. Thursday was knitting club – she didn't knit but it was good to catch up with some of the locals over coffee and cake.

There was also a playgroup that Lizzie forced herself to go to once a week. It got them out of the house and it was pleasant enough to chat with other parents, just slightly annoying that all the conversations revolved around kids.

Lizzie greeted Josie cheerfully when she answered the door to her in the middle of the afternoon. Her wonderful border collie, Tilly, came to the door too and wagged her tail furiously as Josie made a big fuss of her. The poor dog didn't get as much attention as she used to.

"Sorry," Lizzie said as Josie shrugged her coat off and draped it over the baby gate at the bottom of the stairs. "I've been meaning to call since the last time I saw you. I don't know where the days go."

"I know how it is," Josie said. "Where are my beautiful nieces?"

"Maya's having a nap," Lizzie said as they moved into the living room. Tilly headed back to the kitchen – her safe space where there were no children to pull on her tail and ears. "Phoebe's refusing to nap today."

Phoebe was definitely the more spirited of the twins. In the living room, she'd pulled herself to standing while holding onto the couch. She looked like a little angel as she grinned at them.

"Ooh look at you, standing up," Josie cooed.

"I'm sure she thinks she has too much to learn to bother with sleep. I can't believe she's already pulling herself up. I swear she'll be walking before we know it."

"Come here," Josie said, picking her up for a cuddle.

Lizzie was just about to make drinks when Maya started crying upstairs. She fetched her down and then got to work on the coffees.

"We're having a book launch tomorrow for Emily's new book," Josie said when they were finally settled. The babies played happily on the floor. "Do you want to come? It starts at 6 p.m."

"I'd love to. It depends what time Max gets home, though. Emily must be excited."

"I'm not sure that's the right word," Josie said dryly. "She doesn't like the attention."

"It'll be fun. I'm glad the writing is going so well for her. I was sad I didn't get to edit this one." Lizzie had enjoyed editing Emily's previous books, but with the twins she didn't have time for this one. "Hopefully by the time the next book is ready I might have more time."

"At the rate Emily's going the next one will be finished soon too. She's slightly obsessive about it all."

"I think you need to be to write books," Lizzie mused. And she completely understood Emily's dedication. When it came to work, Lizzie had often fallen toward the obsessive side herself. She'd always been driven in her career.

"If I don't make it tomorrow, can you ask Emily about the christening? I keep meaning to email her but haven't got round to it."

"I think she'll be keen to come. It'll be fun to show her Hope Cove."

"Do you think Jack will come with her?"

Josie smirked. "Jack's a nice guy you know."

"I didn't say anything! I only asked if he would come."

"Yeah but you had that look in your eye that you always get when Jack is mentioned. Your nostrils flare and your eyes turn green and start swirling . . ."

"Shut up!" Lizzie laughed. "I don't have a problem with Jack. Don't you find it weird, though?

Seeing them together. Was it awkward that weekend at Annette's?"

"No. It's nice to see them. And they're a lovely couple. Jack's great – me and him just weren't meant to be." She paused. "It'd be good if Jack did come for the christening. I might have a word with him. He'll probably need a bit of encouragement, and Emily's not very good at nagging him. Like this weekend I had to call him and tell him to lend her his car because she didn't want to ask him."

"She's independent." Lizzie admired that about Emily. Nothing like Josie. "And I'm not sure you should be interfering in their relationship. Does Emily know you talked to him?"

"No! Sometimes she doesn't know what's best for her."

"Well thank goodness she has a friend who knows what's best for everyone!"

Josie grinned cheekily and nodded. "She's very lucky."

"Is everything okay with you and Sam?" Lizzie asked. "You seemed stressed last time I saw you."

Josie set her coffee aside and sat down on the floor with the babies. She picked Maya up and bounced her on her lap. "Everything's fine." She kept her attention on Maya so it was hard to tell, but Lizzie caught the hesitation and the flash of uncertainty in Josie's eyes.

"I know how stressful it is organising a wedding. Make sure you let me know if you need any help."

Josie looked pointedly at the babies and then around the messy room. "Yeah, right. Because it seems like you spend most of your time bored with nothing to do. I'm sure you could use more jobs!"

"Well, I *am* bored," Lizzie said with a chuckle. "But not because I have nothing to do."

Josie gave her a funny look and she realised how she sounded. Part of her wished she was one of those mums who was excited by every tiny thing their baby did and felt the constant need to snap pics and videos for social media. Truthfully, she found it all pretty mundane. She adored the girls, of course; she just didn't quite feel fulfilled as a stay-at-home mum.

When she fell pregnant, Lizzie was self-employed and working from home, so it seemed to make sense that she stay home with the girls. At the beginning she'd been quite happy with the arrangement, but the more time went on, the more she envied Max when he left for work in the mornings.

They'd decided to put the girls in nursery when they turned a year old. That would be in November, but the local nursery that Lizzie had her heart set on didn't have spaces until January. When they'd booked them in, the extra couple of months had felt irrelevant, but Lizzie was starting to feel like every day would make a difference now.

The day the girls started nursery and she went back to work would be a day for celebration. She definitely couldn't imagine being a mum who was upset about leaving their kids in childcare for the first time. In fact, she suspected it would take a lot of restraint not to dance around the streets screaming 'freedom'.

The conversation moved on. Josie wanted to hear all about the new house, and Lizzie agreed she'd take Josie up there when Max got home. It was a bit of a state and not really an ideal playground for crawling babies.

In the meantime, they took the twins out for a walk into the village. They hadn't been back long when Max got home. He came into the living room, saying a vague hello to Lizzie and Josie and then smothering the girls with kisses and cuddles. At least he was always happy to see them.

"I'm going to take Josie up to Lavender Lane to see the house. We'll leave the girls with you, okay?" She chastised herself for asking if it was okay. Why did she have to ask? She'd spent all day with them; she shouldn't need to ask permission to go out.

"Yeah, but I just want to have a shower first."

Lizzie was fuming when he walked out and headed upstairs. "He does that all the time," she told Josie through gritted teeth.

"What?"

"Just goes off for a shower. I haven't had time to shower today. But he had one this morning before work and now he's having another."

"You're annoyed with him for showering too often?" Josie squinted in confusion.

"No. I'm annoyed that he gets to shower whenever he feels like it. And generally he does what he wants. He never asks my permission to go out. But I just asked him if I can leave the girls with him. That's my fault, obviously." She shrugged. "Why do I ask him?"

"I didn't really notice you did . . ."

Max came back down five minutes later dressed in jogging bottoms and an old T-shirt. "Do you know where all my socks are?"

Lizzie scanned the living room as she and Josie moved to the doorway. "Probably in the washing basket over there. If you get time you could fold it and put it away."

He nodded and sat on the floor with the girls.

"You don't have to," Lizzie snapped. "There's no need to look at me like that."

"Like what?" he asked, irritated.

"Like you wonder what I do all day." The washing basket on the desk was overflowing with clean washing. It had been there three days. The washing basket upstairs was full of dirty washing and she was fairly sure she'd put a load of washing in the machine that morning and then forgotten all about it. She'd have to put it on to wash again tomorrow.

"I wasn't . . ." Max sighed. "Do the girls need feeding?"

"They just need milk at bedtime."

"Okay. You won't be long, though, will you?"

"Probably not." She clenched and unclenched her fists. "I don't know." She noticed Josie looking slightly uncomfortable as she waited in the hallway. "Come on," Lizzie said, ushering her to the front door. Josie shouted bye to Max, while Lizzie shook her head in annoyance and closed the front door heavily behind her.

"I think he might actually drive me mad one of these days."

Josie chuckled as though she found their life

very amusing. "You guys are fine, though, aren't you? I mean aside from the sleep deprivation and bickering . . ."

"Aside from those two things . . . probably. It's hard to say for definite seeing as sleep deprivation and bickering make up most of my life."

Josie chuckled again. It annoyed Lizzie. She couldn't see how it was the least bit amusing.

Chapter 13

The sisters wandered slowly up the road, and after five minutes turned left onto Lavender Lane. Their house was the first one you came to on the quiet little street. It was just like Lizzie and Max's place in that the back garden led onto the coastal path and had a wonderful sea view. In fact, the garden was potentially even nicer than theirs. It was bordered by a low wall as opposed to their high hedge, which provided privacy but hindered the view.

"It's cute." Josie surveyed the place from the small front garden.

"It's a mess," Lizzie corrected her, battling the front gate which had come off the hinges in her hand. She propped it up against the wall.

"It's got potential, though. Let me in – I want to see the inside." Once they were in, Josie turned her nose up. "It smells like old people!"

"Dead old people maybe," Lizzie said. "I think it was a while before they found the previous owner."

"Really?" Josie asked.

"Well a couple of days, I think. It's a good job Tammy is a nosey sort of postwoman or it could've been a lot longer." Lizzie was good friends with Tammy so she'd had a first-hand account of how she'd noticed the post still dangling in the letterbox and had peered in the window to see the poor old lady lifeless in her armchair.

"That's creepy." Josie looked around. "The fireplace is lovely."

"The chimney's blocked so you can't use it," Lizzie said glumly. There wasn't much about the house that did work as it should.

"Oh, but look at all the books," Josie said. "Emily will love it." One whole wall was covered from floor to ceiling with bookcases, all filled with dusty old books.

Lizzie led Josie on a tour of the house, ending in the wonderful big front bedroom with the most spectacular view of the sea.

"Oh my gosh." Josie gasped as she stood at the bay window. "It's like a little reading nest." There was a wide window seat surrounded by little nooks dug into the wall for bookshelves. "I definitely have to get Emily to come. She'll be in her element here."

"I'll just need to get the place tidied up a bit," Lizzie said, wondering when she would fit that in. She'd have enough to do getting her own house clean for the christening. They were having a little party after the ceremony at the church so she'd need to try and get the place looking decent.

"I wouldn't worry. No one will mind. And it's really not too bad. Just a bit of dust."

Lizzie ran a finger along a shelf and then held it up to Josie. "If you think this is a *bit* of dust, you've got very low standards."

"Well maybe I can come over and give you a hand sometime," Josie offered.

"Thanks. I was thinking of telling Max to take a

day or two off to tidy the place up. It was his bright idea to buy it."

"It's lovely, though." They walked back down the creaky staircase. "I should come over and help with the kids more anyway. You don't rope me in for babysitting duties like I expected you would."

"I generally don't have the energy to go out."

"Why don't I babysit tonight?" she said enthusiastically. "You and Max can have an evening out. Do you guys ever go out these days?"

"Not really." More like not at all, if she were honest. "The girls aren't easy to put to bed."

"I'm sure I'll manage if you want to go out."

Oh God, it was actually a serious offer. Lizzie fought for an excuse. "I don't think I feel like it. Another time."

"Go on. You were just saying you never get to go out."

"To be honest, I don't even want to go out with Max. He drives me crazy most of the time."

Josie held her gaze for a moment and then burst out laughing. "You crack me up. Just call him and tell him he's taking you out tonight."

Why Josie assumed she was joking was a mystery to Lizzie. It didn't seem worth arguing so she wandered into the kitchen to call Max.

"Is Maya okay?" she asked as the baby screamed in the background.

"Fine. Phoebe just hit her with a toy."

"Oh, okay. Josie just offered to babysit if we want to go out tonight."

"Erm . . ." He seemed to be mulling it over as he soothed Maya. He was looking for an excuse and

Lizzie hated him for it. It was unfair since she didn't want to go out either. "I'm happy to stay with the girls if you want to go out with Josie . . ."

"Okay." She sighed. "I'll see you later then." She ended the call without saying goodbye and then walked back into the living room. "He's got some work to do."

Josie huffed. "You should have insisted! How often do you get to go out? You'd think he'd jump at the chance."

"I'm tired anyway. It seems like a lot of effort."

"You only need to go to the pub. It doesn't need to be a wild night. Walking into the village isn't much effort."

No, walking into the village was definitely the easy part. It was talking to Max for an hour or two that would be hard work. She didn't have the energy.

"Thanks for offering anyway."

Josie's phone rang then and she smiled as she answered it. Lizzie listened in on her conversation with Sam. He was obviously just calling to check on her and find out when she would be home. Lizzie felt even more deflated. She and Max used to be like that too.

"I better get back," Josie said when she finished the call. "If you're sure you don't need a babysitter."

"No, thanks. You get back to Sam." Make the most of the time when you enjoy each other's company.

They walked back to Seaside Cottage and Lizzie waved Josie away. Then she turned to the house. All the lights were on and she could hear one of the girls crying. It sounded like Maya again.

Lizzie felt awful when it occurred to her how much she hated the thought of going inside. She should have gone for a drink with Josie like Max had suggested.

She even contemplated going down to the pub alone. But that was sure to set tongues wagging in the village. Instead, she turned and walked back the way she'd come – back to Lavender Lane.

Walking around the back of the house, she traipsed through the overgrown garden and sat on the low wall at the end. The view was stunning. The sea stretched as far as you could see along the craggy coastline. The rocks were pounded by fierce waves, but every now and again they gave way to beautiful little beaches where the waves rolled peacefully onto the shore. The hum of waves was hypnotic and the salty air was intoxicating.

Lizzie didn't take advantage of the incredible surroundings as much as she used to. The double buggy and the narrow path along the coast weren't compatible. Winter had kept them inside too, but now that the weather was better she was determined to make the most of their wonderful location.

Lost in a trance, she sat for an hour – until her bum went numb on the wall and she suddenly couldn't bear to sit there a moment longer.

It was creepy in the house alone at night. Lizzie found herself wondering about the woman who'd lived there before. An image of a dead body in the threadbare armchair gave her the shivers, and she forced herself to think of something else. There was an old TV in the corner and Lizzie found the remote. Nothing happened when she pressed the button so she peered down the back to find it wasn't plugged in.

It was awkward to get her arm down the back of the TV, but she finally managed to wrangle the plug into the socket. She felt the surge of electricity and saw a quick flash by the socket. There was a brief moment of panic when she thought she might be the next corpse in the room. Dropping the plug, she fell back onto her bum as the lights went off and the house descended into darkness.

Her eyes adjusted after a moment, and the darkness faded with the gleam of nearby streetlights and the gentle glow of the moon.

It was probably a sign that she should go home, but instead she flopped onto the couch and leaned her head back, telling herself she would go in a minute. She told herself that for over an hour. It was nice to sit in absolute silence for a while. Unfortunately, it was broken by a scratching noise coming from the kitchen. Lizzie listened hard and heard the definite sound of tiny feet scurrying around. Time to leave.

Her phone vibrated in her pocket as she stood, startling her so much she almost hit the ceiling. She answered as she walked outside, cradling the phone between her ear and her shoulder as she locked the door behind her. It was Max.

"Where are you?" he asked.

"Just on my way home."

"I thought you were out with Josie."

"Yeah."

"I was just chatting to Sam and he said Josie came home hours ago."

"Yeah," she said again. She didn't even have the energy to feel guilty for not going home. "I'll be home in five minutes."

She definitely didn't hurry, and when she arrived home she braced herself for the inevitable shouting match. Max appeared at the top of the stairs. Maya was nestled in his chest and he gently rubbed her back. "Are you okay?" he asked in a loud whisper.

"Fine." She peeled her jacket off and hung it over the banister.

"Where were you?"

"Up at Lavender Lane."

"Why?" he asked, puzzled.

She was hoping he wouldn't ask because she couldn't be bothered to lie. Maybe it was best to ignore the question.

"Lizzie?" he called when she took steps towards the kitchen.

Backtracking, she craned her neck to look up the stairs. "I didn't want to come home," she said flatly before walking away.

The kitchen was a mess, and she assumed the living room was in a similar state of disarray. It all made her feel like crying.

As she wiped down the high chairs, which were encrusted with dried food, she heard Max's footsteps overhead and then the creak of the stairs as he came down.

He hovered in the kitchen doorway. "I thought you were going out with Josie."

Lizzie rinsed the dishcloth and half-heartedly wiped down the sideboard. It was a pointless task, seeing as most of the sideboard was covered in dirty dishes and baby bottles and discarded dummies.

"She wanted to get back to Sam."

"I'm sorry," he said. "We should've gone out."

"Except you didn't want to go out with me," she said tersely.

"It wasn't like that," he said with a sigh.

She threw the cloth into the sink and turned to face him. "It *was* like that," she snapped. "I know because I didn't want to go out with you either."

He closed his eyes as he squeezed the bridge of his nose.

"I really hate this." Her voice was thick with emotion. "I hate the mess we live in and I hate the constant arguing." She wiped tears from her cheeks with the back of hand. "I hate all of this. I'd rather spend the evening sitting in a house with no heating or electricity than come back here."

He came and put his arms around her and she felt utterly defeated as she rested her head on his shoulder.

"Sorry," he whispered into her hair.

Pulling out of his embrace, she moved across the kitchen. "I'm going to bed."

"Lizzie?" he called after her. She paused. "There's supposed to be electricity in the house."

"Well there isn't." After having had doubts about whether or not buying the house was a good idea, she felt slightly smug about what a disaster it was turning out to be. "But if it's any consolation I'm fairly sure it's got mice."

Chapter 14

The spare room had become a sort of refuge. Lizzie or Max would sleep in there to get a good night's sleep while the other got up with the girls. On this occasion, Lizzie just wanted to be away from Max. The girls slept reasonably well – she was only up with them twice. The third time they woke, she heard Max go into them and left him to it.

At 8 a.m. she woke with a start. It was quite a lie in for her. Even after a decent amount of sleep she was still exhausted. It was as though all the months of sleep deprivation had accumulated and now she'd never catch up. Her whole life would be led in a zombie-like state.

It was tempting to roll over and go back to sleep, but she felt a pang of guilt as she heard Max in the kitchen with the girls.

"Morning," she mumbled when she padded down in her pyjamas. Something was weird. "You're all dressed already," she said in surprise. Usually if the girls were dressed by midday they were doing well.

"Morning!" Max handed her a coffee and caught her by surprise when he dropped a gentle kiss on her lips. "I thought we could take coffees down to the beach, like we used to." They'd done that all the time in their pre-baby days – sat on the beach and watched the sunrise with their morning coffee.

"What about work?" she asked.

"I can go in late."

The girls were banging happily on their respective high chairs. "Come on," Max urged. "Grab a baby and let's go."

"I'm not even dressed." She couldn't fathom whether it was a lovely idea or an utterly stupid one.

Max grabbed his hoodie from the back of the kitchen chair and told her to put it on. She pulled it over her head. "Should we take the buggy?"

"No. Let's just be spontaneous and go."

"You know there's a reason why we don't do anything spontaneous any more." She pushed her feet into a pair of shoes by the back door regardless. Tilly had been lazing in her dog bed, but stood and wagged her tail excitedly.

"*Two* reasons," Max corrected her. "But I'm sure we can manage ten minutes sitting on the beach that is right at the end of the garden."

Lizzie pulled Phoebe from her high chair, balancing her on her hip before picking up her coffee. Swept up in Max's enthusiasm, she suddenly liked the idea of coffee on the beach. Tilly seemed just as excited and barked as Max opened the door. She was off like a shot down the garden.

Halfway down the garden, Maya threw up her morning milk all over Max's T-shirt.

"That's why we don't do spontaneous," Lizzie said with a smirk.

"We're going to get changed and then we'll catch you up . . ."

Lizzie had to put her coffee down on the grass

to open the door at the end of the garden. It was a quirky feature – an old wooden doorframe firmly placed in the hedge with its green door. The paint was cracking and it was getting a bit overgrown. Lizzie missed her long walks with Tilly. Recently, Tilly got her exercise trailing along the pavement beside the buggy. The poor dog really didn't get walked as much as she used to.

As soon as Lizzie got the gate open, Tilly ran straight down to the beach, chasing off a pair of seagulls who squawked indignantly as they were forced to take flight.

Lizzie paused to admire the view, then crossed the narrow path and descended the few stone steps onto the perfect little sandy cove. The small stretch of beach was deserted.

Phoebe wriggled in her arms. She was getting heavy, and Lizzie didn't go far before stopping to sit with Phoebe between her legs. The happy child patted the sand, and Lizzie had just taken a mouthful of coffee when Phoebe threw sand in the air with a jerky arm movement. Peering into the coffee mug, Lizzie decided a bit of sand wasn't so bad. She was about to take a sip when Phoebe repeated her new trick, showering them both and getting even more sand into the cup of coffee.

Lizzie laughed and gave up on the coffee. The waves rolling gently into the shore were mesmerising. They really were lucky to have such a view on their doorstep. Now the weather was picking up, Lizzie was determined to get out there more.

As Phoebe happily explored the damp sand,

Lizzie twirled the blonde curls at the back of her daughter's neck. After ten minutes and several sand showers later, she gave up waiting for Max and went back to the house.

"Sorry," he called from the living room. "I just got us changed and then there was a nappy incident. We're almost clean."

Lizzie dumped her coffee in the sink and dampened a flannel to try to wipe the sand out of Phoebe's eyes. She was screaming and rubbing more sand into them.

In the living room Max was on the floor with Maya, wrestling her into fresh clothes.

"We ended up with sand in my coffee and in Phoebe's eyes."

"Sorry," Max said again. "It probably wasn't the best idea."

As Phoebe calmed down, Lizzie lay her on the floor and took a seat on the couch. She trailed her fingers through Max's hair. "It was a lovely idea," she said.

He finished off Maya's buttons and pushed himself up onto the couch, planting a kiss on the side of Lizzie's head.

"I'm sorry for being in such a bad mood yesterday," she said.

"That's okay. I was thinking you should take some time for yourself – just go off on your own one day at the weekend." He smiled cheekily. "Or half a day."

"It doesn't seem very fair on you."

"I get to go to work five days a week," he said sheepishly.

"That's true." She leaned into him. "I'd really love to go to work five days a week. One day would even be lovely."

"They'll be in nursery before you know it and you can start taking on projects again."

"I can't wait. Does that make me a horrible mother?"

"No," he said, chuckling. "Not at all."

Tears sprang to her eyes. She hated her constant emotional state. "I feel like every moment of my day is about the girls, and it drives me crazy. But then I feel so guilty for feeling like that."

"Don't. I'm fairly sure it's normal to want time to yourself."

Lizzie had an idea. "Josie and Tara are throwing a book launch party for Emily tonight. I think I might go."

"Sounds fun," he said. "I've got a meeting in Plymouth this afternoon but I shouldn't be too late."

She frowned. "It starts at 6 p.m."

"Oh." He looked thoughtful. "You could ask Dotty to come and watch the girls until I get back."

"No." Their lovely neighbour would definitely be willing to help, but Lizzie didn't feel she could ask. "It's too much for her. I know she offers to help, but she couldn't actually manage them. And it's dinner time, and they always get grumpy around then. No, it doesn't matter."

"Sorry." He grimaced and kissed her head again.

Lizzie wished the idea hadn't popped into her head at all. Now she felt like she was missing out.

Chapter 15

The drive from Oxford seemed to fly by, and Emily arrived in Averton late on Friday morning. When there was no sign of Josie at her place, she left the car and walked round to Annette's, assuming Josie would be at the kennels.

"She was here earlier," Annette said, in the kitchen. "But she said she was going home to wait for you. Who knows what's happened to her. She's hard to keep up with. Stay and keep me company for a while. I'll put the kettle on."

"Thanks." Emily took a seat at the table and ran the pendant along the chain of her necklace. It was a dainty silver sun and was a gift from Jack to congratulate her on the book release. It had come with a card with a line from an E.E. Cummings poem: *You are my sun, my moon and all of my stars.* She had a sickeningly sentimental boyfriend, and of course her worries about any feelings he may have for Josie vanished in an instant.

But now she was worried about her friend. It was so strange for her to disappear when she knew Emily was arriving.

"Is everything okay with Josie?" Emily asked. "She seemed a little out of sorts last time I was here."

Annette took a seat and seemed to mull the

question over. "She's been a bit quiet. I think it's all the wedding planning getting to her. Even though it's quite a small do, there's still a lot to organise. And she works hard too. I keep telling her she should take a holiday."

Emily nodded, and Annette got up again as the kettle clicked.

"I might go back and see if I can find her," Emily said, standing abruptly. "Do you mind? Maybe she didn't hear the door. I only rang the bell once and then assumed she was here. She was probably in the shower."

"Of course. You get on. I bet you've got lots to prepare for the big party tonight. Congratulations on the latest book!"

"Thank you. Will you be coming to the launch party?"

"No. I don't like to be out in the evenings. Bring me a copy, though, won't you?"

"I will," Emily agreed happily. "See you later."

Back at Josie's house, she rang the bell again, then banged loudly on the door. She was just peering in the front window when she heard footsteps on the stairs.

"I'm sorry," Josie said, blinking as she opened the door. "Have you been here long?"

"Not really. I went up to Annette's when you didn't answer the first time but she said you should be here. Are you okay?"

"Yes, fine." Josie led the way into the living room.

"Are you sure?"

She looked terrible – pale with dark circles

under her eyes.

"I was out with the dogs early this morning. When I got back, I sat down and must have fallen asleep."

"You look awful."

"Thanks." She forced a laugh. "This is just how I look when I wake up."

Emily had seen Josie getting up after all-night partying sessions and she'd never looked this bad.

"Should I call Sam or something?"

"What?" Josie asked, shocked. "No. Why?"

"You look ill. I'm worried about you."

"I've not been sleeping well. The wedding planning is giving me insomnia. Stop fussing. I'll be fine once I've properly woken up. How was the drive?"

"Easy, actually. Hardly any traffic, which was nice."

"And Jack was fine with you borrowing the car in the end?"

Emily bristled slightly. She knew Josie had had a hand in that. "Fine," she said quickly, hoping to skim over the matter. "So what's the plan today? When do we need to be at the bookshop?"

"Late afternoon. I think around five or so will be fine."

"I'm really nervous." Emily stared out of the kitchen window. It was a lovely garden, with scattered wildflowers growing in the grass. "I might have to have a drink beforehand."

"You'll be fine," Josie assured her. "Once we're there, you'll relax. And Tara will take care of you. She knows you need lots of hand-holding."

"Good," Emily said, feeling marginally better.

After a cup of coffee and some lunch, Josie seemed to perk up. They walked back up to Annette's place and spent the afternoon roaming the countryside as they walked the dogs.

Annette insisted they eat with her before they left for the evening. Sam wasn't home from work when they set off to Tara's bookshop in the small town of Newton Abbot. It was only a twenty-minute drive from Averton, and Emily was mesmerised as soon as she saw The Reading Room.

It was magical even from the outside. She stood holding her box of books as her eyes roamed the wonderful shopfront. The royal blue signage gave it a regal feel and the old-fashioned train set gently stuttering around a display of children's books in the window gave her goosebumps. It was adorable.

"This is all down to Tara," Josie said proudly. "Apparently it was quite drab and rundown before she came along. She does all the displays. And she set up the kids' corner. You'll love it."

The tension that Emily had been feeling about the book launch diminished as she stepped inside. Any bookshop tended to cast a spell on Emily, but this one was utterly delightful.

"I love it," she said as Tara approached her. She was rooted to the spot as she took in the neat rows of books and the scattered reading nooks. Tables and chairs were carefully arranged, making you want to grab a book and sit down in one of the shabby chic armchairs. "Does anyone buy anything?" she asked. "Or do they just come in to escape the world?"

Tara took the box of books from Emily.

"Luckily they usually do both."

The kids' area was tucked away at the back of the shop. It was vibrant with brightly coloured bean bags. Cuddly toys adorned the lower shelves, set up holding books as though they were happily reading away.

"That's so cute!" Emily exclaimed.

Josie grinned. "You'd never know Tara hates kids, would you? Not with all the effort she goes to draw them in."

"It's a good business plan." Tara moved over to a table decked with snacks and picked a crisp. "Kids nag their parents to buy things. And I don't hate kids," she said pointedly to Josie.

"Yeah, right," Josie said. "Anyway, the food looks great."

"It's only a few nibbles and dips," Tara said. "The Prosecco should be a big hit, though! Shall we have a cheeky glass before things get hectic? Toast the success of the new book?"

"I'd love one," Emily said. "I need something to calm the nerves."

"There's nothing to be nervous about," Tara said. "All I put on the flyers was meet and greet with the author. So there's no pressure to do anything other than chat to people and sign some books." She paused. "It would be fab if you did a little reading, though!"

They'd discussed the format of the evening via email. Emily had agreed it would be good to read an excerpt from the book, but she was concerned she might have an attack of nerves and not even be able to say her own name. Tara had kindly suggested that they play it by ear and see how Emily felt on the day. She'd prepared something to say and hoped she'd be brave enough to go through with it.

"I think I'll read a couple of pages," she said. "Except I've made myself nervous now just thinking about it!" Public speaking was her nemesis at the best of times – reading part of her book was about a million times worse.

"You'll be fine," Tara said. "I bet your nerves will disappear with a glass of this . . ." There was a short hiss as she unscrewed the top of the Prosecco.

"Real wine glasses," Emily said. "I'm impressed."

"Andy let me borrow them. I hope no one orders wine in the Bluebell tonight!"

"Cheers!" Josie said, holding up her glass.

"To the new book," Tara said. "And a wonderful author. I hope you remember us when you're rich and famous!"

Emily laughed at her enthusiasm. They clinked their glasses together and had just taken a sip when a guy walked out of a back room.

"Starting already?" he said.

"The author requested a glass of fizz," Tara said with a shrug and a mischievous smile.

"Well if the author requests it . . ." He walked confidently over and offered his hand to Emily. "I'm James," he said. "Nice to finally meet you."

"Thanks," she muttered, trying to figure out who he was. It seemed as though she ought to know, but the only other person she'd expected might be there was Tara's boss.

"We'll have to behave now the boss is here,"

Tara said with a twinkle in her eyes.

Emily blinked a couple of times. She'd heard James mentioned a few times in conversation and emails, but he was nothing like she'd imagined. In her head she had a very clear picture of a middle-aged man in brown corduroy trousers and a grey cardigan. But this guy was young and athletic-looking. His attire was smart casual – jeans and a nice shirt with a pair of Nike's. She'd definitely put him as the owner of a gym rather than the owner of a bookshop. In fact, she decided she was probably confused about him owning the place. It just didn't quite fit.

"I might have a glass with you, if you don't mind?" He looked at Tara, waiting for her approval.

She didn't reply but poured him a glass.

"Actually, I thought I might hang around for the thing if I'm not in the way?"

"It's not a *thing*." Tara passed him the glass. "It's a book launch. Congratulate Emily on her new book."

"Sorry." He turned and held his glass up to Emily's. "Congratulations!"

"Thank you." She took another sip, hoping the alcohol would drown her nerves.

After a few minutes chatting about the book, they went over to the table Tara had set up for Emily to sign books. It was fun arranging the books and promotional materials.

"If you decide to read something you could sit at the table," Tara said. Glancing around, she caught James's eye. "We still need to get the chairs out of the back room."

He gave a quick salute and disappeared into the back. The atmosphere between them was so strange. It seemed more like Tara was the boss. Emily could see why Josie thought he was in love with Tara. He had the look of a man who was smitten. She was eager to talk to Tara about him, but he kept coming and going, bringing chairs out. Tara arranged them around the space at the back of the shop.

"I want it to be casual," she said. "So when you're reading, people can sit or stand, or lounge on a beanbag. Nice and informal. Not rows of people staring at you."

Emily didn't comment on the fact that she was talking about the reading as though it was definite. The wine had calmed her down and she was even getting excited.

"I think I *will* talk," she said. "So long as there aren't too many people."

"You'll be great. Just remember they're mostly a bit star struck to meet a real-life author. They think you're a big deal. It hardly matters what you say, they'll lap it up."

"Oh God, you've made me nervous again now. They're expecting someone who knows what they're talking about and they get me instead."

"You do know what you're talking about!" Tara rolled her eyes. "Just tell them what it's like being an author. It's fascinating."

Emily snorted a laugh. "I think you're drunk already."

"Not yet. But ask me again at the end of the night." She gave a discreet wink. "Anyone want a top-up?"

"No," Emily said. "That's enough for me. I'm worried about making a fool of myself as it is. Getting sloshed at my own book launch wouldn't be very classy, would it?"

"Maybe not as people are arriving," Tara agreed. "Later, though." She looked questioningly at Josie, holding up the bottle.

"I've got to drive later," she replied. She'd barely drunk any of her first glass either. It was strange how Josie suddenly seemed overshadowed by Tara's outgoing personality. Emily couldn't remember Josie ever being so quiet.

"This is the last of them," James said as he brought out two more chairs. Tara indicated where he should put them with a discreet nod.

"We're all set then?" Josie said.

"Oh God." Emily groaned, glancing towards the door. "This is the bit where we wait and see if anyone turns up."

"I think it'll be a nice little crowd," Tara said firmly.

Emily looked to Josie. "Is your friend Amber coming?" She'd seemed pleasant when Emily had met her in the pub. Whenever Josie talked about her friends it was always Tara and Amber so Emily had thought she might be there.

Josie glanced at Tara and they both laughed.

"Amber can't make it," Tara said, grinning widely. "But her mum's coming . . ."

"Amber wanted to come," Josie explained, "but her mum refused to babysit because she wanted to come. Amber's furious with her. Her husband's away and she couldn't find anyone else to look after

Keiron. She said to tell you she wanted to be here. And we have to take her a book."

"I'll see her tomorrow anyway, won't I?"

"Yes!" Tara bunched her shoulders up and clapped her hands excitedly. "Dress shopping!"

"I can't wait to see you in a wedding dress," Emily said.

James stood by the table of nibbles, munching away. "When's the big day, Josie?"

"End of August. I thought we were keeping it simple but there still seems to be a million things to plan."

"It'll be amazing, though," Tara said. "I can't wait."

The bell tinkled over the front door and they exchanged excited glances before Tara scuttled away to greet the first arrivals.

Over the next half hour, the shop steadily filled up. Emily got swept up in it all and the nerves soon faded. It was fun talking to people who were so interested in her books. The atmosphere was very relaxed, with people chatting and browsing the shop. James and Tara were excellent hosts, topping up drinks and passing round nibbles.

Josie stayed close to Emily, and a few times Emily worried about how subdued her best friend was. It was unusual for Emily to be the centre of attention and overshadow Josie. There was even a brief moment when Emily wondered if Josie was jealous, but she quickly brushed it aside. As much as Josie generally enjoyed being the centre of attention, she'd never begrudge Emily her evening in the spotlight.

When it seemed like everyone had arrived, Tara tapped her wine glass with a spoon and then proudly introduced Emily. The first moment in front of her audience was daunting, and she nervously fingered the pendant on her necklace as she smiled at her audience.

Once she got going, it really wasn't so bad. She spoke about herself at first, mainly talking about her job in Oxford Castle and Prison and how it had inspired her to write a book about it, and how that book turned into a series which was keeping her very busy.

Her friendly audience nodded and smiled, seeming genuinely interested, just like Tara had said. After her little talk, she read the first chapter of the book. That was the most nerve-wracking bit, and she was relieved when she finished, then blushed bright red at the gentle round of applause.

The rest of the evening went by in a blur of signing books and chatting to people, and drinking probably a little more fizzy wine than she should have done.

By the time they said goodbye to the last guest, Emily's cheeks ached from smiling.

"That was amazing!" She hugged Tara excitedly. "Thank you so much."

"My pleasure," she said. "I had a great time."

"The books are all sold and the Prosecco's all gone." James was collecting up empty glasses. "That makes it a success, doesn't it?"

"Definitely," Josie piped up. She was nestled in a bright green beanbag in the children's corner. "We should do this for every book!"

"Fine by me," Tara said.

"Let me get the next book finished before we start making plans!"

"I'm going to start washing glasses," James called. "I don't mind tidying up if you want to go out and celebrate."

"You should go home," Tara said to him. "We can tidy up."

"I don't mind doing it." James smiled at Tara. The atmosphere was slightly uncomfortable for a moment.

"Why don't you do the glasses, James?" Josie walked over to them. "And we'll get everything straightened out here. It won't take long if we all help."

"Great." James disappeared into the back with a tray full of wine glasses.

"Do you want us to go?" Josie asked Tara quietly.

Tara glared at her. "What?"

"Should we leave you and James to tidy up alone?"

"No! Don't you dare. Shut up and start tidying."

Josie dutifully picked up a couple of chairs. "I don't know why you won't give him a chance. He's so lovely."

"And I don't know why you won't drop the subject. How many times do I need to tell you it's never going to happen?"

"Okay!" Josie rolled her eyes and Emily followed her lead in taking the extra chairs back into the store room.

It didn't take long to get the shop looking neat

and tidy again, and they said goodbye to James before the three of them got into Josie's car. Tara asked if they wanted to go to the Bluebell Inn for a quick drink, but in the end they all agreed it would be best not to be hungover for the big shopping trip the next day. They dropped Tara at her place.

Back at Josie's house they sat in the living room and excitedly gave Sam a rundown of the evening. Emily went up to bed before Josie and Sam and was sitting in bed with her laptop, trying to catch up on social media, when Jack called.

She launched into another account of the evening at the bookshop, proudly telling him how she'd talked in front of everyone and read part of her book. He sounded happy for her as he congratulated her.

"And how are the book sales?"

"Good." She clicked back onto the sales report on her laptop. "It's amazing being able to see as soon as I sell anything. I've sold more than I expected to during release week so that's good. Fingers crossed it keeps going like this."

"I'm sure it will," he said. "How's Josie?"

She paused, thinking. "Quiet," she said finally. "I'm not sure what it is, but she definitely doesn't seem herself."

"That's weird. Maybe she'll talk to you at some point over the weekend."

"Maybe," Emily agreed. Although there'd been plenty of time to chat as they roamed the hills in the afternoon and she'd not said anything. "I better get some sleep. I've got a big day of wedding dress shopping tomorrow."

"That shouldn't take long. Josie hates shopping." He'd echoed Josie's sentiments exactly.

"I think wedding dress shopping is a bit different!"

"I wouldn't know," he said, chuckling. "Have fun anyway. I love you."

"Love you too."

She wished him goodnight and hung up with a contented smile.

Chapter 16

Amber picked Josie and Emily up on Saturday morning. Then they collected Tara before driving to Exeter for a day of wedding dress shopping. The plan was to choose a bridesmaid dress for Emily too. Lizzie would be maid of honour. One of the twins was ill so she couldn't make the shopping trip, but apparently she was happy to choose a dress later in the colour they chose for Emily.

The four women were greeted in the fancy wedding dress shop by a tall, haughty-looking shop assistant who introduced herself as Polly. She immediately offered them champagne, and Emily could almost hear Tara and Amber wondering whether Josie would accept or not.

Surely Josie was aware that her sudden move to teetotal had everyone speculating? She seemed quite oblivious, as though the wedding diet was a real thing. Did she really think they were so gullible? Emily chastised herself; maybe the reason Josie was sticking to her diet story was because it was the truth. A bit of healthy living had everyone gossiping.

"Thanks," Josie said, taking the glass of champagne that was offered to her.

Emily caught Amber's eye and quickly looked away again.

"Thank you." Tara winked at Polly as she took a

glass. "I've only come along for the free drinks!"

Polly looked less than amused but forced a polite smile nonetheless.

They clinked their glasses together and made a toast to Josie.

"May she find the perfect dress," Amber said.

"And may it take all day so I can get nicely sloshed on free champagne," Tara added with a mischievous glint in her eyes.

"I hope it doesn't take all day," Josie said. "You know I'm not a fan of shopping."

"Do you have an idea of the style you'd like?" Polly asked. She'd been hovering nearby.

"Something that will go with a pair of Converse," Josie said flatly.

Polly really needed to work on the fake smile.

"Is it okay if we just have a browse?" Amber asked.

"Certainly. Shout if you find anything you'd like to try."

"I don't even know where to start." Josie scanned the sea of white dresses, then looked to her friends. "Help me!"

They got to work searching out the perfect dress. Josie seemed entirely half-hearted about it.

"At least pretend to be excited," Tara said, holding up a big, puffy dress.

Josie laughed and shook her head.

"What about this?" Amber said, with a simpler but elegant dress. It was white satin with intricate beading in the bodice.

"I'll try it."

Polly jumped to action, and Josie followed her

to the fitting room.

She came out a few minutes later, holding the top part of the dress up until Polly fastened it up. Then Josie walked over to the mirror and her friends gathered around her.

"What do you think?"

Amber's eyes glinted with tears, and Emily felt she wasn't far behind with the emotions.

"Love it," Amber sniffed.

Josie turned for a side view. "I'm not sure. I feel so restricted. And doesn't it look too mermaid-y?"

As soon as she said it, Emily looked at it completely differently. It did in fact look very much like a mermaid tail – flaring out from the knees. Josie's legs weren't long enough to pull it off.

"I don't like it," Josie said, firmly. She winced then and wriggled her shoulders, taking a deep breath. "I can't breathe." Panic washed over her features and she reached a hand behind her in a desperate attempt to get to the zip. "I need to get it off."

Stunned, no one reacted immediately.

"Get it off me!" Josie said, her voice high-pitched.

Polly appeared and quickly unzipped the back. Josie's eyes shone with tears as she held the dress on and shuffled back to the fitting room, leaving the rest of them exchanging puzzled glances.

"Are you okay?" Emily asked, poking her head into the changing room.

"I'm fine." Josie smiled tightly. "It was a bit stifling. Can you show me some more?"

Polly arrived with a dress in her arms. "What

about this?" she asked.

"That's nice."

"This one's gorgeous," Amber said from the other side of the shop.

Josie stepped out to look. "I'll try them both."

She spent the next hour trying on dresses while the rest of them cooed around her. Tara made good progress on the bottle of champagne.

"Do you think she's okay?" Emily whispered to Tara while Amber helped Josie into another dress.

"She's definitely lacking some enthusiasm," Tara agreed.

That was exactly right. Josie didn't seem the least bit excited – it was as though the shopping trip was a chore that she wanted to get over and done with.

"You don't think she's got cold feet?"

Tara shook her head. "No way."

"You're right. She just seems so . . ." Emily struggled to find the right word.

"Depressed?" Tara suggested.

Emily's brow furrowed, but she quickly flicked a smile on when Josie made her way out of the fitting room in a classic A-line dress in ivory. It was strapless with a sweetheart neckline and a delicate lace overlay on the bodice. The full skirt flowed from her waist to the ground. She looked like a princess.

Emily joined Josie and Amber in front of the mirror. Tears filled her eyes. "I love it."

"Me too." Josie turned to inspect it from every angle. "This is the one."

"It's perfect," Tara said.

Nodding to herself in the mirror, Josie suddenly bit down on her lip and her chin began to wobble.

Emily put a hand on Josie's elbow. "Are you all right?"

"Yes." She turned to Emily just as the tears spilled down her cheek. "It's all bit emotional."

"I want to give you a hug," Emily said. "But I'm scared I'll crumple your dress."

"I'm fine." Josie swiped at the tears and forced a smile. "Did you see anything you liked?"

She'd told Emily to have a look round for a bridesmaid dress but hadn't give her any direction about what to look for.

"I saw a lovely one but you didn't even tell me what colour scheme you want."

"Show me," Josie said, picking up the bottom of her dress to follow Emily.

"If you don't like it just say . . ." She held up the pastel pink dress. It was simple but elegant – strapless with a fitted bodice, it flowed gently from the waist to the calf.

"I love it," Josie said. "Try it on."

Emily beamed and hurried to the fitting room. When she came out again, she stood in front of the mirror beside Josie. The dress fitted perfectly and was a flattering cut.

"How did you find the perfect dress first time?" Josie asked, grinning.

"It is perfect, isn't it?"

Amber squealed. "You both look amazing."

"Is the colour really okay?" Emily asked.

"Yes," Josie said. "We can go a shade darker for the men's ties so it's nearer maroon than pink."

She looked to Tara. "That would work, wouldn't it?"

"Definitely."

"Are you really going to do your whole colour scheme around my dress?" Emily asked, smiling.

"Yes!"

"Are you sure you didn't have anything else in mind?"

"I just wanted you to choose. And I love it."

"I'm going to hug you now." Emily had tears in her eyes as she embraced Josie.

"I thought this was an all-day event," Tara said, finishing her glass of fizz. "I suppose we'll have to hit up the pub instead!"

Chapter 17

In the end, they went back to Josie's place and ordered pizzas. Amber went home but arranged to meet up with them in the evening.

She was already at the bar when they arrived. Sam had joined them for pizza and then went with them to the pub. He went to play pool almost as soon as they'd got drinks. It seemed to be his usual routine.

Once again, Emily was surprised by the number of people in the pub. It wasn't packed by any means, but it was such a small village and the pub was so unassuming. From the outside you wouldn't imagine there'd ever be more than a handful of customers.

They were just about to find a table when a middle-aged woman at the bar leaned over to Josie.

"Are you on orange juice again?" she asked. "What's going on with you? You're not pregnant already are you? Get the wedding out of the way first!" Her laugh came out part cackle. She seemed to think she was hilarious.

Josie's face fell and her gaze moved quickly to the floor.

"Shut up, Belinda!" Tara snapped. "Come on." She ushered Josie to a table at the back of the pub. Emily and Amber followed.

"She's such a nightmare," Tara said, taking a

seat. "Bigmouth Belinda! I know I can be a bit tactless but she's unbelievable. Asking if you're pregnant." She clicked her tongue with a quick shake of the head. "How rude."

Silence fell around them and Josie nervously took a sip of her orange juice.

"It's pretty funny, though," Tara said, "that you can't go a few weeks without alcohol without people assuming you're pregnant."

"I'm not pregnant," Josie said quietly, pushing a wayward strand of hair behind her ear.

Tara gulped her wine and the atmosphere was uncomfortable. It would be easier if Josie just admitted she was pregnant. If she was. Emily was fairly sure she was.

"Can you all stop looking at me?" Josie took a deep breath. "You're almost as bad as Belinda. I already told you I'm not pregnant."

"Hmm." Tara didn't hide her scepticism. "Okay."

"Oh my God," Josie snapped. Her gaze locked on Tara. "I'm not pregnant."

Emily put a hand on her arm. "Are you okay?"

"I'm fine. I'm just not pregnant." Her chin quivered and tears pooled in her eyes.

"Sorry," Tara said quickly, her features full of concern. "What's wrong?"

Emily noticed the look of sympathy on Amber's face as though she'd figured out what Josie was going to say before she said it.

"I'm not pregnant." Josie's voice was choked with emotion and fat teardrops spilled down her cheeks. "I was. And now I'm not."

Tara bit on her lip. "Josie . . . I'm so sorry."

Josie stood and took off quickly across the pub. Emily chased after her. She caught up with her on a bench outside the pub. Her head was buried in her hands and her shoulders jerked as she cried.

"I'm so sorry." Emily wrapped her arms around her and began to cry herself. "Why didn't you tell me?"

"I don't know." Her words were muffled. "I wasn't even very far along. I'd just known for a few weeks when I lost it." She broke down in more sobs. "I feel like I shouldn't be so upset."

"Of course you're upset." Emily squeezed her shoulders. "I wish you'd told me."

The door to the pub opened and a concerned-looking Sam stepped out. "You okay?"

Josie sat up straighter and took a deep breath. "I'm fine." She pushed her hair back off her face and forced a smile.

He cocked his head to one side. "Are you sure? Shall we go home?"

"I'm just going to talk to Emily for a bit," she said with a sniff.

"Okay." He flashed a crooked smile. "Let me know when you want to leave."

The door swung shut behind him. "He's been so sweet," Josie said. "I'm not sure he knows what to do with me, though." She laughed without humour and more tears welled in her eyes. "I'm so sad all the time. I can't help it. I'm supposed to be excited about the wedding, but I just can't bring myself to care very much."

Emily couldn't find any words. She felt so

awful for Josie.

When the pub door opened again, Tara appeared. She looked absolutely distraught. "I'm sorry." Her voice came out a croak when she crouched in front of Josie. "I'm a horrible, insensitive person." Tara's face crumpled and her already damp cheeks were flooded with more tears. "I'm so sorry."

Josie shuffled along to make room for her on the bench. "It's okay."

"It's not," Tara said firmly. "I'm a horrible friend."

"You didn't know." Josie managed a small smile. "And to be fair, if you stopped drinking, I'd assume you were pregnant too."

Tara smiled sadly as Amber came and sat beside them, leaning over Tara to squeeze Josie's hand. "Are you okay?"

"I feel stupid now." Josie dabbed at her eyes with her sleeve. "I've not been drinking because I knew it'd make me an emotional wreck but I'm blubbing away anyway. Always the drama queen, aren't I?"

"No." Amber shook her head. "You're not being dramatic. Of course you're upset. That's normal."

"Now I can't stop crying," Josie said. "Everything just seemed so perfect. It wasn't planned but we were so happy about it. I'd just taken a test on the day Sam proposed. I was going to tell him as soon as he got home from work, but he surprised me by showing up at the kennels and asking me to marry him." She paused, taking a tissue from Amber and wiping her eyes. "I thought he must have been home and found the test, but he swore he had no idea and it was a coincidence."

They smiled sympathetically and waited for her to go on.

"So we planned the wedding for before the baby . . ." She swallowed hard as she battled her emotions. "When I was trying on dresses today all I could think was how thin I look. I thought I was going to have a big bump for the wedding. I must be the only bride wishing they weren't so slim on their wedding day."

"You should have said something," Amber said. "You don't need to go through all this alone."

"Sam's been amazing," she said. "But I feel so guilty too. He was so excited."

"Don't feel guilty," Amber said. "It's not your fault."

"I know that really. It's hard, though – it was my body that failed."

"You couldn't do anything," Amber said.

Josie nodded, then blew her nose. "I'm sorry. I feel stupid getting so upset. But I spent those few weeks thinking we were going to have a baby, and it's amazing how much you can plan in a few weeks. I was already thinking about how to decorate their room, and how I could take them to work with me and it would be so lovely for them growing up around the kennels. I even imagined them playing with Lizzie's girls." She stopped and took a deep breath. "I was so wrapped up in it all, I didn't think anything could happen . . . But I keep thinking some people have much worse to deal with . . ."

"It's normal to be upset," Amber said. "And it doesn't matter how many weeks you were or what anyone else is going through – you lost your baby and you're grieving. You shouldn't apologise for that."

Emily was thankful Amber was there. She seemed to know the right thing to say, whereas Emily couldn't think of anything at all to make Josie feel better. And she really wanted her to feel better. An image of how upset she looked trying on dresses that afternoon made tears well in Emily's eyes.

"What about the wedding?" she said quietly. "I'm sure if you don't feel up to it you could postpone it."

"No." Josie sat up straighter. "We talked about that but we want to go ahead with it. I want to marry Sam and I don't want to put it off."

"Okay," Emily said. "But you just need to tell us whatever you want us to help with. We could take over all the organising if you want . . ."

Josie smiled and the colour came back to her cheeks. "Thanks. It gives me something to focus on though. Besides, everything seems to be under control."

"I wish you'd told us sooner," Tara said, draping an arm around Josie's shoulder and touching her forehead to hers. "We should've been looking after you."

"I didn't want to talk about it."

"You didn't need to," Tara said. "We would've just sat and cried with you."

They huddled together on the bench and sat in silence for a few minutes. One of the streetlights was broken and let out a quiet buzzing noise as it flickered on and off.

Josie gazed at it for a moment and then turned to Tara with a hint of smile. "Are you dying to make a joke about the village flasher?"

"It's killing me," Tara said, chuckling and wiping away tears. "I know I've made it before, but it's a great joke."

The tension was broken and they all seemed to relax a little.

"Sorry for ruining the evening." Josie stood and beckoned to Sam through the pub window.

"You didn't at all," Amber said, giving her a big hug. Tara squeezed her tightly too.

When Sam came outside, they said goodbye to Tara and Amber, and Emily linked arms with Josie as they set off home. She was emotionally drained when she finally crawled into bed that night.

When her phone rang she was almost tempted not to answer. She wanted to tell Jack all about the events of the day, but it didn't seem appropriate in a phone call.

"What's wrong?" Jack asked when her voice came out strangled with emotion. She felt so sorry for Josie and annoyed with herself for not being more supportive sooner. It had been obvious something was wrong.

"Nothing," she said, sniffing. "I'm okay. Just had a weird day. I'll fill you in when I get home."

"Do you need me to drive down there and give you a hug?" he asked mock-serious.

She couldn't help but giggle. "I've got your car!"

"That's true," he said. "Otherwise I'd be on my way already."

She grinned into the phone and idly fingered the pendant on her necklace. He was joking around, but she had the feeling that he really would drive all that way if he thought she needed him.

"I love you," she said.

"I love you too. And I'm really bored without you here."

"What have you been doing?" she asked.

A feeling of contentment washed over her as she listened to him tell her about his day working with his uncle at the Boathouse.

They chatted for a long time, but she didn't mention anything about what was going on with Josie. She'd tell him later. For now, she felt better hearing his voice and knowing he was just at the other end of the phone.

Chapter 18

Sunday with Josie and Sam was wonderfully relaxed. They went to Annette's place for a lunch of roast chicken and all the trimmings. It was delicious and Emily could see why they liked to eat there. Then they played with dogs and walked them over the lovely picturesque countryside.

Josie talked to Emily a little more about the miscarriage and how she'd been feeling. It was so hard to know what to say, and Emily felt so useless. She hoped that listening was enough, and Josie would feel a bit better for talking about it.

They were having a quiet evening in front of the TV when Jack called. Emily was sitting in the armchair and Josie had fallen asleep on the couch with her feet in Sam's lap.

"You're early for your goodnight phone call," she said quietly, smiling into the phone. "Can I call you back when I'm snuggled up in bed?"

"Yes." He sounded cheerful. "Talk to you later."

"He must be missing you," Sam remarked.

"I hope so."

"He was saying you guys are moving in together soon."

Emily tensed. She still had to tell Jack that she wanted to wait a while. It would definitely be an uncomfortable conversation. He wouldn't be at all concerned about the money, and she wasn't sure how to explain that it was an issue for her even if it wasn't for him. She told herself she was working herself up over nothing. Maybe he'd be fine with it.

"Yes. That's the plan," she said to Sam. "I suppose it's about time I move out of my mum's place."

"Josie said you and your mum are really close."

"We are." She couldn't help but smile. She and her mum had a great relationship. "We're good friends."

"She'll miss you then."

"Yeah. Luckily Jack's place is close by." She glanced at Josie, fast asleep. "I think I might head up to bed and call him back . . ." Really she just wanted to avoid any more talk of moving in with Jack.

She'd half thought that if she didn't mention it, it might take a while for the subject to come up again, but if Jack had even talked to Sam about it, she guessed it would come up sooner rather than later. After wishing Sam goodnight she went up and got her pyjamas on and slipped into bed to call Jack.

She was missing him and it was lovely to hear his voice. He was his usual jokey self as he asked about her day and told her about his morning helping Clive at the boathouse. Then his voice turned strangely serious.

"I was talking to my mum this afternoon." He paused. "Her car broke down again. It'll be in the garage for a few days."

"That's annoying," she said, trying to figure out why he sounded so nervous. "Is she okay?"

"A bit stressed," he said hesitantly. "I was thinking of giving her the money for the car repairs. Money's a bit tight for her."

Emily wasn't sure what she was supposed to say. It sounded like he was asking permission.

"I'm sure she'll appreciate it," she said.

"Yes."

"What's wrong?" she asked.

"It'll mean I need to keep doing extra work for Clive at the weekends. And I was hoping to take some weekends off to spend with you over the summer."

"I can come and hang out at the Boathouse." It was one of her favourite places so it wasn't exactly a hardship. "It'll be fun."

"Thank you." He sounded relieved. "I better let you get to sleep. I can't wait to see you tomorrow."

"I can't wait to see you." She hugged the phone even after they'd ended the call.

He was so generous, always putting others before himself. Of course he'd help his mum if he could. It was hard not to feel sorry for him, though. Seemingly, all the women in his life were a financial burden. Emily was furious with herself. If she hadn't been so relaxed about money recently, she'd be able to move in and help him with the rent so he wouldn't have to work so many hours.

She hated the thought of being yet another burden to him.

***

It was an emotional goodbye the next morning. Emily promised to be in touch more and made Josie promise to call if she needed anything or simply wanted to talk.

"I'll see you at the christening, won't I?" Josie said. "That's only a few weeks away."

"Are you sure it's okay for us to come? I didn't know if Lizzie was just being polite . . ."

"I spoke to her about it. She said she's been meaning to get in touch with you but she's not very organised these days. You'll probably get an email from her."

"Okay." Emily smiled. "I'll wait until I hear from her and then see if I can convince Jack to come."

"He'll come," Josie said confidently. "You have him wrapped around your little finger – he'll do anything you ask!"

"I'm not so sure about that," Emily said. "But I hope he'll come."

"Me too. It'll be fun."

"I can't wait to see Hope Cove." Emily put her arms around Josie and hugged her tightly. "And in the meantime, call me any time, okay?"

Josie promised she would and thanked her for coming before waving her off.

As she drove through the village, Emily decided she'd call at the bookshop and see if Tara was there for a quick chat. It would be good to talk to someone about the events of the weekend. Her thoughts were all a bit jumbled.

When she arrived in Newton Abbot she found a parking spot right in front of the bookshop. It wasn't open yet but Emily could see Tara inside and knocked on the window. She smiled when she saw her and came to let her in.

"I thought you'd be on your way back to Oxford by now."

"I am," Emily said, walking inside. She loved the smell of the bright and airy bookshop and was mesmerised by the beautifully displayed books. "I just wanted to come and say thank you again."

"You're very welcome. Have you got time for a coffee?"

"That would be great. If I'm not disturbing you?"

"Not at all. I was just going to have one myself."

"Are you on your own?" She glanced around as they reached the coffee machine at the back of the shop.

"Yeah. James will be in a bit later. My turn to open today. I actually enjoy opening up. It's lovely and peaceful in the morning."

"I'm quite envious," Emily said. "It's such a lovely working environment."

"I like it," Tara agreed. Her features turned serious. "How's Josie?"

"I'm not sure. I think it probably did her good talking everything through. I can't believe she kept it to herself."

"I couldn't stop thinking about her yesterday," Tara said. "And I feel so awful. All this time I've been making stupid comments and winding her up about not drinking."

"You couldn't have known."

"I knew something was off with her, though." She passed Emily a steaming mug of coffee and gestured to the beanbags in the kids' corner. "I'm sure if I'd thought about it more I could've guessed."

"Hindsight's great," Emily said. She put her coffee on the floor while she got comfy in the bright orange beanbag. "This is a nice way to start the week."

"Not bad at all," Tara agreed. "Josie and Amber will probably be in to see me later this morning too. I like Mondays."

"It's amazing to have a job you enjoy so much," Emily said. "And great that you have such a good boss. James seems lovely."

"He is," Tara said with a crooked smile.

Emily's curiosity got the better of her. "Is it true what Josie says about him being in love with you?"

"No," Tara said firmly. For a moment she seemed lost in thought, then she bit her lip and concentrated on her coffee. "Sometimes Josie gets things completely back to front."

"Oh." It took a moment for Emily to fully digest the comment. "Oh," she said again, with understanding.

"Yeah. It's a little awkward."

"Wow. That must be . . ."

"Torture?" Tara blew lightly on her coffee before taking a sip. "Yes. Every day is torture."

Emily was surprised by the revelation and even more intrigued by the dynamic between them than before. "So you won't date him because he's your boss?"

"I did date him. Not for very long. I tried to resist for a long time but . . ." She sighed and wriggled into the beanbag. "It's a long story. I should have stuck to my guns and not dated him in the first place. I knew it would never work."

"I don't understand why it didn't work if you're in love with him. I didn't meet him for long but it seemed as though he likes you too."

"If I tell you the whole story you'll think I'm a complete weirdo." Tara's tone was light but her eyes were veiled in sadness.

"I think you have to tell me now. I can't imagine I'll think you're weird."

Tara pursed her lips and seemed torn as to whether or not to say anything more. She took another sip of her coffee before she spoke. "I don't want kids."

"Okay," Emily said slowly.

"When I mention this to Amber she pats me on the arm and tells me I'll change my mind one day. When I meet the right man, apparently." She paused, staring into her cup. "I've never wanted kids and I'm absolutely sure I never will. No one understands that. I guess I'm wired wrong or something."

Emily was lost for words, as she so often was. If only she was one of those people who always knew the right thing to say. Honestly, she struggled to get her head around the idea of never wanting children. She often thought about having kids with Jack. Not that she was in any rush, but kids were definitely in her plan – somewhere on the horizon. It felt more like instinct than anything, and she couldn't imagine not having any desire to have children.

"I told you you'd think I'm weird," Tara said.

"I don't think that," she replied. "I think it must

be really hard, though." They sat in silence for a moment. "So James wants kids and you don't? That's why you're not together?"

Tara frowned. "That's the short version."

"And the long version?"

She puffed out a humourless laugh. "He said he loved me and wanted to be with me, and if it meant never having kids he was okay with that . . ." She chewed on her lip as tears pooled in her eyes. Her head tilted slightly. "But I wasn't okay with it. I love him. I can't ask him to not have children for me."

"But you weren't asking, were you?"

"No. But I knew he'd end up resenting me. Or he'd spend the next ten years hoping I'd change my mind. So I ended it. I don't know why I agreed to date him in the first place."

"So now you work together and pretend everything is fine?"

"Oh, no." She raised an amused eyebrow. "You wanted the long version didn't you? I'm not finished yet!"

"What happened?"

"It was very heated when I ended things. It was horrible between us. He was angry. After a few weeks of me stubbornly telling him it would never work, he got back together with his ex-girlfriend. I thought he was just trying to get back at me or make me jealous . . ."

"But?"

"But now they're engaged." Her voice was raw with emotion and tears streamed in a steady flow down her cheeks. "And the icing on the cake . . . she's pregnant."

"Oh my God." Emily's heart broke for her. "I'm so sorry."

"Sometimes I think I should have said I'd have a kid. Then I could be with him. I mean it's only eighteen years before the child moves out anyway!" She chuckled through her tears.

It took a moment for Tara to wipe her tears and get herself under control. Emily felt terrible for her.

"How on earth do you manage to work with him? Don't you want to leave?"

"I've had my letter of resignation in my handbag for a while now." She managed a sad smile. "I can't bring myself to actually go through with it. If I leave I'd have no reason to ever see him again. I *couldn't* ever see him again . . . he's getting married and he'll have his little family. This way I get to spend every day with the man I love."

Emily grimaced as she felt an overwhelming sorrow for Tara. How on earth could she live like that? It reminded Emily of when she was in love with Jack and thought she could never be with him. But she got as far away from him as possible in an attempt to move on. How could Tara see James every day, knowing she could never be with him?

"I know," Tara said as though she could read minds. "I'm torturing myself. Part of me knows I should leave. I keep thinking he might ask me to. But he just treats me like an employee now. He's polite and kind. He stopped flirting with me so it doesn't feel particularly inappropriate. We don't talk about our personal lives. It's all very professional."

"But how could he just go back to his ex?" Emily was stunned by the conversation.

"I've thought about that a lot. My only conclusion is that he was never really in love with me."

"I don't believe that. Not if he was ready to give up on having kids for you."

Tara wiped at her eyes and took a deep breath. She stood and took Emily's empty mug from her. "There's not much point dwelling on it. He's getting married and starting a family and I will be forever on my own." She flashed an awkward grin.

"Don't say that." Emily followed her to the counter.

"Please don't try and tell me everything will work out okay in the end. It's not that kind of situation."

Emily looked sheepish. She always believed everything would work out okay. Not necessarily exactly how you wanted it, but things usually worked out somehow. "You don't know what's going to happen in the future," she finally said. "But I know you won't always feel like this."

"I really hope you're right about that." Tara smiled. "Sorry to dump all this on you."

"I don't mind. If you ever need someone to talk to, you can always give me a call."

"Thank you." She let out a long breath. "Josie and Amber don't know any of it. I didn't even tell them when I was dating him."

"I won't say anything," Emily promised. "It might be easier if they knew though. Josie would be mortified about teasing you if she knew the truth."

"I know. I feel bad for not telling them. It seems easier to shut off from it when no one knows about it. And sometimes teasing is easier to handle than sympathy." She glanced at her watch. "Anyway, enough of that. It's almost time to open up."

"I'll get out of your way. Thanks again for organising the book launch. I really do appreciate it. And I mean what I said . . . If you need someone to talk to just give me a call."

They hugged each other at the door.

Emily couldn't stop thinking about Tara and Josie the whole drive home.

Suddenly she felt overwhelmingly thankful for all the good things in her life. And she was desperate to get back to Jack.

Chapter 19

Emily was emotionally drained when she arrived home. She contemplated getting her laptop out to do some work on the next book, but she had the feeling all she would do was stare at the screen. Instead she made a conscious decision to keep the laptop firmly packed away. She wasn't even going to think about writing.

She'd offered to pick Jack up from work, but he'd organised a lift with a colleague so she arranged to meet him at his place that evening. In the end she went over early and cooked a shepherd's pie. It was his favourite and she knew he'd appreciate the effort. Even though he'd most likely joke that it wasn't as good as his mum's.

It was in the oven when he arrived home, and the delicious aroma filled the apartment. Emily felt very domesticated as Jack grinned and wrapped her in a big hug before flopping onto the couch. He looked exhausted.

"How was the weekend?" he asked as she snuggled beside him.

"Pretty eventful," she said.

"Really? How was the book party?"

"It was great." Although it felt like a long time ago what with everything else that had happened. "I'm really happy I did it. And Tara's lovely when you get to know her."

"That's good. How's Josie?"

She moved her head from his shoulder. "Not so good really."

Jack looked concerned as she filled him in on everything. "Poor Josie." He rubbed at the stubble on his jaw. "Do you think I should call her?"

Emily raised her eyebrows. Of course he shouldn't call her. It was completely inappropriate. But all she could do was stare at him.

"I'll give her a quick call," he said. "Check she's okay."

Emily sat in a daze for a moment as he walked towards the bedroom. "Jack . . ."

He was in the doorway, head down as he scrolled through his phone. "Mmm?" He didn't look up so he didn't see the tears in Emily's eyes.

"I don't think you should call her." Maybe she should see his concern as sweet, but she couldn't. All she could see was a guy who clearly had feelings for his ex.

His gaze met hers. The intensity made her think he was annoyed with her. Then he looked toward the kitchen. "Is something burning?"

Swearing under her breath, she ran to the kitchen. Smoke billowed out as she opened the oven door. With a tea towel, she took the dish out of the oven. Heat burned through her thumb and she instinctively let the dish go. It landed with a crash at her feet, and she swore some more and stuck her thumb in her mouth.

"Are you okay?" Jack led her to the sink and ran the water cold before sticking her hand under it.

"Yes." More tears came as she looked at the mess on the floor. "I made you shepherd's pie. It's ruined."

"It doesn't matter." He moved to the freezer and wrapped some ice in a clean tea towel. "Are you okay?" he asked again as he put the ice on her thumb.

"Yeah." She sniffed. It wasn't the pain that was upsetting her. Could he really not see it was inappropriate to call Josie? Or was she being overly sensitive? They were still friends, after all. If he had feelings for Josie they were purely platonic. Should she really be upset about him calling her? She was anyway, whether she should be or not.

"Go and sit down," Jack said. "I'll clean up."

She didn't argue. On the couch, she cradled her thumb and forced herself to think clearly. It was completely irrational of her to be jealous of Jack's relationship with Josie. She'd known what she was getting into when she got together with him. And it really wasn't a problem if he was in touch with Josie now and again.

"What's going on?" Jack asked when he joined her five minutes later.

"Nothing."

"You're upset because I was going to call Josie?"

There didn't seem much point denying it. "She's your ex-girlfriend. Of course I'm not keen on you disappearing off into our bedroom to call her."

"You know it's not like that. She might be my ex, but she's also my friend."

"I realise that, but can you think about it

objectively? It's not your job to comfort her. How do you think Sam will feel if you start calling to see how she is? You're going to cause problems in their relationship, and I don't know how you can't see that."

He pushed his head back into the couch. "And in our relationship."

"I'm not worried about our relationship." That wasn't even close to the truth. "But I hate how you look at me like I'm being neurotic and jealous when you want to call your ex-girlfriend."

"I don't think you're neurotic. But sometimes I have the feeling that you don't trust me."

"Of course I trust you, but it doesn't mean I'm happy with you calling other women. I don't like it. Maybe it's me being insecure, but I don't think it's okay. Would you really be fine with it if my ex was calling me for chats?"

"No." He rubbed the back of his neck. "Am I an idiot?"

She chuckled. "Yep."

"I love you so much." He reached for her good hand. "You don't think I have feelings for Josie?"

"No." She paused. "At least not when I'm thinking rationally. If I'm honest, I'm a bit insecure about the situation. But that's my problem. You shouldn't have to keep reassuring me."

He put his arm around her and pulled her close. "I can spend forever reassuring you if that's what you need."

"Hopefully not." She smiled as she kissed him. "I ruined dinner," she said as she pulled away.

"Yeah, you did. Is your hand okay?"

"Yes." Putting aside the ice, she inspected her red thumb and sighed. "I broke that nice dish too."

"It's amazing I put up with you at all, really!"

She gave him a friendly shove before he got his phone out to order a takeaway.

Chapter 20

Emily knew it wouldn't be long before the subject of moving in with Jack came up. They'd been together three months and that's when they'd agreed they would move in together. She'd decided to be honest with him about her financial situation but was dreading the conversation.

It turned out she didn't have to wait long for him to bring it up. They'd been out for dinner on the Wednesday after Emily got back from visiting Josie. Jack had insisted on taking her out even though she'd tried to persuade him they could eat at his place. She was trying to be careful with money and hated him paying for everything.

"Are you coming back to mine?" he asked when they got into his car after the delicious Chinese meal.

"No. I should go back to my mum's tonight."

"Why?"

"Because I've stayed at yours the last two nights. Mum might report me missing soon."

His lips curled upwards. "You could just move in with me. Then she wouldn't have to wonder where you are."

"Soon." She nodded, then diverted her gaze to the steering wheel, hoping he might get the hint and start the engine to drive her home.

"I thought you were going to move in after three months?"

"Yes." She smiled nervously. "I meant approximately three months. I didn't think we were planning things to the day . . . I'll move in soon."

"Right." He reached for the key in the ignition. Pausing, he shifted in his seat so he was looking squarely at her. "I thought we were being pretty literal with the three-month plan. And the proposal. I really thought we were going to get engaged on a specific day. Did I misunderstand?"

"Well, no," she said flustered. If she wasn't careful she was going to lose out on the romantic proposal. Okay, some people might say it wasn't romantic to have everything planned out, but she thought it would make a great story. "I was being specific about the proposal. A year to the day."

"Right," he said slowly. "But moving in together is flexible?" He squinted in confusion.

"The thing is . . ." She took a deep breath. "I have a bit of a cash flow situation so I was thinking I'd stay at my mum's a little longer."

His eyebrows knitted together. "I don't understand."

"I can't afford to pay you any rent at the moment, so I want to wait a while."

"It doesn't matter if you can't pay me any rent . . ."

"I knew you'd say that." She felt panicked and was talking fast. "That's why I was avoiding the subject. But I really feel uncomfortable about you paying for everything."

"But I honestly don't mind."

"I mind," she said wearily. Reaching for his hand, she looked pleadingly at him. "Please can we just keep things as they are? Just for a month or two."

He smiled sadly and moved in to kiss her. "Of course. If that's what you want."

"It is." She stroked his cheek and kissed him again. The conversation hadn't been anywhere near as painful as she expected. "Thank you."

Jack pulled his seatbelt round him and switched on the ignition. It occurred to her as they drove that maybe the conversation hadn't really gone as smoothly as she thought. At least judging by the awkward silence that had enveloped them.

"You do want to live with me, don't you?" Jack asked when they pulled up at her mum's house.

"Of course." She was slightly high-pitched, but she quickly leaned over and kissed him.

"Good." He smiled. "Say hi to your mum."

She smiled tightly as she stepped out of the car and turned to wave from the front door.

It was a relief to find her mum at home. She'd half expected her to be out at the gym or something. Emily really needed to talk.

"Jack asked me to move in with him," she said after a quick hello.

Her mum muted the TV. "It's not exactly big news. I'm fairly sure he asked you months ago."

"I know but I told him I can't because I don't have any money . . ."

"What did he say?"

"He told me the money doesn't matter."

"Fairly predictable." She sat up straighter. "So

you're moving in with him?"

"No. I said I want to wait a while."

"And he's okay with that?"

"He said so. But then he was acting a bit strange. It felt awkward."

"Can't you just move in with him? You do want to live with him, don't you?"

"Yes." Her voice lacked conviction and her mum gave her a look that told her to keep talking. "I'm not sure if it's just the money situation that bothers me. There's the Josie situation too." She chewed on her thumbnail. "You know, he wanted to call her the other day for a chat. He didn't realise it was inappropriate."

"Did you tell him?"

"Yes."

"And?"

"And he didn't call her."

Her mum looked a little smug. "You see what happens when you're honest about things?"

"You're not going to help me with this situation are you?"

"I am helping. I'm telling you to be honest with him."

"So I should tell him I'm a crazy jealous person and I'm uncomfortable moving into the apartment where he used to live with Josie?"

She shrugged. "Yeah."

Emily frowned and went over to kiss her mum's cheek. "I'll think about it. I'm going up to bed."

***

That night she could hardly sleep. Everything felt a

bit of a mess. She'd spent so long thinking that if she could be with Jack, life would be perfect, but now she was with him and life was more complicated than ever.

When he called her the following afternoon she was tired and grumpy.

"I finish work in an hour," he told her. "Do you want to come to my mum's for dinner? I can pick you up on the way."

"I said I'd have dinner with my mum." She wasn't sure why she'd said that. Her mum wouldn't care either way. She just felt like getting lost in her writing for the evening and not worrying about real life.

"Okay," he said, coolly.

"What's wrong?"

"Nothing. I was just hoping to see you tonight."

"You saw me the last three nights," she pointed out, sounding more harsh than she intended.

There was silence down the line.

"I didn't mean . . ." She had no idea what she meant, and why she was being so frosty with him.

"It's okay," he said. "I've got to get back to work. I'll talk to you tomorrow?"

"Yeah. Say hi to your mum."

He ended the call abruptly after a curt goodbye and she was left feeling awful. She really hadn't intended to be so abrupt with him.

Feeling entirely unsettled, she suffered another sleepless night. When Jack didn't call her the next day she began to panic. Usually, he'd message or call her throughout the day when he had a spare few minutes at work.

"Are you out with Jack tonight?" her mum asked, coming up to Emily's bedroom when she came home from work.

"I don't know. He hasn't called. I think he's annoyed with me."

"Why don't you call him?"

"Because I think he's annoyed with me."

Her mum shook her head. "For a rational person you do a good impression of someone completely unbalanced."

"I only want to postpone moving in with him. Why is that such a big deal?"

"It's not," her mum said with a sigh. "The big deal is you not being honest with him about why."

"I told him about the money situation."

"But that's only half of it."

"I can't tell him the rest. He'll think I'm crazy."

"You are crazy," her mum said dryly.

"Are you going out?" Emily asked as her mum moved to the landing.

"Yeah. I'm meeting the girls from work for dinner and drinks." She was in her bedroom when she called out to Emily. "Just call Jack!"

Emily picked up her phone. After a moment of staring at it, she put it down again and went back to her writing. At least the book was going well. Another couple of hours passed with her lost in the lives of her fictional characters.

It was getting late when she checked the time. Her phone was right beside her on the desk, but she glanced at the screen as though she might somehow have missed Jack's call. Why hadn't he called her? Taking her phone over to the bed, she finally called him. It took him a few rings to answer and then it was hard to hear him.

"Where are you?" she asked.

"In the Fox and Greyhound. Having a few drinks with Lee and the lads."

"You could have told me."

There was a short pause before he spoke. "We didn't have anything planned did we?"

"No. Are you annoyed with me?"

"No. Lee invited me out and I haven't been out with them in ages."

"That's fine."

"Is it? Because now you sound annoyed with me and I feel like I can't win."

"What's that supposed to mean?"

"We were supposed to move in together but now you don't want to. You think I'm being too intense so I back off, and now you're annoyed with me for going out with my friends without asking your permission?"

"I didn't say you need my permission. And when did I say you're being too intense?"

"Hmm . . ." His tone was part mocking, part angry. "Maybe yesterday when you told me seeing me three nights in a row was your limit."

"I did not say that," she insisted. "Are you drunk?"

"I really wanted a stress-free night," he said wearily.

"Well I'm very sorry to have ruined that for you. Go and have fun! Don't worry about me." She pressed end and then summoned a lot of willpower to stop herself from throwing the phone at the wall.

Chapter 21

Emily barely slept again and wasn't quite sure how she would manage the two tours she was taking round the castle that afternoon.

It was a relief when Jack called the next morning. He sounded as though he was moving around as he spoke. "I just woke up. I said I'd help Clive at the Boathouse today." There was a short pause. "Sorry about last night."

"I've got two tour groups booked in this afternoon." It was too early to get into any deep conversations so she decided to ignore the apology. "Do you want to meet after?"

"Yeah. Give me a call when you've finished. I'm not sure what time Clive needs me till. Depends how busy it is."

"The weather forecast is good," she said. "Sunny."

"I was hoping for rain so I can leave early."

"Hungover?" He definitely sounded weary.

"Very. Sorry, I've got to get organised and get to work."

"I'll see you later."

"Bye."

She was left holding the phone to her ear, wondering why he hadn't told her he loved her like he normally did.

Pulling herself together, she tried not to dwell on it and got showered and dressed for work. Thankfully she was so used to taking the tours now she could almost do it on auto-pilot. Both groups were American tourists who were engaged and interested in everything she said. It was always easier when people were enthusiastic. She made good tips too and was happy to have something to put towards her publishing costs. Book sales were also going well, so she was hopeful that her financial situation would improve soon.

The weather forecast turned out to be spot on for once, and it was a wonderfully warm, sunny day. When Emily finished at work, she didn't bother to call Jack but walked to the river instead. At Folly Bridge, she took the footpath along the pretty little stretch of the River Thames until she came to the Boathouse.

It was a while since she'd been there, and it brought back some wonderful memories of when she and Josie would visit Jack at work and spend all day lying in the sun. With a sigh, she wondered if she'd ever be able to go more than five minutes without a reminder that her boyfriend and her best friend used to be together.

The tables outside the cafe were mostly taken, and there were a few groups of people standing around eating ice creams. More people occupied the stretch of grass alongside the cafe. They basked in the warmth of the sun as Emily and Josie had so often done.

Inside the cafe, Emily squeezed past the queue

of people and slipped behind the counter to where Jack was manning the till.

"Hey!" He gave her a quick peck and then reached into the freezer and pulled out Cornettos for the woman waiting in line. He took her money before focusing on Emily again.

"I'm guessing you can't get away any time soon?" she asked.

"There's another waitress coming in soon. I can leave when she arrives."

"Great. I'll hang around then."

"Do you want anything? Coffee? Ice cream?"

"No, I'm fine thanks. I might have a wander along the river." She began to move away as a middle-aged man impatiently shouted his order to Jack. "Come and find me when you're done."

He smiled ruefully and went back to serving customers.

Emily didn't get very far in her walk along the river. Her favourite bench was surprisingly unoccupied so she took a seat. It was the bench she and Jack had been on when he'd asked her to move in with him. They'd only just got together and Emily had insisted they wait three months. At the time, he'd also said he was going to propose to her on that bench. She'd responded that he had to wait a year to propose.

The memory made her smile. It had been such a happy day, and she'd been so excited about her future with Jack. She still was, of course, but life wasn't always perfectly romantic like that day had been. There were money problems and ex-girlfriends to complicate matters.

A goose pecked in the long grass by the leg of the bench and Emily stamped her foot in an attempt to shoo it away. It didn't work. She turned her attention to the river in front of her. The slow-moving water glistened as the sunlight hit it. A few houseboats bobbed on the opposite bank. They were permanently moored there and were all very familiar to Emily. One in particular she loved – it was brightly coloured and adorned with hanging baskets and potted plants. Emily knew the owner by sight and would always wave and call out a greeting when she saw her.

It was a relaxing spot to sit and watch the world go by. The beautiful scenery was abuzz with life. Ducks and geese roamed freely. Cyclists and joggers hurried along the path, while others wandered slowly, taking their time to enjoy the surroundings.

It was half an hour later when Jack joined her. He was smiling as he approached her, and she felt a surge of butterflies in her stomach.

Standing, she pulled him into a tight hug.

He kissed the top of her head. "I love you."

"I love you too."

"Sorry about last night . . ."

"You're allowed to go out with your friends."

"I shouldn't be allowed." He slumped onto the bench beside her. "My head's killing me!"

She trailed her hand through his hair and leaned her head on his shoulder.

He pushed her hair behind her ear. "Everything's okay between us, isn't it?"

"Yes," she said hesitantly.

"But I should stop asking you about moving

in?"

"It's not that I don't want to live with you," she said slowly. "But I need to be able to pay my own way . . . I promise I'll move in as soon as I can pay you some rent."

"Okay. I'll stop mentioning it. I just got worried. I presumed I did something, or you're not sure you want to live with me."

"It's definitely not that."

He squeezed her hand as he kissed her. "Shall we go?"

"You look tired," she remarked as they stood.

"I'm not used to big nights out with the lads any more." He smiled lazily. "I much prefer staying home with you."

Chapter 22

With the subject of moving in dropped, Emily and Jack managed to get back to some sort of normality. Unfortunately, it only lasted a week.

Emily arrived at Jack's place on Friday afternoon. He wasn't home from work yet so she made a cup of tea and sat down to wait for him. When her phone rang with a call from Josie, she was pleased. She'd messaged Josie a couple of times during the week but hadn't actually spoken to her since she'd seen her a fortnight earlier.

"How are you?" she asked.

"Busy," Josie replied. "With work and the wedding, I'm constantly occupied. I think it's a good thing though."

"That's great." She definitely sounded more upbeat.

"Did you decide about the christening? Lizzie said she'd been in touch with you."

"Yeah, we've been emailing a bit. I think I'll come, but I've not had chance to speak to Jack about it." When they were only just back on an even keel, she was reluctant to rock the boat. She really wanted Jack to go too, but she wasn't sure how to broach the subject after he'd initially been so against the idea.

"You should definitely get Jack to come. I'm really looking forward to it. It'll be fun, all of us

169

being in Hope Cove together. You're going to love it. And the house Lizzie and Max bought is gorgeous."

"It all sounds amazing. I'll try and convince Jack."

"Are you living at his place now? I was thinking the other day, you said you were going to move in with him after three months. You've been together three months, haven't you?"

Emily's heart rate increased. There was something about Josie's voice that made her wary. It was hard to put her finger on it, but Emily had the feeling that it was more than just an off-hand remark. She almost sounded rehearsed.

"Technically, I'm still living at Mum's place," she replied slowly. "I spend a lot of time at Jack's, though."

"So are you going to move in with him?"

"Yeah. You know me, I like to take things slow."

Josie chuckled. "Yes. Not like me!" There was a pause as the laughter faded. "You guys are okay though? Everything's going well?"

The muscles in Emily's neck tensed and her shoulders hunched slightly. Josie was fishing for information.

"Yes. We're good. Why do you ask?"

"No reason." Considering Josie had once dreamed of being an actress, her acting skills were pretty poor. She sounded so far from casual it was almost funny. "I've been a bit self-involved recently and I realised everything's been about me and the wedding. I felt bad I've not really asked about you."

"Nothing new here. Everything's fine." Emily was sure she was a far better actress than Josie and her casual tone was perfectly convincing.

"Happy to hear it," Josie said. "And speaking of the wedding, I need your opinion . . . I was thinking of inviting James. Tara's boss. I feel like they need some sort of push to get them together—"

"No," Emily said forcefully.

"That was Sam's reaction too. He told me not to play matchmaker. But I think they'd make such a great couple."

"They work together," Emily said. "They see each other every day. If they wanted to date each other they would. I don't think they need you setting them up."

"I'd just really like to see Tara settled."

"She seems pretty settled to me," Emily said.

"I think I'm going to invite him."

"Do you know where he lives?"

"No. I thought I'd just give him the invitation when I see him."

"That's not my point. Do you know his phone number?"

"No," Josie replied hesitantly.

"If you don't know a person's phone number or where they live, you don't know them well enough to invite them to your wedding."

"What if I casually invite him to the evening do? Just mention it in passing when I see him?"

Emily sighed. When Josie had an idea it was hard to get her to let it go. Although she supposed it wasn't really an issue. James was getting married himself. There's no way he'd turn up and cause an issue with Tara.

"I guess that would be okay," she said. "If you really must. Tara won't like it though. Just to warn you."

"I told you she needs a little push in the right direction." Barking began in the background. "I'm at the barn. I need to feed the dogs before they turn on me! Let me know about the christening weekend."

Emily promised she would. The call left her feeling deflated. Apparently Jack hadn't dropped the moving in subject after all. He was just approaching it from a different angle. When he got home and kissed her cheek, she was tempted to ask him directly. It all felt exhausting, though. He'd said he wouldn't raise the subject with her again, and Emily supposed there was a chance that Josie's phone call was purely coincidental.

But much as she tried, she couldn't quite put the conversation out of her mind. It niggled at her while they ate and when they curled up on the couch together. Emily was reading while Jack watched TV with his legs draped across her lap. He seemed as though he'd probably fall asleep any minute, and Emily was all set to switch the TV off as soon as he did. The noise was annoying her.

Jack's phone buzzed on the coffee table, and he blinked as he read the message then tapped out a reply. Emily glanced at him occasionally as he continued to exchange messages.

"Is that Lee?" she asked when curiosity got the better of her. Jack wasn't usually one for messaging.

There was the briefest pause before he replied without looking at her. "Yeah"

It was a lie. She could tell straight away. His face gave it away even if it weren't for the fact that she knew Lee would never send more than a meme or message requiring a yes-no answer.

Emily tried to go back to her book, but she knew her mind was only going to whir into a frenzy if she didn't say something. When Jack finally pushed his phone back onto the coffee table, she put her book aside, balancing it on the arm of the couch.

She nudged him until he moved his legs off her.

"What's wrong?" he mumbled.

"It wasn't Lee, was it?"

He made a vague attempt at looking puzzled. "What?"

For a moment she stared at him, then shifted her focus to his phone. The silence was loaded as she waited for him to say something. Emily was almost certain he'd been messaging Josie. She just wasn't sure he was going to admit it. If he kept up with the lies, she'd walk out, and she really wasn't sure where that would leave them.

He lowered his head to his hands, rubbed at the bridge of his nose. "No," he said quietly. "It wasn't Lee."

"Was it Josie?"

He closed his eyes as he sighed. "It's not what you think?"

"Really?" she said bitterly. "Because I think you're messaging your ex-girlfriend while you're nice and cosy on the couch with me. Feel free to enlighten me if that's not the case."

"It's not like that."

"No. I'm sure it's all very innocent. That's why

you just told me it was Lee!"

"Because I knew you'd be upset."

"That's very perceptive of you."

She stood abruptly, not quite sure where she was going but needing to move.

"Where are you going?"

"I can't believe you're messaging Josie and lying to me about it."

He put a hand on her arm. "Just sit down and talk to me, please."

"So now you want to talk to me? Josie busy is she?"

He raked a hand through his hair. "I've been talking to Josie because you won't talk to me. I don't know what's going on with you and I thought Josie might have an idea . . ."

"There seems to be a bit of a theme here, because when you were with Josie you found it very easy to talk to me. But now you're with me . . ."

The hurt in his eyes made her stop in her tracks. He didn't say anything. After a moment, he walked over to the bedroom, closing the door softly behind him.

Emily dropped back onto the couch, hating herself. Why had she said that? She was angry with him for talking to Josie, but the anger was evaporating quickly. Suddenly she was terrified she was going to lose Jack and all she felt was sick. And she couldn't stand the way he'd looked so hurt.

The rational part of her brain knew he wouldn't do anything to hurt her. She knew there was nothing going on with him and Josie. But there would always be a part of her that was jealous of their bond. And there would always be a part of her that wondered if she really was Jack's first choice or if he was just making do because he couldn't have Josie.

When she pushed the bedroom door open a couple of minutes later, Jack was perched on the edge of the bed, bent over with his elbows on his knees, hands clasped together.

"Sorry," she said weakly.

"I'm not cheating on you," he said flatly.

Emily sat beside him, trying not to cry and hating how sad he looked.

"I called Josie a couple of days ago to ask her advice." He didn't look at her as he spoke. "She messaged me this evening to see how things were. That's all."

Emily puffed out a laugh. "That and the time she got you to offer to lend me your car . . ." Her voice was soft and not accusing. They may as well get everything out in the open.

He sighed. "That was nothing."

"It was nothing to you, but to me it was you and Josie keeping secrets from me. And now you're doing it again. I don't like it."

He nodded his understanding.

"What did you want her advice about?" she asked.

"You." Finally, he looked up at her. "I feel like I'm losing you and I don't know why." Tears glistened in his eyes just before he shifted his gaze away. "I thought Josie might know what was going on."

"Of course you're not losing me," she said with

a sniff. "Why would you think that?"

"I don't know what to think. One minute everything is fine and then suddenly you're distant. And if I mention you moving in, you freak out." He looked at her sadly. "I love you so much and I started to think maybe that's the problem – that I'm too intense and I'm scaring you away . . . But when I back off you also seem annoyed with me . . ."

"You're not scaring me away." Tears dripped down Emily's cheeks and she couldn't stop them. When she squeezed Jack's hand he didn't react, just waited for some sort of an explanation.

"I'm so jealous of you and Josie," she said. "I hate hearing anything about when you and her were together. And I realise that's my insecurities, but you secretly messaging her doesn't help."

"Okay. I get that. But it doesn't explain why you don't want to live with me."

"I do want to live with you."

He sat up straight. "Then why don't you?"

"I told you: I can't move in because I can't afford to pay you rent. I've hardly been working because I wanted to do more writing, and then I had all these costs for releasing the book . . ."

"I don't believe you," he said softly.

"You don't believe I'm skint?"

"I don't believe that's the real reason you won't move in with me."

She stared at him until he went on. "Come on, Em. I asked you to move in as my girlfriend not as a housemate to share costs. You knew I wouldn't care about the rent . . ."

"But I care." She sighed. "You're always

looking after everyone else. You're working extra so you can help your mum. And I think it's great that you do that for her. But I don't want you to have to pay for me too. It's not fair."

"I'll be paying the same as I already do." He looked genuinely puzzled. "It makes no difference."

"But it will be like it was with Josie . . ." She blurted the words out, surprising herself as much as Jack. "Josie didn't pay rent when she lived with you," she reminded him. "And it annoyed you. I don't want to be like that."

After a short silence he threw his arms up in the air. "I don't know how I'm supposed to argue with that. It was a totally different situation, but everything always seems to come back to Josie. You can't keep comparing the relationships." He stood and paced the room. "I don't know what to say. Don't move in." He shrugged. "Let me know when you can afford to pay me rent and maybe you can move in then."

"Jack," she said desperately. "Don't be like that."

"What am I supposed to do? Beg you to move in? I've been doing that for a while and it doesn't work. You said yourself, moving in together should be something exciting, not something we rush into. You're clearly not excited by the idea."

"I don't know what to say." She looked at him gravely. "Should I leave? Are you splitting up with me?"

His eyes were wide and sorrowful. "No." He shook his head and sat beside her again. "Of course not."

He wrapped an arm around her and kissed her forehead. "Sometimes I feel like I'm more invested in this relationship than you are. And it scares me."

"That's not true." She hated that he could ever think that. She loved him so much.

"If you'd talk to me, instead of shutting me out, I wouldn't need to ask Josie what's going on."

"Okay," she agreed. "I'll try."

She wiped tears from her cheeks, then reached up to kiss him. The thought of losing him terrified her. And he was right, she wasn't great at communicating with him. She wasn't used to having to communicate with anyone apart from her mum.

"Can I stay here tonight?" She looked at him hopefully, not sure whether he might want some space.

"You don't have to ask," he said. "You can stay whenever you want."

It took her a long time to fall asleep that night. Her mind whirred through their argument over and over again. She kept coming back to the same conclusion: she was an idiot.

When Jack's alarm sounded the next morning, Emily was already wide awake. She wrapped her arms around him as he reached out to silence the annoying beeping.

"Can I ask you a favour?" she said.

He rolled onto his back, blinking his eyes open and looking at her questioningly.

"Can I drop you at work and borrow your car today?"

He stretched as he untangled himself from her and sat up. "Yeah."

She waited but he didn't say any more. Sitting up beside him, she rested her chin on his shoulder. "Don't you want to know what for?"

"What for?" he asked flatly.

"I thought I might move my stuff over here," she said. "If it's still okay for me to move in?"

He smiled but didn't look quite as happy as she'd expected. "You don't have to move in just because we had an argument."

"I'm not." She frowned. She'd really expected him to be delighted. "I was worried about the money. But I can pay you as soon as I get some money. I wouldn't be living here forever without paying. Just temporarily. If that's okay with you?"

"It's fine with me."

"Okay. So I'll move in today?"

He nodded. "Good."

"Jack?" She called him back when he stood up from the bed.

"Hmm?"

"I thought you'd be more excited . . ."

He laughed and strained his sleepy eyes to look at her. "I'm getting a coffee." He went back and kissed her. "Then I'll be ecstatic, I promise."

Chapter 23

"I'm leaving you," Emily announced loudly when she walked into her mum's house.

"Good morning to you too," she called from the kitchen. "What are you talking about?"

"I'm moving in with Jack."

Her mum wandered out of the kitchen with a coffee in her hand. "Really?"

"Yes!" Emily remained at the foot of the stairs, poised to go up and start packing. "We had a huge argument last night but everything is out in the open now. I told him about the money situation and my feelings about Josie."

"And you're okay about the fact that she used to live there now?"

"I didn't mention that to Jack," she confessed.

Her mum laughed. "I thought everything was out in the open?"

"Most stuff." She screwed her face up. "What's the point in telling him I hate moving into the place he lived with his ex-girlfriend? It's not like he can do anything about it. And I can hardly suggest we find a new place when I have no money."

"It might be good if he knows how you feel, though . . ."

"Maybe I'll talk to him later. But I actually think that once I've moved my stuff in and got used to living there, I'll forget that Josie used to live there."

"If you say so." Her mum sounded dubious. "Do you want help packing?"

"Haven't you got Pilates this morning?"

"I can skip it," she said. "It's not every day my only child moves out of home." She followed Emily up the stairs. "I'll probably have a house party tonight to celebrate. I can get completely drunk and dance on the kitchen table without you here to judge me."

"Ha ha!" Emily shook her head. "Can you get the suitcases out? I'll start sorting through my clothes."

They spent most of the morning sorting through Emily's bedroom and loading up the car. They'd just sat down for a coffee and a sandwich when the doorbell rang.

"What are you doing here?" Emily asked when she saw Jack on the doorstep.

"I got off work early so I could help you move." He beamed at her and put his hands on her cheeks as he kissed her.

"Hi, Jack!" her mum called from the kitchen.

He walked through and wrapped her in a hug.

"You're stealing my baby girl?"

"I am," he said with a smile. "I promise to look after her and send her back to visit from time to time – probably when she annoys me!"

Emily gave him a playful shove. He turned to make himself a coffee.

"Help yourself to a sandwich," her mum offered while Emily sat back down to finish her lunch.

Jack didn't need any more encouragement and loaded bread up with ham and salad, then leaned casually against the sideboard to eat. It was nice how at home he always seemed there.

"I'll be honest . . ." He swallowed a mouthful of his sandwich. "I'm worried you're going to be lonely, Alison."

"I'll be fine, Jack," her mum said.

"I was thinking – we go to my mum's for dinner on Thursdays so it's probably only fair that we come here for dinner one night too."

"Do you ever stop thinking about food?" her mum asked.

"Rarely." He flashed a cheeky grin. "How's Tuesday for you?"

"Tuesday's fine," her mum said with a wide smile. She stood and kissed the top of Emily's head. "I'll fetch those last couple of bags down."

"Thank you," Emily called after her. Then she moved to Jack and snaked her arms around his waist. "You're so sweet with my mum."

"Well you're not the best cook so I need to organise something . . ."

She jabbed him in the ribs. "You can pretend the suggestion was all for your benefit but you forget how well I know you."

He turned and hooked his hands behind her back. "I love you."

"I love you too," she said. "Shall we go home now?"

He beamed down at her, nodding eagerly.

***

Emily was glad Jack had managed to finish work early as they lugged her stuff from the car to the apartment. Thankfully there was a lift in the building.

"There should be room for everything." Jack surveyed her suitcases and boxes scattered over the floor in the living room.

If Josie had managed to fit her stuff, surely Emily wouldn't have a problem. But she managed to keep that thought to herself. The less said about Josie living there, the better.

"There are some drawers free in the bedroom, and there's loads of space in the wardrobe."

She dragged a suitcase to the bedroom and set it down beside the drawers.

"What do you want me to do?" Jack asked.

"I'm not sure," she said. "You could unpack my books, if there's space on the bookcase. Maybe I should have brought my bookcase too." She'd been considering bringing a couple of items of furniture but decided to bring the small stuff first. She surveyed the bedroom, wondering how they could rearrange things. "Do you think if we move the bookcase right up to the wall, we could fit my desk in? Otherwise I could use the kitchen table, but I like working at my desk."

"I think it'll fit," he said. "Should I go and fetch it?"

"If you don't mind."

She sent him off with her house key and instructions on how to take it apart if it didn't fit in the car.

It was easier unpacking without Jack around.

There wasn't much he could do to help, and Emily felt better about rearranging his things when he wasn't there. It was quite fun finding places for everything. There were candles and framed photos that she spread out around the apartment, giving it a more homely feel. Jack always kept the place fairly bare.

For the time being, she jammed books haphazardly into the bookcase, but she was determined to arrange it neatly later.

She ignored thoughts of Josie as she neatly arranged her clothes in the drawers that used to hold Josie's clothes. As she hung items in the wardrobe, she noticed a scruffy old pair of Josie's Converse lying at the bottom. She had them in her hand when Jack walked back in.

"Oh," he said, sheepishly. "I think they can go in the bin."

Out with the old, in with the new! Again, Emily was proud that she managed to keep that thought to herself. "Did you get the desk?"

"Yeah. I nearly killed myself getting it down the stairs."

"Mum not there?"

"Nope. You better message her and tell her we've taken it. Can you help me carry it in?"

She nodded and followed him outside.

It was amazing how comforting it was to have her desk there. It fit perfectly in the space in the bedroom, and she set up her laptop on it and filled the drawers with all her notebooks. With her own things around the place it felt much more like home.

She was completely content when they sat on

the couch eating pizza that evening. "I can't believe we live together now," she said happily.

"I know." He wiped tomato sauce from his chin. "I was starting to think it would never happen."

"There's something else I wanted to ask you about . . ." Immediately, she kicked herself for bringing the subject up when everything was going so well.

"What?" He looked unnerved by her hesitation.

"I was wondering about going down to Hope Cove for the twins' christening . . . remember Lizzie invited us?"

"I remember she invited *you*."

"She invited us both," Emily insisted.

"Don't ask me to go, Em." He sighed and put his plate down.

"But I really want to go. I don't want to go on my own, though."

"Why not? You know everyone. You'll have a good time. If I'm there it will make everything awkward."

"No it won't." She hated how whiney she sounded, but she really wanted him to go with her.

His features softened. "I think, when it comes to Josie and her family, you might need to compartmentalise your life a bit."

"What's that supposed to mean?" she snapped.

"I mean *you* go to events involving Josie and her family, and I don't."

She dropped the cold pizza in her hand back onto the plate. "I want you in every part of my life." It was true. If that meant she'd be seeing Jack around Josie regularly, she was going to have to get used to it. "And what about Josie's wedding? Are you planning on going to that?"

"Yes. The wedding's different. But this is Lizzie and Max's thing. I'd feel really uncomfortable."

"Okay," she said. "I probably won't go either then."

He laughed. "You're not allowed to guilt trip me! If you want to go, you should go. Don't let me stop you. You can even borrow my car," he added with a cheeky grin.

"I'm not trying to guilt trip you," she said. "I was thinking we'd go for a long weekend. Lizzie said we could use the house for as long as we want. I always wanted to go to Hope Cove, and it seems like the perfect opportunity. I thought it would be a nice little getaway for us. It wouldn't be the same on my own."

He stared at her with a flicker of amusement in his eyes. "I thought you weren't trying to guilt trip me?!"

"I'm not." She laughed and fluttered her eyelashes shamelessly.

"Okay," he said.

"You'll come?"

"If I can get time off work . . ."

"You're the best boyfriend in the world!" She hugged him hard.

He rolled his eyes. "I can't believe you got me to agree to this."

Chapter 24

The house on Lavender Lane continued to be a subject of contention between Lizzie and Max. He'd been up to get the electricity back on and set live traps for the mice, but it was a few days before the christening and they still hadn't managed to get any cleaning done. Max mentioned it a couple of evenings, but Lizzie had only snapped at him, sure he was trying to get out of helping her put the twins to bed. She would've preferred to go up and do it herself, but she was always so tired at the end of the day.

In the end, Max took a day off work on the Wednesday before Emily and Jack were due to arrive. He was going to spend the day at the house, getting it straightened out, but Lizzie had bickered with him again, saying he got the easy job and she'd much rather clean the house herself while he looked after the girls.

So she was sitting on the couch in the dusty old house trying to find the energy to clean. The trouble was, the house was in such a state she didn't know where to start.

Dragging herself up, she took her cleaning supplies to the kitchen and got to work. After a couple of hours, she'd managed to get the kitchen and bathroom looking decent enough.

The patio furniture was weathered and worn but she sat out in the sunshine for a break. All she could rustle up for refreshment was a glass of water. Her stomach growled with hunger, and she contemplated nipping home for lunch. The thought was unappealing, and instead she set off down the garden and turned right on the path along the coast. It was a wonderfully bracing walk, and an hour later she arrived at Thurlestone Golf Club absolutely famished.

The restaurant there was stunning, set high up on the cliff overlooking the English Channel. She followed the waiter to a table on the terrace and ordered a glass of red wine while she happily perused the menu. Finally, she settled on the salmon, knowing that whatever she chose would be delicious. She and Max used to eat there often. In fact, it was one of the first places they ate together, before they were even a couple. It was funny to think that the first time she'd walked up to the golf course and seen the beautiful restaurant, she'd been too nervous to dine in a restaurant alone. Now, it seemed like utter bliss.

The wine and food relaxed her, and by the time she made it back to the house in the middle of the afternoon, the last thing she felt like doing was cleaning. She stalled a little by sitting on the patio, enjoying the sunshine and the view.

Forcing herself back to work, she made an attempt at getting rid of some of the dust, and then vacuumed the whole house.

There was still plenty to be done. The windows definitely needed a good clean, but there was no way she had the energy for that. She couldn't even be bothered to make up the beds so she left bedding and towels on each bed and decided her guests could manage that for themselves.

She'd been out too long and really needed to get home, yet she found herself taking the scenic route. Anything to put off returning to the chaos her house would undoubtedly be in.

***

Emily and Jack set off to Hope Cove early on Thursday morning. The christening was on Sunday and Josie and Sam were arriving on Saturday to spend a night in Hope Cove. It would only be a short break, but Emily had been looking forward to the change of scene and the time away with Jack. She was full of excitement on the drive down there.

It was almost lunchtime when they pulled up in front of Seaside Cottage – Lizzie and Max's house.

"It's so lovely," Emily said as she walked through the front gate and along the little path to the front door. She spied Lizzie through the front window and waved.

Lizzie beamed when she opened the door. "You made it!"

"Yes." Emily stepped in and gave her a big hug. "I can't believe I'm finally in Hope Cove. It's so exciting."

"I just hope it lives up to your expectations." She ushered them inside and Jack kissed her cheek in greeting.

"Thanks a lot for inviting us," he said.

"You're very welcome. I did mention the house

is a bit of a mess, didn't I? I hope you're not expecting a luxury getaway."

"We're easy to please," Emily said. "It's just nice to have a weekend away."

"Oh God, it's a mess in here," Lizzie said as they walked into the living room. "Maybe the Lavender Lane place will seem quite pleasant in comparison."

Emily wanted to say something reassuring, but she was quite surprised by the state of the living room. Lizzie had always come across as a bit of a neat freak, but there was nothing neat about the living room.

"The babies are getting so big." Emily stroked the cheek of the one in the jumperoo. She had no clue which was which, but the baby was bouncing excitedly and banging her fists.

"They've just started crawling," Lizzie said. "Maya can only go backwards. The other day I came in and found her stuck under the desk. I'd only gone to put a nappy in the bin and when I came back I thought I'd lost her. Do you want a coffee?"

Emily looked around for somewhere to sit but the couch was piled with washing and the armchair was littered with toys. "If you've got things to be getting on with, don't feel you have to entertain us . . ."

Lizzie sighed. "I'm happy to have company. These two aren't the best conversationalists . . ."

"Coffee would be great," Jack said.

"Make yourselves at home," Lizzie said as she headed for the kitchen.

"It's chaos," Emily whispered to Jack. She

really didn't know where to sit.

He laughed and piled up the folded washing into the basket and put it aside.

"Do you know which is which?" She took a seat on the space he'd cleared and watched as he knelt down on the floor beside the baby.

"I think this one's Maya. She can crawl backwards anyway." When she backed into the wall, Jack picked her up.

"Careful," Emily said.

He laughed. "Did you just tell me to be careful with the baby? What do you think I'm going to do with her?"

"They're delicate. You have to be careful with their heads and stuff . . ."

"They're not newborns." Jack stood and held Maya over his head, making silly noises. "They're pretty sturdy."

"Put her down," Emily hissed. "You're scaring me."

He pretended to drop her, catching her at the last moment. Emily gasped and felt stupid when he laughed at her. "Just stop it, will you? You're like a big kid yourself."

When he blew raspberries on Maya's belly, she laughed and banged him on the head. Phoebe was watching intently and began to cry.

"Here, take this one." Jack handed Maya to Emily and lifted Phoebe out of her seat. "You want to play too?" he asked in a silly voice. After he threw her up in the air a few times, he swiped some toys off the armchair and took a seat with Phoebe in his lap. Emily didn't have much experience with babies and felt uncomfortable holding Maya.

"I'm not good with babies," she said as Maya arched her back. She was surprisingly strong.

"Put her on the floor again," Jack said, bouncing his leg up and down with Phoebe on it.

"I can't just put her on the floor."

"Why not?"

"I don't know. It feels rude."

"It's not rude. Look at her – she wants to go down."

She was wriggling a lot. Emily sat her gently on the floor and she immediately pushed forward onto all fours.

"Turn her around," Jack said when she reversed into the couch.

"They're not toys!"

Lizzie came back in looking flustered. "Oh good. You found some space. The washing is never ending." She held a mug out to Emily. "You don't take sugar do you? Because I think we've run out."

After handing the coffee over, Lizzie reached down and pulled on Maya's legs, swinging her round to face the opposite direction. Emily was quite shocked – why was no one being gentle with the poor babies?

To be fair, Maya seemed quite happy as she crawled backwards across the room.

"This is a great game." Jack turned her so she could go back the other way. He set Phoebe down on the floor and took the coffee from Lizzie. Phoebe sat looking at Jack for a moment, then began to whine until he abandoned his coffee and picked her up again. She settled happily in the crook of his arm and rested her head on his chest.

"She likes you." Lizzie sat beside Emily and sank heavily back into the couch.

"Looks like you've got your hands full," Emily remarked.

"It's amazing how much work two tiny people create." She reached to turn Maya around when she bumped into the couch again. "Anyway, tell me about the book. Josie said the launch party was a big success."

"It was really lovely," Emily said. "And the book is selling well. I guess I'm doing something right. I'm spending a bit of money on advertising. Plus the gift shop at Oxford Castle is selling it and has a big display about it so that's great exposure."

"Your colleagues at the castle must be really proud."

"They've been great." They'd all been wonderfully supportive, and Emily was convinced no one made it through a tour of the castle without hearing about her book.

As they chatted, Phoebe fell fast asleep in Jack's arms. Emily could hardly take her eyes off the two of them. It was odd seeing Jack with a baby. There was something very attractive about it. She was pathetic, she told herself, feeling her cheeks heating up and dragging her gaze from Jack.

"I'll put her in her bed," Lizzie said, taking the peaceful baby from Jack.

He immediately got down on the floor with Maya, passing her toys and shaking a rattle in front of her.

"We should go soon," Emily said. "I'm dying to

explore."

Lizzie arrived back a moment later. "I might try and get Maya to sleep too. If I could get them both to sleep at the same time it would be lovely."

"I bet you never get a rest," Emily said. "You must spend all the time they're sleeping trying to tidy up . . ." Emily's smile faded when she saw Jack's expression. He didn't look up from playing with Maya, but she caught the way he winced as though she'd said something stupid.

"Not that I'm saying it's a mess . . ."

Jack winced again and stood, handing Maya to Lizzie. "I can't wait to have a look around Hope Cove after I've heard so much about the place. And Josie tells me the fish and chips here are the best."

"They're delicious," Lizzie said. "I recommend eating them on the beach with the sea air filling your lungs! I have to limit myself these days – it's definitely not the healthiest dinner."

In the hallway she handed Jack a set of house keys along with instructions on how to get to the house. "Like I said, it's a bit run-down," she added.

"It'll be fine," Jack said.

"I took sheets and towels up there, but I was rushing and didn't have time to make up the beds."

"No problem," Jack said. "I'm looking forward to seeing the place."

"The garden takes you to the path along the coast. There are beautiful walks in either direction."

"We'll get out for a walk this afternoon," Emily said enthusiastically.

"Max's nephew will turn up at some point. I think he'll arrive on Saturday but he's a bit unpredictable and hard to pin down. Anyway, if you need anything just give us a shout."

"Thanks so much," Emily called as they stepped out onto the front path. At the car she turned and waved. Her forced smile was becoming painful. "Did I just tell her she had a messy house?" she asked Jack in the car.

"Yep." He turned the key in the ignition.

"Oh my God." She put her hands to her flushed cheeks. "Why do I just blurt things out? I'm so awkward."

"You forgot about thinking before you speak. I thought you'd been doing better at that recently."

She punched his arm as the car moved off down the road. "Don't tease me. I'm so embarrassed. I can't believe I said that." They were silent for a moment. "It's a complete mess, though, isn't it?"

Chapter 25

They were still chuckling when they turned onto Lavender Lane. Number two was the first house they came to on the left and there were only a few other houses to be seen further up the road.

A crumbling wall ran around the stone cottage. The front gate had come off its hinges and was leaning at an odd angle. Emily ran her gaze quickly over the unkempt garden as they walked to the front door. "I thought they were probably exaggerating about it being run-down," she remarked as Jack jiggled the key in the lock. "But now I'm starting to think they may have underplayed it."

With a shove, the door juddered opened, making the cobwebs on the windows quiver. "I'd have booked a hotel if I'd known how bad it was."

"You sound a bit uppity today, you know." Jack planted a kiss on her cheek as she walked past him into the house. "It's an adventure."

"It's creepy," Emily countered, taking in the faded couch in the dull shade of pink. She had a glimmer of excitement at the large fireplace until she saw the piece of paper in the grate which read 'Do not use' in big black letters.

Then she noticed the old mahogany bookshelves which took over one wall from floor-to-ceiling. Her eyes widened as she went over to them. "Wow!"

"I feel like I might just have lost your attention for the weekend," Jack quipped before wandering through the living room to what Emily presumed was the kitchen at the back. She couldn't drag her gaze from the shelves, which were packed full of a variety of books from trashy old romance novels to beautifully bound hardbacks of classic works of literature. When she blew on the shelf in front of her, she sent a plume of dust flying all around. It sparkled in the sunlight which cut from the front window across the living room.

Pulling out a withered old hardback, she opened it and put her face between the pages to inhale the wonderful scent of aged paper.

"You're weird," Jack said affectionately. He continued upstairs to explore while Emily was awed by the beautiful books.

"Em!" he called out from upstairs.

Dragging herself away, she followed his voice up the carpeted staircase. The banister wobbled unnervingly when she touched it.

"What?" she called from the landing.

"Come and look at this."

He was standing at the window of one of the back bedrooms.

"Oh my goodness." Emily didn't know where to look – the sea view, or the gorgeous cosy window seat. She actually thought she might cry. "I love it so much."

Taking a seat, she pulled her legs up onto the cushioned alcove. Only then did she notice the shelves dug into the walls bordering the window, filled with even more books.

Turning her attention out of the window, she watched a seagull sore high over the house and then glide along the length of the garden, finally hovering out to sea. Its wings flapped for a moment before it leaned to one side and took off on a course along the craggy shoreline which stretched as far she could see.

The sky was bright blue and dotted with puffy white clouds.

"I want to live here," Emily said.

Jack's laughter rattled around the sparse bedroom. "A few minutes ago you were ready to check into a hotel."

"The view has sold it to me."

"And the books," he said, settling beside her.

"It's a fascinating collection." She pulled a hardback copy of *Vanity Fair* from the shelf beside her. "Look how covers have changed over the years." The midnight blue cover was embossed with a delicate gold pattern. "I wonder what Lizzie and Max are planning on doing with all the books . . ."

Jack raised an eyebrow. "Our apartment is cramped enough as it is."

Settling her feet in his lap, she brought the book up to her face. Then she held it up to Jack.

"Smells musty," he said.

"Not musty! Magical."

"If you say so." He chuckled and pushed her legs gently away. "Let's go."

"Go where?" She turned her nose up. "I was thinking I'd just sit here all weekend."

"I need to get out in the fresh air. All this dust is setting off my asthma."

"You don't have asthma!" She poked him in the ribs.

He faked a wheeze. "I can feel it developing. And look at that view – we should be out in it, not sitting here looking at it."

"Okay but fetch the bags in first and put them on the bed. I want this room!"

"No one else is arriving until Saturday," Jack said.

"Josie and Sam aren't, but no one seems to know when Max's nephew is arriving. I don't want to come back and find he's pinched the best bedroom."

"Fine." Jack sighed cheerfully. "I'll get the bags."

***

They walked north along the coastal path in the opposite direction of Hope Cove. They were planning to explore the village later and have a fish and chip dinner.

The sea air was exhilarating, and Emily's hair whipped around her face as the gusty winds blew over the headlands. It was absolutely stunning. They passed dog walkers and hikers, and everyone exchanged friendly greetings.

After half an hour they reached South Milton Sands – a popular tourist beach. There they ate sandwiches outside a wonderfully rustic café before walking down to sit on the beach. The waves were busy with surfers and body boards.

Emily wasn't sure it was really warm enough to swim, but apparently a lot of people did as they splashed in the shallow waters.

"So did you find me really attractive holding the baby earlier?" Jack asked out of the blue.

Emily cracked up laughing.

"You did, though," he insisted. "I saw you looking at me with your big soppy eyes."

"You're so full of yourself sometimes." She couldn't bring herself to admit he was spot on with this comment. She loved seeing how natural he was with the babies.

"I can't wait to have kids," he said with a cheeky grin.

"Oh my God! You can't go near the twins again. I can't cope with you getting broody."

He bent his legs and wrapped his arms around his knees. "You want children, though? One day?"

Gazing at him, she felt her cheeks heat up and butterflies flutter in her stomach. Sometimes, she felt like she was living in a dream. She really was going to marry him and live happily ever after. Leaning into him, she rested her head on his shoulder. "I love you so much."

He shrugged her away from him and raised an eyebrow. "You just avoided my question."

"Yes." Her grin was so wide she thought it might damage her face. She fell into gentle laughter and hugged Jack's arm. "Yes. Of course I want kids with you."

He faked a dramatic look of surprise. "I didn't say anything about having kids together. It was just a general question!"

"You're such an idiot!" She pushed him back onto the sand and he pulled her down with him.

"Fine," he said between kisses. "We'll have kids together. Whatever!"

She sighed contentedly as she nestled her head under his chin. "One day."

"When?" he asked quickly.

She had to look at him to see if it was a serious question but she still couldn't tell.

"Don't look so worried," he said. "I'm not suggesting we have kids immediately. I just wondered what sort of timeline you're thinking . . ."

Puffing out a breath, she gazed over the water. "Five years." It came out more like a question.

"I can live with that." There was a moment of silence. She stared at him. "Why are you looking at me like that?" he asked, chuckling.

"Are you thinking that if I say five years you can probably get me down to three with some nagging?"

He attempted to look innocent before flashing his boyish grin. "Are you a mind reader or what?"

She gave him a playful shove, then shook her head, beaming. "I can't believe we're talking about kids."

"Blame Lizzie." He scrunched his features. "Her babies are just too cute."

***

They stayed at the beach for an hour, enjoying the mild weather and watching all that was going on around them. Then they set off the way they'd come, ambling back along the path until they reached Hope Cove. It was a sleepy little village, almost exactly as Emily had imagined. The white houses with thatched roofs were quaint and adorable.

They stood looking out over the bay. It was so picturesque with the perfect crescent beach bordered by rocks, which gradually made way to the craggy cliffs. Boats bobbed a little way out to sea and the sunlight made the surface of the water shimmer beautifully. A few kids were building a sandcastle and alternated between bickering and laughing together.

A man walked past with a fishing rod and cheerfully said hello with a nod of the head.

"Everyone's so friendly," Emily said quietly to Jack. "And everyone seems so happy. Do you think it's the sea air or what?"

"I think it's probably you romanticising everything," Jack said. "What about the guy who told you off for stroking his dog earlier? He didn't seem overly cheerful."

"Oh, he was okay. I really shouldn't have stroked the dog without asking. It was rude of me."

Jack snorted a laugh. "Can we get chips now?"

Chapter 26

Lizzie was concerned that the desire to scratch Max's eyes out was getting harder to quell. It was Friday evening and she was sitting opposite him at the kitchen table. Phoebe was on her lap and Lizzie was tugging her little arms into her jacket.

"I only asked you to do one thing," she hissed at him.

"And I'm quite happy to take the girls for a walk," Max replied angrily, wrangling Maya into an identical jacket. "I'm just not going up to Lavender Lane."

"All you have to do is stop by and ask if everything's okay. See if they need anything."

"They're adults – if they needed something they'd ask, not sit there hoping we might stop by to check on them."

"That's not the point, Max! It's just polite. They're going to think we're really rude."

"We let them stay in the house. How is that rude?"

"But we've not made any effort to see them."

"Why would we? They're Josie's friends."

"I'm friends with Emily," Lizzie said adamantly. Even if Josie was their main connection, she and Emily had bonded through their work too. She'd intended to call over and see them, but the day had got away from her and now she was exhausted and still had to get the house straightened out before her parents arrived the next day.

Max shook his head. "I'm really uncomfortable around Jack. We don't have anything in common. It's always been weird between us, and since he jumped from Josie's bed to Emily's I lost any scrap of respect I had for him."

"I'm fairly sure it's not as simple as that." Again, she was trying to defend Jack, but she could definitely see Max's point. "No one else seems bothered by it."

"That's all right then," he said mockingly.

They headed to the front door and strapped the two wriggling girls into the double buggy in the front garden. "Will you please go up there? You don't have to stay and socialise. It'll only take five minutes."

"No! I already told you, I'm not going up there."

"Fine!" She was absolutely seething as she elbowed him out of her way. The poor kids jolted in the buggy as she set off hastily down the path. "I'll go! And I'll take the kids for a walk . . ." She turned and nodded to Tilly, who was waiting at the front door. She trotted obediently down the path. "And the dog," she snapped. "Just like I have to do everything round here. You can't do one simple thing for me!"

"Okay, I'll go."

Lizzie was all set to storm off up the road, except the house was a mess and she really needed to start cleaning to get the place decent for the christening on Sunday. "A minute ago you were acting like I'd asked you to stick your hand in the fire . . ."

He inhaled deeply and took over the buggy. "I'll go."

"And try and be nice to Jack," she said as he walked away.

He turned and opened his mouth before clamping it shut again and smiling tightly. She might have been pushing it with that comment. Back in the house she surveyed the carnage in the living room. The kitchen was no better. She blew out a long breath and headed upstairs. The mess would still be there after a nap.

***

Emily and Jack had spent the day at the beach and even braved a swim. The water temperature was actually quite pleasant once you got over the initial shock. Then they'd gone to the village to explore some more.

Emily remembered Josie telling her about a gallery which sold art by local artists. It was only a small shop but it was packed full of the most wonderful treasures, and Emily spent a good while browsing and finally bought a small print of the bay at Hope Cove. She would have liked a larger picture but she was trying to be careful with money.

They ended the day with dinner at the local pub and then walked slowly back up to the house. There was some worn patio furniture out the back and they sat outside for a drink while daylight slowly faded.

"You're such a cheap date." Jack took a swig of his beer and eyed Emily with amusement. "Two glasses of wine and you're all giggly."

"I'm not giggly," she insisted. She almost got the words out without laughing but not quite. "You're just being silly and making me laugh!"

"I haven't said anything funny."

"You told me not to down neat vodka." She laughed again. "It's funny because it's just a glass of water."

"But all that joke deserved was an eye-roll, not a full belly laugh."

"I thought it was funny."

"Which brings me to my original point – you're drunk!"

"I am not." She leaned her head back and felt a little dizzy. She really couldn't take her alcohol. "Was that the door?" She craned her neck to look into the kitchen as though that would bring answers.

"What?"

"Someone was knocking."

"I didn't hear anything."

"Go and have a look," she said.

"No. You're drunk and imagining things. Or maybe it's the ghost of the woman who died here . . ."

"Don't say that. You'll give me the creeps. Answer the door, will you?"

"There's no one at the door!"

She shook her head and walked through the house. Max was standing on the street as though he was about to leave again.

"Hi!" she called. "Sorry, we were sitting out the back."

He rocked the buggy back and forth. "We were

out for a walk and thought we'd say hello and see how you're getting on."

"We're fine, thanks. Having a great time." Oh God, she was drunk and overly cheerful.

"Got everything you need?" he asked.

"Yes." She'd only met Max a few times and felt awkward, as she generally did around people she didn't know well. Conversation suddenly felt as easy as astrophysics. "You should come in and have a drink." She smiled, happy that she'd managed to say something normal. "Bring the buggy round the back. You can have a beer with Jack."

"I was trying to get these two to sleep, really . . ."

"You'll have to come and see Jack, though, or he won't believe you were here." Apparently one normal sentence was all she could manage.

Max gave her a wonky smile. "Okay."

She stood back as he manoeuvred the cumbersome buggy through the gate and then strained to get it through the long grass beside the house. The dog followed after him. "I should have sorted the garden out a bit."

She laughed nervously and moved in front of him. "Look who's here!" she said to Jack.

"Oh hi!" He grinned. "So you weren't hearing things."

After shaking Max's hand, he bent to the girls and tickled their knees as he said hello in a silly voice. Emily hadn't even thought to say hello to the babies. She frowned, thinking she'd been really rude.

"Hello!" She waved at them but they were too

busy grinning at Jack. "I'll get you a beer," she said to Max.

"I'm okay. I really wasn't going to stay. I don't want to disturb you . . ."

"Oh, you're not. He's not, is he, Jack?" She didn't wait for a reply as she nipped into the kitchen and took a beer from the fridge. Scanning the room for something more to offer, she grabbed a packet of Pringles from the kitchen table. Then she put them down again, realising the packet was already half empty and it wasn't a very elegant snack.

At the door she dithered again and went back to pour some of the crisps into a bowl – that looked better. Why she was treating Max like visiting royalty she had no idea. Although she probably wouldn't offer Pringles to royalty. She took a deep breath and promised herself that in future she'd stick to her one-glass-of-wine limit.

Max and Jack were sitting on the patio chairs, discussing the weather and the local beaches. Max thanked her as she gave him the beer. Emily shot Jack a look when he took a handful of Pringles. His eyebrow twitched slightly in confusion and he nodded at a chair. She sat down quickly, wondering why on earth she was so socially inept.

"So how's the new job going?" Max asked Jack.

"It's good. Not that new now, really."

"Sam was saying you might get promoted to paramedic?"

"It wouldn't be a promotion. It's a different job. I'd have to go through all the training. I haven't really decided. It'd mean going back to studying, which would be difficult financially. I'll probably stay where I am, to be honest."

"It's a good job," Emily said quickly. "It's not emergency care but he makes a big difference in the lives of a lot of really ill people . . ." She trailed off. Jack was giving her a look.

"It sounds rewarding." Max reached behind him to pick up a toy one of the girls had dropped.

"How's Lizzie?" Emily asked. "We were going to call in today, but I thought she'd be busy with the girls and I didn't want her to think she had to entertain us."

"She's fine." He stretched his legs and leaned back into the chair. "Busy trying to clean up and get the house in order for the party on Sunday."

"Oh gosh, she's got her work cut out then." Heat rose from Emily's chest and crept up her neck. "I mean I guess it's hard to keep the place tidy with the kids . . ." Oh no, she was digging herself a hole.

"How many people have you got coming on Sunday?" Jack asked, redirecting the conversation. Really, Emily should just never speak. Ever.

"It's only family and a few close friends. And you," he added with a smile.

Emily wasn't sure what he meant by that. They didn't fall under the category of friends or family? What were they? Gate-crashers to a christening?

There was an awkward silence and all three of them reached for their drinks. Emily wished it was vodka now and not water.

"Hello!" They all turned to see a guy gradually appearing around the side of the house. "I tried knocking . . ."

"Hey!" Max stood and gave him a hug and a

slap on the back. "I didn't think you were arriving until tomorrow."

"I felt like getting out of the city." He approached Emily with an outstretched hand. "I'm Conor."

"Sorry," Max said. "Conor's my nephew."

After shaking Jack's hand, Conor moved to coax Maya and Phoebe into high-fiving him.

"I went to your place first," he said to Max. "I feel bad – I think I woke Lizzie up."

"Oh, really?" Max's lips twitched to a smirk.

"She said you were up here." He glanced at Jack, eyeing his beer. "Don't suppose you've got another cold one?"

"In the fridge. Help yourself."

"Thanks." He headed inside. "I've got a crate in the back of the car. I'll fetch it in a bit."

"No uni today?" Max asked when Conor stepped back outside. He clinked his beer bottle against Jack's and then Max's before sitting down.

"No." He bent to stroke Tilly, who lay calmly under the table. "But if you speak to my dad don't mention I was here today."

"So you're supposed to be in uni today?"

"It's a stressful environment. I needed a break."

Max took a deep breath. "I feel like every time I see you, you want me to lie to Jim about something."

"Not lie," Conor said. "Just don't mention you saw me. He's not going to ask."

"No." Max sounded disapproving. "Because he assumes you're in uni . . ."

"It's just one day," Conor said.

"Last time I spoke to him he said you'd had some run-in with the police and would probably get kicked off your course . . ."

Conor chuckled and flashed Emily a cheeky grin. "My dad's prone to exaggeration. I may have had a few too many beers and got caught using a wall as a urinal. I'm not exactly a hardened criminal. I got a fine. Dad should never even have known about it. A friend of mine is doing an internship at Dad's firm and somehow it became office gossip. Now Dad reckons I'm going off the rails."

"Don't get kicked off your course," Max said with a sigh. "And what's the situation with Jim? You *are* speaking to each other, aren't you? Lizzie's panicking that there's going to be an atmosphere on Sunday."

"Nah, it's fine." Conor turned and pulled a face at the girls. "Dad seems to have calmed down again. I think we're good."

"I hope so," Max said. "Just remember you're the godfather and try not to cause any drama."

Conor gave a frustrated sigh before pointedly turning his attention to Jack and Emily. "So how do you like Hope Cove?"

"It's gorgeous," Emily said.

"It's really not a bad spot," Conor agreed. At the end of the garden, the sun touched the horizon, turning the sky a delightful shade of pink.

"I better get these two home to bed," Max said, standing. "Have a nice evening."

"You too," Emily mumbled as the others said goodbye.

There was a silence as Max pushed the buggy

round the side of the house.

"He used to be really chilled out before he had kids," Conor said after a moment. He shook his head slowly. "It's like he's turning into my dad – nagging all the time."

"What are you studying?" Emily asked.

"Law." Conor grimaced. "It's like I've sold my soul to the devil."

Emily couldn't help but chuckle. "Why do you do it, if you don't like it?"

He looked slightly sheepish, picking at the label on the beer bottle. "My dad wanted me to."

Confusion wrinkled Jack's brow. Emily also didn't get it. "But . . . why would you study something just because your parents want you to?" she asked.

There was mischief in his eyes. "They bought me an Audi and set me up with a really sweet apartment."

"Oh . . ." That made more sense.

Jack snorted a laugh and soon they were all chuckling. The atmosphere relaxed and Conor turned the conversation to them, asking where they lived and what they did, how they knew Lizzie and Max. He seemed like a lot of fun, and it was refreshing after Max's awkward little visit.

"I'm going to go up to bed," Emily said a little while later. The sun had set and the air was chilly. Conor and Jack had finished off the beers in the fridge and were making a start on Conor's supply.

Standing behind Jack, Emily dug her fingers into his hair, massaging the back of his head. "I might try and get a bit of work done before I go to sleep."

"Okay." He took her hand and kissed it. "I'll be up in a bit."

"Night," she said to Conor. Their laughter followed her up the stairs, and she suspected it might be a while before Jack came to bed. In the bedroom, she got her laptop out, determined to get some words down. She couldn't resist sitting in the window seat.

Pushing open the small window at the top, the hum of Jack and Conor's conversation drifted up to her. Glancing down, she could just make out their silhouettes in the glow from the kitchen lights. In the background she could hear the lull of the waves. It was all very serene.

She gave up on the laptop before she even opened it, suddenly sure she wasn't going to get any work done. Instead, she pulled an old paperback copy of *Little Women* from a shelf and shuffled to get comfy.

It was almost midnight when Jack stumbled into the room. Emily had heard him coming long before he burst in with a big grin on his face.

"You're so drunk," she remarked as he fought to get out of his clothes. He tripped with his jeans around his ankles and landed ungracefully on the bed, where he kicked himself free of his trousers.

"Just a little bit," he mumbled, laughing. "Conor's a good laugh."

"Yes." She smiled as he made a meal of getting under the covers. "I could hear you laughing all evening. It's a good job there aren't any neighbours nearby."

"Come to bed," he said, patting the mattress

beside him.

"If you're aiming for a smouldering sexy look, you've got it a bit wrong!"

"You love it." He chuckled to himself. "Come on, come to bed." He patted the pillow this time.

"Two minutes," she said. "I'm just finishing the chapter."

She watched contentedly as his eyelids drooped. He was fast asleep about twenty seconds later, and she finished the chapter in peace.

Chapter 27

In the morning, Emily assumed Conor and Jack wouldn't be awake for a while and set off into the village to get breakfast supplies. There was a chill in the air and the wind whipped around her as she made the exhilarating walk into the village. It was impossible not to linger by the beach as the waves rolled gently onto the shore. If she could start every morning that way she'd be happy.

When she got back to the house it was mid-morning, and she put the bacon on to fry, presuming the smell would rouse Jack and Conor. She was right; a few minutes later, Jack arrived in the kitchen in a pair of boxer shorts and a T-shirt. His arms snaked around her waist as she stood at the cooker. He brushed her hair back to kiss her neck, then rested his head on her shoulder.

"Morning," he mumbled.

"Good morning! How are you feeling?"

"Not very well," he complained pathetically, snuggling into her.

"I'm not surprised." She shrugged him off. "How much did you drink?"

He glanced through the open back door at the patio table, which was covered in empty beer bottles.

"A lot." Taking a seat, he dropped his head onto

the kitchen table.

Emily filled the kettle for coffee. Upstairs, she heard the shower being turned on. "Bacon and eggs will sort you out," she said, going over and stroking his hair.

He grunted an unintelligible response.

Conor had perfect timing and arrived downstairs just as Emily was plating up the bacon and eggs. He was showered and dressed and looking far more energetic than Jack.

"It smells amazing," he said after a cheerful good morning.

Jack stared at him as though he'd arrived from Mars. "How are you so lively? Aren't you hungover?"

"Not really." He sat opposite Jack and grinned at Emily when she put a plate of food in front of him. "Thanks."

"How is that possible?" Jack bit gingerly on a rasher of bacon while Conor tucked in with gusto.

He shrugged. "Practice!"

"This is your fault." Jack pointed his rasher of crispy bacon accusingly at Emily. "I don't go out enough since we got together. You're hampering my drinking abilities."

"Or you're getting old," she suggested.

"I'm not old," he said firmly.

"Can't you even eat?" she asked with amusement. She'd never known Jack so cautious with food.

"I'm going to be doing everything slowly this morning if that's okay with you." He took a bite of toast. "And you could be a bit more sympathetic."

Shaking her head, she tucked into her own breakfast. True to his word, Jack ate his breakfast at a snail's pace and then slowly took himself upstairs to get showered.

Conor was easy to be around, and she was telling him about her current writing projects when Josie and Sam wandered in the front door.

The atmosphere was immediately livelier as they greeted each other with a flurry of hugs, kisses and handshakes. Emily squeezed Josie tightly and was happy to see she looked brighter than the last time she'd seen her.

"I didn't think you'd be here until later this afternoon," Emily remarked.

Josie rolled her eycs. "Apparently the men are off to play golf this afternoon."

"No one said it was exclusively the men," Sam insisted. "Everyone's welcome."

"Max didn't mention anything to me," Conor said.

"I think your dad suggested it this morning," Sam told him. "We're booked on the first nine at 2 p.m."

"I've not checked my phone." Conor wandered over to the bookcase where his mobile lay. "No doubt my presence will be requested." He tapped wearily on his phone. "Yep!"

Jack wandered down looking slightly more chirpy after his shower. He gave Josie a big hug and then shook Sam's hand.

"We're playing golf this afternoon if you want to join," Sam offered.

"No, thanks. Golf's not really my thing."

"The rest of the guys are going," Emily said, creeping an arm around Jack's waist.

"And what are you ladies doing?" he asked.

"Well I'm definitely not playing golf," Josie said. "Although it might actually be the preferable choice." She grimaced as she looked at Emily. "I volunteered us to help Lizzie get ready for the party."

"That's fine," Emily said. She looked up at Jack. "You should go and play golf."

He chuckled as though she'd said something very amusing. "No."

"Don't blame you," Conor said. "I wish I could get out of it. We'll meet up after and go to the pub."

Jack winced. "Let me recover before you suggest more drinking."

"Did you guys have a session last night?" Sam asked.

"Yeah," Jack said. "It seems I'm not used to drinking so much any more."

They drifted into the kitchen and Conor made drinks and kept them all entertained with his lively banter about his crazy student lifestyle.

After five minutes, Emily noticed Jack had slunk away and went in search of him. He was lying on their bed and his eyes flickered open as she opened the door.

"Are you okay?"

"Fine. It was just a bit loud for me."

"I think Josie and I are going down to Lizzie's soon."

"You're going to spend the afternoon tidying her house, you know?"

"It'll be okay." She sighed and lay down, snuggling up to Jack. "What are you going to do?"

"Hang out here . . . nap . . . maybe go down to the beach for a swim."

"It seems a bit anti-social if they're all going to play golf and you don't go."

"You can say what you want – there's no way I'm going to play golf."

"It'll probably be fun."

"No. It won't. For a start, I can't play golf. But I also don't want to spend the afternoon with my ex-girlfriend's family."

"Okay," she said wearily.

"Oh, what now?" he said. "You're annoyed with me because I forgot I'm not supposed to mention the fact that Josie's my ex!"

"I didn't say anything," she said. "I'm not annoyed with you. I'm not sure why you're in such a bad mood."

"I'm in a bad mood because I'm hungover and you're nagging me because for some weird reason you want me to go and play golf."

"I just think it would be nice if you made more effort to get on with people."

"I get on with everyone fine," he said, sitting up.

"Not Max."

"I get on fine with Max. And even if I don't, no one cares except you. You're making issues where there aren't any. I don't know why."

"And I don't know why you turn grumpy every time we meet up with Josie."

He swung his legs off the bed. "Do we really

have to do this again? Now?"

Tears stung her eyes and she knew she was being crazy and irrational. She couldn't help it, though, and Jack clearly wasn't in the mood to discuss it.

Shaking her head, she crossed the room. "No. We don't need to talk about it. I'm going out with Josie. You do whatever you want." She didn't look at him and was surprised when she opened the bedroom door to find Josie on the landing.

Josie looked as startled as she was. "I was just coming to see if you're ready to go?"

"Yep." Emily tried to sound cheerful. "I'm ready."

"Is Jack going to hang out here? I think Sam and Conor are leaving soon too."

"Yeah," Emily said. "I think he's going to have a nap."

"Okay."

Downstairs, they shouted goodbye to Conor and Sam and wandered out the front door.

"Is everything okay?" Josie asked.

"Yeah," Emily said with false cheer.

"With you and Jack I mean?"

She nodded. "Of course. Why?"

"Things seemed a little strained, that's all."

Josie didn't miss much and Emily didn't feel she had the energy to lie. The problem was she also couldn't tell the truth – that they were absolutely fine as long as Josie wasn't around or mentioned.

She was still searching for the right thing to say when a voice called out to them. They stopped and turned. Jack was jogging down the road.

Emily eyed him warily. "Everything okay?"

As he took Emily's hand, his eyes were on Josie. "Keep walking," he said, tipping his chin. "She'll catch you up."

Josie chuckled and carried on down the road.

"What?" Emily grumbled.

With his fingers creeping into her jeans pocket, he pulled her close to him. "You can't leave without kissing me goodbye."

She sighed heavily and then relaxed into him, snaking her arms around his neck. "Sorry," she whispered.

"Can you try and look at it from my point of view . . . I'd have no problem if we were just hanging out with Josie and Sam. But this is all a bit awkward for me. Josie's parents will be there tomorrow so that's going to be weird."

"I didn't think about that," Emily said sheepishly.

"It'll be fine." His arms tightened around her waist. "But I only came because you wanted me to. I love you and I would do anything for you, but please let me blend into the background as much as possible while everyone's around."

"Okay." It sounded very reasonable when he said it like that. Her fingers trailed over his neck and she lightly brushed her lips against his. "I better go and find Josie," she whispered.

"Mmhmm," he mumbled. But he kissed her again. And again. Until she squirmed to get away from him with a huge grin on her face.

"I'll see you later."

"Have fun cleaning," he called as she hurried

away.

By the time she caught up with Josie, she was already outside Lizzie's house. "Sorry," she said breathlessly.

"Don't worry about it."

"I wanted to ask how you're doing," Emily said, touching Josie's elbow and giving her a meaningful look.

"I'm doing okay."

"Really?"

Josie had a hand poised to knock on the door. "We can talk properly later."

Emily nodded her agreement as Josie knocked then immediately opened the door. "It's just us," she called.

***

It was bliss having the house to herself, and after a quick tidy round, Lizzie lay on the couch enjoying absolute silence. It lasted about five minutes, until there was a knock at the door and Josie shouted a greeting as she let herself in.

"Come in!" Lizzie shouted. She couldn't be bothered to get up.

"Where are the girls?" Josie asked when she and Emily wandered into the living room.

"Max's mum took them out for a walk so I can get tidied up. I don't know what happened – I cleaned yesterday and then this morning it was a mess again."

"Charlotte's here already?" Josie asked.

"Yeah." Lizzie was so relieved when her mother-in-law offered to take the girls for a walk.

She always felt a little on edge when Charlotte was at their house. It had previously been her house before Lizzie bought it from her. She always had the feeling that Charlotte was scrutinising the place, seeing how they were looking after it. And since the arrival of the twins it was a constant mess.

"She drove down with Jim and Sarah," Lizzie said. "They're all staying in a hotel. What is it about in-laws that's so stressful?"

"No idea," Josie said, dropping onto the couch when Lizzie sat up to make space. Emily took the armchair.

"There's always some feud between some members of Max's family," Lizzie went on. "Conor's been having issues with Jim – which is nothing new really. I'm just hoping they all behave for the christening."

"I'm sure they will," Josie said.

"I feel sorry for Conor, really." Lizzie had always had a soft spot for Max's nephew. "His parents put him under so much pressure. If he does what they want, they throw money at him. If not, they practically disown him. And they're always having a go at him regardless. It's a wonder he's not rebelled more than he has."

"I like Conor," Josie said. "He's fun."

"He's a bit reckless these days, from what I hear." Lizzie sighed. "I hope he's okay. He was here when I first met Max . . ." She smiled at the memory. "That seems like forever ago. Was he okay last night?"

"He was fine," Emily said. "I thought he was very entertaining. And he and Jack seemed to hit it off. They stayed up drinking until the early hours."

"Hopefully he'll get it out of his system and not get drunk tomorrow. Every time I've seen him recently he's either drunk or hungover."

"He's a student," Josie said, rolling her eyes. "And you sound old." Lizzie threw a cushion at Josie. She caught it with a giggle and set it aside. "You do!"

"He's studying law. He'll never manage if he spends all his spare time drinking."

"I thought law students were notorious for partying," Josie said. "Give the guy a break."

"I'm sure it'll all be fine. Family gatherings make me nervous, that's all. With Max's family anyway." She glanced around the room. "It looks tidy enough, doesn't it?" So long as you didn't open any cupboards or drawers – her tidying up involved a lot of shoving things out of sight.

"It looks good," Josie mused. "I thought you were getting us here to help clean up."

"I had a whizz round before you got here. It'll do. Shall we open a bottle of wine and sit outside?"

"That sounds way better than cleaning," Josie said.

Chapter 28

The patio was a fantastic little sun trap. It was so calm and peaceful, and Lizzie felt wonderfully relaxed as she sat with Josie and Emily. If only her mother-in-law would visit and take the kids out more often. She rarely came to Hope Cove since she didn't like to drive any more. Max and Lizzie would visit her in her residential home every few weeks. The twins were always a big hit with the old people, and it was pleasant enough to visit. It would be far better if she would come to them sometimes and help with the girls. She was very good with them.

"This is bliss." She took a long sip of the crisp white wine. "I wish we could do this more often. Sometimes I feel like I never get any peace. The girls seem to need constant attention, and I'm forever snowed under with housework." She glanced at Josie with a smirk. "Remember when I was a workaholic and thought I'd never have kids?"

"Yes." Josie chuckled. "You thought it was degrading to be a stay-at-home mum."

"Did I?" She didn't remember saying it, but she was fairly sure she'd thought it occasionally.

"To be fair," Josie said, "you looked down your nose at most people back then."

"I did not," she insisted.

"You did." Emily snorted a laugh, then took

another sip of wine. She seemed giddy already after just a few mouthfuls. "When I worked at the magazine with you, you thought you were above everyone."

"You can't really blame her," Josie said with a mocking tone. "It's difficult when you know everything and you have to work with a load of people who are basically clueless. Poor Lizzie!"

"Hey! I was very good at my job. And part of my job was telling people what to do. Why are you picking on me?!"

"It's just too easy," Josie said.

"Turns out I didn't know everything." Lizzie laughed. "It's amazing how much I've learned in the past year. I really had no idea how hard it was being a mum." Her wine sloshed in the glass as she pointed at Josie and Emily. "I can give you some advice . . . you should wait a while to have kids. Don't rush it. I mean, don't get me wrong, I wouldn't change anything, but there are definitely times when I feel like I missed out on that honeymoon phase with Max."

Josie and Emily fell silent and Lizzie had the impression they thought she was spoilt and ungrateful. She didn't mean to complain, but they had no idea how much work it was with twins and what a strain it was on her relationship with Max.

Emily glanced around awkwardly and then gave Josie an odd look as she stood and muttered that she needed the bathroom.

"You think I complain a lot, don't you?" Lizzie asked Josie. "I don't mean to. Everything is fine, really. It just feels like Max and I don't have any time to ourselves."

"I don't think you complain a lot." Josie took a sip of her drink. Tears glistened in her eyes.

"What's wrong?"

"Nothing."

"Don't say nothing." Lizzie bit her lip as Josie wiped tears from her cheeks with the back of her hand. "Tell me what's going on."

Josie put her glass down. "I had a miscarriage. A couple of months ago."

Lizzie's insides seemed to twist and constrict. She knew something had been going on. Quickly, she moved to the chair beside Josie and took her hand. "I'm so sorry. Why didn't you tell me?"

"You have enough going on." She shook her head. "That's not really why. I know you'd always make time. I just didn't want to tell anyone for a while. It felt like I should be able to forget about it and move on. I didn't want to make a big deal of it."

"It is a big deal." Lizzie put her arms around Josie and hugged her tightly. "I'm so sorry. I wish I'd known."

"It's okay." Josie gave her a quick hug and then shrugged her off. "Don't hug me too much. When I start crying, it's hard to stop."

"I can't believe I've been complaining about the twins to you. You must want to shake me."

"Sometimes." Josie laughed and wiped away more tears.

"I'm sorry," Lizzie said again. "How far along were you?"

"Seven weeks." She sniffed. "Can we not talk about it now? I'll get upset again. I'm sick of being upset all the time."

"Okay." Lizzie squeezed her hand. "But if you ever need anything, let me know."

"You could let me look after my nieces sometimes. Whenever I offer, you make some excuse."

"That's true. But you always offer to babysit in the evenings. I'm too tired to go out in the evenings." She sighed. "I'm complaining again, aren't I?"

Josie chuckled. "Why don't Sam and I come over one weekend and you and Max can go on a lunch date . . ."

"That sounds perfect." It really did sound good. She and Max should spend some time together without the girls. Things hadn't between good between them, but she was sure it was only because they didn't spend any quality time together. And she felt awful now, knowing what Josie was going through. It put things into perspective.

Emily appeared in the kitchen doorway. "There's someone at the door. Do you want me to get it?"

"It'll be Max's mum bringing the girls back." Lizzie smiled as she went to let them in. Her peace and quiet was over, but she definitely wasn't going to complain about it.

**

It was late in the afternoon when Emily and Josie left Lizzie's house. Emily was relieved that they hadn't been roped into cleaning. It would have been slightly unfair if the women were all cleaning and looking after the children while the men went off to play golf. Some of the men anyway. She wondered what Jack was up to. Probably relaxing on a beach somewhere.

She wished she'd been with him, but wine and sunshine and a good catch-up with Lizzie and Josie had been fun too. And she was glad that Josie had told Lizzie about the miscarriage. Some sisterly support would be good for her.

When they set off back to Lavender Lane, they took the path along the coast. There was a gate in the tall hedge at the end of the garden and Josie led the way through it.

"That view is fantastic," Emily said as they stepped out onto the path at the other side. "And I love the smell of the sea air," she said, inhaling deeply. "All that salt and seaweed!"

They followed a sandy path onto the small stretch of beach and Josie stamped her foot to chase off a lone seagull. She laughed as it took flight. "So what were you and Jack arguing about?" She slipped off her shoes and Emily did the same.

"We weren't arguing,"

"Yes you were!" They fell into step and moved towards the water. "When we left he came out to apologise, or make up. Jack doesn't like leaving things on an argument." She paused and glanced at Emily. "You forget how well I know him."

Unfortunately, that statement was about as far from the truth as you could get. She wished she could forget how well Josie knew him.

"I was annoyed he wouldn't go and play golf," she said finally. "I thought he was being anti-social."

"Jack can't play golf."

"You hit a ball with a stick," Emily said. "How hard can it be to learn?"

They'd just reached the water when Josie started giggling. "You've never played golf, have you?"

"No. But it looks pretty easy," she said with a smirk.

"I almost wish we'd gone with them now!"

"Shut up!" Emily gave Josie a friendly nudge into the water, and in return Josie kicked water up at her.

"You seem happier than last time I saw you," Emily ventured when they stopped messing around.

"Yeah." They walked until they were above the water line and then sat in the sand. "Tara and Amber have been great. I should have told them sooner. And Annette knows now as well."

"She's so lovely. It's good that you told Lizzie too."

"I wasn't planning on it. She's got enough to worry about already. And I think I made her feel guilty for complaining about the twins." She paused, looking out over the water. "It was really good talking to Amber. It turns out she's had two miscarriages." Her eyes clouded with tears. "She's really easy to talk to."

"I'm glad you have someone to talk to," Emily said, tearing up herself. "Sorry I'm a bit useless."

Josie leaned her head on her shoulder. "You're not useless. I'm so glad you came this weekend. It's so great being here with you. I love Hope Cove."

"I love it too," Emily said. "And the house is

gorgeous. I'm hoping I'll be able to come back for little writing retreats when Lizzie and Max start renting it out."

"I think you should write a book about Hope Cove. It would fit really well with your historical romance stuff. Basing it on smugglers is a great idea."

Emily shook her head. "Don't give me ideas. If I get ideas they niggle at me until I write them, and I've got enough ideas to deal with at the moment."

"I think this one's going to niggle at you," Josie said with a mischievous glint in her eyes.

Chapter 29

When they arrived back at the house, Sam and Conor had just got back from golf. Apparently the plan was for everyone to have dinner together in the village. They got ready and made the twenty-minute walk together.

"This is getting a bit awkward," Jack whispered to Emily as they approached the pub.

"Because we had dinner here last night too?"

He flashed a boyish smile. "I also had lunch here."

"You'll be getting a reputation."

Inside, she and Jack said hello to everyone and then lingered at the edge of the small group. Max's mum was there, and his brother and sister-in-law. Apparently the twins were at home with Lizzie's parents.

There were only small tables left in the pub so everyone naturally split off. Emily was happy to just be with Jack and not have to make polite conversation. After ten minutes, Conor joined their table. "I hate these family things," he said. "Golf was a nightmare. Be thankful you didn't come, Jack. Although, there's a bar there so I suppose it could have been worse."

That's why he seemed drunk, then. He'd had a couple of beers at the house too.

"It's all a bit sedate around here." He scanned the pub. "We've seriously lowered the average age. You know what we should do? Get a taxi into town and find somewhere decent to party."

"I'm looking forward to my bed," Jack said.

"Come on," Conor coaxed. "Let's get some shots in. That'll perk you up."

Jack shook his head. "We've got to be up for the christening tomorrow. I'm already done in."

Conor rolled his eyes. "Emily?"

"I can't drink shots. I'm a lightweight."

"I'll be back in a minute," he said and wandered off.

"That's not good," Jack remarked.

"He's hammered," Emily said, watching him lean on the bar. "Do you think we should convince him to stop drinking and go home?"

"Yeah," Jack said flatly. "I'm sure if we tell him he's had enough to drink he'll go straight home to bed."

"There's no need to be sarcastic!"

He broke into a grin and kissed her cheek. "You're so adorably naive."

"So what do we do with him?" He was downing a shot at the bar but no one else seemed to notice.

"I don't see how he's our problem. Besides, he doesn't seem that bad. And he's an adult. If he wants to get wasted, he's allowed to."

"I feel like it's going to be an issue."

"Maybe." Jack took a sip of his Coke. "But not our issue."

Over the next hour or two, Emily and Jack ate and chatted and occasionally glanced around to see what Conor was up to. It didn't seem as though he had anything to eat – just drink. They were talking about leaving when he stumbled over and sat heavily on the stool, swaying so much it seemed as though he'd fall.

"Do you know what I noticed earlier?" he said with a grin. "The boats on the beach are just tied up with a rope. So I was thinking . . ." He slurred his words as he leaned closer to Jack. "We could borrow one!" He put a finger to his lips and giggled.

"Borrow a boat?" Jack asked.

"Yeah! You up for a bit of joyriding?"

Jack pretended to mull it over. "I can't say I am."

"Come on." He narrowed his eyes and almost fell off the stool again. "It'll be a laugh."

"It's really dangerous," Emily said.

Conor stared at her for a moment, then stood up. "You're right," he said, apparently trying to mock her. "It's very, very dangerous. And a very silly idea!"

They watched him stumble through the pub without stopping to talk to anyone and disappear from view through the front door.

"What do you think the chances are he's gone home to bed?" Jack asked.

"He's gonna drown," Emily said flatly.

Jack stood and kissed her head. "I'll see if I can steer him away from the water."

For a moment, Emily sat alone, until Josie called her over to the bar. She and Sam were standing away from the rest.

"Where's Jack gone?" Josie asked.

"He went to check on Conor."

Sam rested an elbow on the bar. "He's so wasted."

"Hey!" Conor's dad, Jim, called to them. "Do you know where Conor is?"

"He went home," Josie said. "He wanted to be fresh for tomorrow."

Jim nodded his approval. "Sensible."

"I'm not sure if he's implying we're not sensible," Sam said.

"He even makes Max look laid-back, doesn't he?" Emily remarked.

They looked at her in surprise before eventually falling into easy laughter.

"Max is all right," Josie said. "Him and Jack still don't get on, do they?"

Sam shook his head. "I don't really get it. I get on with both of them. I don't know what the problem is."

"Everyone should be like you." Josie pinched his cheek. "Friends with everyone."

"Not everyone," he whispered mischievously. "I'm not friends with Jim!"

Lizzie and Max came over to join them. "We're going to go home," Lizzie said. "Sorry to be boring."

"I think we're going in a minute anyway," Josie said.

Lizzie looked away, suddenly distracted by a conversation between the barman and another guy.

"What happened?" Max called over, seeming to know the bearded guy sitting at the bar.

"Someone's messing around with boats. Ken's

down on the beach sorting it out."

Emily's heart rate increased.

"Who's Ken?" Josie asked Lizzie.

"Our local policeman. We can have a nosey on the way out. It'll cause a bit of excitement around here!"

"It's Conor," Emily said quietly to Josie as they went towards the door. "He was talking about stealing a boat."

Josie let out a sigh. "This is going to cause problems."

For Emily, the main problem was that when they stepped outside and saw the police car, it wasn't Conor who was being put into it.

It was Jack.

Chapter 30

Emily stood in shock as the police car drove away with Jack in it. A crowd had formed outside the pub, including Max's family coming out to see what was going on. They dispersed again after the police car left.

"Did Jack just get arrested?" Josie said in disbelief.

"Definitely looked like it." Max didn't seem the least bit concerned. In fact, Emily detected a hint of amusement to his voice.

Lizzie called out to a man walking up from the beach. "What happened?" she asked him.

"I don't really know. Seemed like someone got drunk and decided they felt like going sailing!"

"Did Ken arrest the guy?"

He scratched his head. "I think he was just going to give him a lift home and a talking to. Ken won't want to be driving over to the cells at this time of night."

"It was probably a misunderstanding." Lizzie rubbed Emily's arm reassuringly. "I didn't even notice Jack was drunk."

"He wasn't. He's been drinking soft drinks all evening."

"What was he doing out on the beach?" Max asked.

Emily opened her mouth to speak but Sam beat her to it.

"He had a headache and went out for some fresh air."

"I'm sure it'll all be fine," Max said to Emily. "He's probably already in bed, sleeping it off."

"He's not drunk," she said through gritted teeth.

"Let's get back," Josie said. "See if he's at the house."

They said a vague goodnight to Lizzie and Max, then left them chatting to some locals outside the pub.

"Why didn't you say Jack had gone to look for Conor?" Emily snapped as they walked quickly up the road. "You know this is all Conor's fault."

"It's probably better that Max's family don't know that," Josie said.

"That's not fair on Jack."

"We don't even know what happened," Josie said wearily.

"I know Jack didn't do anything." Emily quickened her pace, leaving Josie and Sam trailing behind her.

As she burst in the front door of the house, she was relieved to see Jack sitting on the couch.

"Hi," he said casually.

"What happened?" She sat beside him on the couch. "I thought you'd got arrested."

"No." He shrugged. "I got a lift home, though!"

Josie arrived, standing in front of them. "Some guy said you were trying to go out on a boat."

He shook his head. "I was trying to stop Conor from going out on a boat."

"What happened to Conor?" Sam asked, perching on the arm of the couch.

"He ran off when the police arrived. I told the policeman I'd seen someone getting in a boat and went to see what they were doing . . . To be fair, he seemed to believe me. Good job I hadn't been drinking." His gaze landed on Sam. "I don't know where Conor is. He didn't come back. And I don't really want to go out looking."

"Of course you can't go out looking for him," Emily said sharply. "It'll look a bit dodgy if that policeman finds you wandering the streets again after he's brought you home. Besides, you almost got arrested thanks to Conor, why should you go looking?"

Jack continued to look at Sam. "I'm a bit worried considering the state he was in."

Sam frowned. "I'll have a wander round. See if I can see him." He'd just stood up when there was a noise at the back door.

"That'll be him." Josie hurried to the kitchen to open the door.

Conor stumbled inside, laughing and pointing at Jack. "How funny was that? I can't believe the police showed up!"

"Hilarious," Jack said flatly.

"It's a good job we're fast." He flopped into the armchair. "They could never catch us!"

"Shame Jack's not as fast as you," Sam said with a smirk.

"What happened?" Conor leaned forward in the chair. "Did they catch you?"

"Jack almost got arrested because of you,"

Emily snapped.

"Wow." Conor blinked rapidly. "I'm really sorry, mate. I thought you ran too."

"Don't worry about it," Jack said. "No harm done."

"Anyone want a beer?" Conor looked between them all.

"Maybe you should go to bed," Jack suggested. "You've got to be up and alert in the morning."

Conor stood. "Oh yeah. The thing . . ."

"Christening," Emily said. "For your nieces. You're their godfather."

"Yep." He pointed at her. "*That* thing! Goodnight."

He tripped on the stairs once but finally managed to make it up and out of sight.

"He's a nightmare," Emily said.

"He's all right," Josie said. "He just has some issues."

Emily nudged Jack. "It's not funny."

He shook his head but the smirk morphed into outright laughter. "If you'd have seen him trying to get the boat in the water you'd laugh too."

"I really thought it was going to be a quiet evening," Josie said, dropping into the armchair.

Jack patted Emily's thigh. "Let's go up. All that excitement has worn me out."

They said goodnight and went upstairs. Emily was still furious as she cuddled up with Jack in bed. And it annoyed her even more that everyone else seemed to think it was one big joke.

"You wouldn't laugh if you'd seen the look on Max's face," Emily said. "It was like he wouldn't expect anything less from you than getting in trouble with the police."

"Who cares what Max thinks?" Jack said idly.

She sighed. "I do." Which didn't actually make any sense – why should she care about Max's opinion? It was more that she hated the thought of anyone thinking badly about Jack. Especially when he'd done nothing wrong.

***

The next morning Jack was already in the kitchen when Emily went down after her shower. He was munching on toast and chatting happily with Josie at the table. The scene immediately put Emily on edge.

"Morning!" She made herself a coffee. "Where is everyone?"

"Sam's gone to collect Annette," Josie said. "And Conor's still sleeping. We'll have to wake him if there's no sign of him soon." She glanced at her watch. "We don't really need to leave for another hour, though."

"Do you think it'll be awkward when his dad finds out about last night?" Emily leaned against the counter and registered Jack and Josie both giving her puzzled looks.

"Who's going to tell him?" Jack asked slowly.

"When anyone asks why you were taken off by the police . . ."

"I'll tell them what I told the policeman: that I saw someone on the beach and they ran away when I went to look."

"But you were just looking out for Conor and you get in trouble for it. It hardly seems fair."

247

Jack wrapped his hands around his coffee mug. "Except I didn't get in trouble."

"Everyone thinks you did, since they all saw you getting taken off in a police car."

"I don't care what any of them think. What's the point in causing problems for Conor?"

"Jack's right," Josie added. "Things are strained enough between Conor and his dad as it is."

"But does no one else think that maybe Conor isn't going off the rails because his parents are too hard on him? Maybe they're hard on him because he's out of control. Perhaps a few consequences for his actions would do him good."

"Emily." Jack's voice was horribly condescending. "Nothing even happened. You're making an issue out of nothing. I already told you I don't care what anyone thinks of me."

"I care!" she said angrily. "It's embarrassing. We have to go to the christening with everyone talking about you getting in trouble with the police."

"It's embarrassing?" Calmly, he set his mug down.

"Yes."

"For who?" His features were tense as his gaze bored into her. She didn't reply. "It's embarrassing for you?" he asked.

Closing her eyes briefly, she let out a long breath. "I didn't say that."

"If you're embarrassed to be seen with me, I can make things much easier and not go today."

"Don't be like that," Emily said.

Jack's gaze had drifted to Josie. "You don't care if I don't go, do you?"

She shrugged in reply.

"Why are you asking *her*?" Emily's voice was an octave higher than normal.

He ignored the question and walked to the back door. "I'm going for a walk. I'll see you later."

"Jack!" Emily called. "You can't just not go to the christening."

He'd already left and was walking away down the garden.

"I can't believe he just did that," Emily said. "He's really not going to go?"

"You were pretty hard on him," Josie said.

"But I don't understand why he doesn't care what people think of him."

"He does care," Josie said. "He cares what *you* think. And you just told him you're embarrassed by him."

Emily stared out the window, hoping he might come back.

"Why should he care what Lizzie and Max think of him?" Josie asked.

"Because we're going to keep crossing paths with them, and I hate that they don't like him when their opinion of him is based on lies and false information."

"But you're the only one who cares," Josie pointed out. "You should apologise to Jack. You've upset him."

Emily shook her head. The last thing she needed was advice from Josie about her relationship with Jack.

"It'll be fine," she said. Though she actually wasn't sure it would be. Her romantic break with

Jack wasn't exactly going to plan.

"But you realise that telling him you're embarrassed by him is pretty much the worst thing you could say to him? And he might seem pretty tough but he's a big softy really—"

"Oh my God! You're talking about *my* boyfriend. Do you think I don't know him? Please stop acting as though you know him better than me."

"I'm not," Josie said. "But he's my friend too . . ."

"And your ex. Yes, I know. It's pretty difficult to forget."

"What is going on with you?"

"Nothing." Quickly, Emily crossed the room, turning back in the doorway. "I assume you won't mind if I don't go to the christening either?"

"Don't be like this, Em."

She carried on through the house and shut herself in the bedroom. Sitting in the window, she looked out at the beautiful sea view and clutched the necklace from Jack. She hadn't taken it off since he gave it to her. Tears welled in her eyes and she couldn't stop them as they fell down her cheeks. Josie was right; she'd been completely unreasonable with Jack. Why on earth did she care so much what anyone else thought? It was so irrational. She shouldn't have had a go at Josie either. That was unfair.

She took a few deep breaths and did her best to compose herself.

Josie was still sitting in the kitchen when Emily went back downstairs. "Sorry. I shouldn't have snapped at you."

"Are you all right?"

"Yeah. I might just be losing my mind." She flashed a sad smile and sat at the table.

"I realise you don't seem to want my opinion," Josie said slowly, "but he really does love you. You are two of my favourite people in the world, and I want you both to be happy."

Emily put a hand to her mouth as a lump formed in her throat. "I'm messing everything up. I'm scared I'm going to lose him."

Josie shook her head and reached across the table to squeeze Emily's hand. "I don't know what's going on between you two. But I'm not sure you could lose Jack if you wanted to. He's so smitten with you it's sickening."

"You think so?" she asked miserably.

"All he can talk about is you! Remember when you came to visit after the dog died? I was in the barn with him. I can't remember where you were. He beamed from ear to ear when he was talking about you. And he was teasing me, saying how ironic it was that I'd wanted to move in with him straight away when he didn't want me to, but with you he was dying for you to move in and you wanted to take things slow."

"He said all that?"

Josie nodded. "I ended up teasing him because he couldn't stop talking about you."

"I'm such an idiot." She'd been so irrational and jealous and it had been over nothing. When Jack wouldn't tell her what they'd been talking about that day it had made her so angry. His secrecy had made Emily paranoid when she really needn't have been.

"I need to go and find him. I'm sorry I've been so grumpy and awful."

"It's fine. See you later," Josie called as Emily left through the back door.

She was certain Jack wouldn't have gone far, but she had to take a guess at which direction and chose to turn right when she came to the path which ran past the end of the garden. After five minutes, she spotted him on a deserted strip of beach. He was lying with one arm behind his head and his eyes closed into the sun. They flickered open when she knelt beside him.

"I'm sorry." She pushed her lips together as she tried not to cry.

Reaching for her hand, he entwined his fingers with hers but didn't say anything.

Emily took a deep breath, filling her lungs with salty air. "I'm not embarrassed by you." She shook her head – it was such a ridiculous idea. "Of course I'm not. I just want everyone to see you the way I do."

"But it doesn't matter how anyone else sees me."

"I know that and I'm sorry."

"It's okay." He tugged on her arm to draw her to him but she resisted.

"I shouted at Josie," she said.

An eyebrow twitched. "Why?"

"Because I didn't like the way she was talking about you."

He sighed knowingly. Clearly he didn't think Josie had been saying anything bad.

"I already apologised. It's all fine." She shifted

her gaze and looked along the peaceful beach. "I didn't used to be so neurotic before I met you."

"Ah, so it's all my fault." His tone was light and jokey.

Emily couldn't look at him. "Do you remember when you were with Josie and I moved to London because I couldn't bear to be around you?"

He sat up and gently ran a thumb over the back of her hand.

"I was so miserable." She sniffed. "But I had this weird sense of calm at thinking things couldn't get any worse. I had nothing to lose." She turned to him and could see the concern etched on his face even through the blur of her tears. "Now I have everything and it terrifies me. I have so much to lose."

"You won't ever lose me, Em." He pushed his hand into her hair. "I promise."

"I don't think I could live without you." She sniffed again, then laughed lightly. "And as someone who's always been very independent, I kind of hate feeling like that."

He shook his head firmly. "I couldn't live without you either so it's perfect."

There were tears on his cheeks too, and she wiped them away before she kissed him, tasting the salt from her own tears.

"I'm sorry for all the stuff about Josie. I got so paranoid when you wouldn't tell me what you were talking to her about when we visited her—"

"I was talking about you!"

"I know that now." She took a deep breath. "Josie told me."

"She never could keep a secret."

Emily grimaced. "Things might be easier if you didn't have secrets with Josie."

"That's true." He hugged her tightly and didn't let go for a long time. "You really don't need to worry about losing me, though. You're stuck with me."

She chuckled. "That's what Josie said."

He pulled back and grinned at her. "I want a whole life with you. Marriage, kids, everything."

"Me too." She kissed him again and hoped she could always feel as happy as she did in that moment.

"Are you going to make me go to the christening now?" Jack asked.

"No." She lay back on the sand and he did the same. "Not if you don't want to."

"I'll go if you want."

She turned her nose up. "How about we skip the church bit and just go for the free food and drinks?"

"I think you're getting a bit rebellious."

She shuffled close to him, tangling her legs with his. "I'd rather lie here with you. I'm sure no one will care."

"No." He stroked her hair, his voice full of amusement. "They'll presume I'm in prison and you're busy trying to bail me out."

Chapter 31

Phoebe woke at 5 a.m. on the morning of the christening. Lizzie was trying hard to get her eyes to focus as she bumped into the girls' room and lifted her from her cot. "Shhh," she whispered as she crept out of the room with her. "Please don't wake your sister."

It was such a stupid time. It felt like the middle of the night but Phoebe obviously thought it was breakfast time. Nudging Max, she set Phoebe down beside him on the bed. "I'm going to get a bottle," Lizzie said. "Maybe she'll go back to sleep."

He grunted a response.

"Max! Don't let her crawl off the bed."

"I've got her." He reached out a hand until he found her on the bed. She sat herself up and grinned at Lizzie. Light poured in from the landing.

"Stay with Daddy," Lizzie said.

"Da da da da!" she babbled happily as she banged on Max's arm. It was the first time she'd said anything that sounded vaguely like a word.

"Morning, princess." Max beamed as he pulled her over to him. His eyes were still closed as he lifted her onto his chest. "Say Daddy . . ."

"Da da da!"

Blinking his eyes, he smirked at Lizzie in the doorway.

"Don't look so smug," she said. "It's the easiest sound to make!"

"Say Daddy," Max said again in a silly voice.

The babbling continued while Lizzie went downstairs to get the milk. When she returned, she propped Phoebe on a pillow to give her the bottle. Her little yellow pyjamas were very cute, and she looked drowsy again as she gulped at the milk. Lizzie was desperate for her to go back to sleep. It was going to be a long day and she needed another hour or two of sleep herself.

"Go and sleep in the spare room if you want," Max said, as though he could read her mind.

"I might. But my mind's whirring with everything I need to do."

"There's not much to do, is there?"

"I don't know." Lizzie sighed. "I can't stop thinking about Josie." She'd filled Max in on Josie's bad news the previous evening.

He lay a reassuring hand on her hip. "She'll be okay."

"I know. I just feel awful. She's lost a baby and all the time I'm complaining about my two happy, healthy babies."

"You didn't know what was going on."

"But even so. I shouldn't complain so much. I have so much and yet I spend most of my time grumbling instead of appreciating it."

"You spend most of your time exhausted. Don't feel guilty for wishing you could sleep more and have some time for yourself."

Smiling sadly, she trailed a hand over his arm.

"I feel bad too," he said. "I've not had a lot of

patience with Josie recently. I thought she was being dramatic about the dog dying. But that was probably right after she lost the baby."

Tears stung Lizzie's eyes. "I wish she'd told us. We could've supported her if we'd known."

"We can support her now."

"Yeah. She wants us to let her look after the girls more."

Max frowned. "That seems like her helping *us* out, but I won't complain."

"I thought they could come over one weekend and we can have lunch at the golf club like we used to."

"Are you also gonna beat me at golf like you used to?!"

"Probably." It would be nice to have a day alone with Max. She really needed to appreciate him more. He tried so hard, and most of the time she had a go at him anyway.

"There's something else playing on my mind," she said.

"Sounds serious."

"It's not. I wondered about offering to edit Emily's next book for her. Just as a favour."

"That's a good idea."

She frowned. "Except I probably don't actually have time . . ."

"If you really want to do it we can make time. I'll look after the girls for a weekend."

"It'd take more than a weekend," Lizzie said. "But I could do it in the evenings and when the girls are napping – if they ever nap at the same time. I don't know, maybe it's too much to take on. I think it's so great how well Emily is doing. I want to get in on the action."

Max smiled sleepily. "Talk to Emily. See what she thinks."

"I will," Lizzie said determinedly. Even the thought of getting back to work – albeit unpaid work – was exciting. "I'll try and catch her today and have a chat about it."

"Poor Emily," Max said. "She looked mortified at Jack getting taken off in the police car."

"I felt really sorry for her," Lizzie agreed. "And it was a bit naughty of Ken, really." The local policeman had come back into the village after he'd driven Jack home and they'd had a chat with him outside the pub. "He said Jack clearly hadn't done anything wrong. If Jack was sober and coherent why did Ken feel the need to take him home? Especially when Ken had seen someone else running away."

"Because he's got nothing to do and wants to be seen to be doing something."

"He could've chased whoever was running away!"

"I'm fairly sure he only wants to be *seen* to be doing something. He definitely doesn't want to chase kids around in the dark."

"You enjoyed watching Jack being escorted away, didn't you?" she asked accusingly.

He chuckled and then switched to a whisper as he glanced at Phoebe. "I found it quite amusing. You never liked Jack either."

"He might be growing on me. I think I mostly disliked him because of how much Josie complained about him. And maybe it was just that they weren't right for each other. He seems very sweet with Emily."

"Maybe you're going soft," Max suggested.

"Maybe." She smiled. "I think I will go and try to get a bit more sleep."

He nodded and puckered his lips until she leaned over and kissed him. When she got into bed in the spare room, it was with a feeling of contentment. She and Max usually only bickered in the mornings. Or any time of day, actually. It was refreshing to start the day on a pleasant note.

She was still feeling chirpy an hour later when Maya's cries put an end to her dozing.

"I'll get her," she said when she met Max on the landing. He looked tired as he turned and went back down to Phoebe. Lizzie followed a moment later with Maya on her arm.

"It's tidy," she said, glancing into the living room on the way to the kitchen. It shouldn't be a surprise since she had spent so much of the previous few days cleaning, but it was nice to get up to a tidy house nonetheless.

Max sat beside Phoebe's high chair, feeding her baby porridge. His hair was ruffled and he had dark circles under his eyes.

"Do you want to go back to bed for a bit?" she asked.

He nodded pathetically. "You're in a good mood," he remarked as he stood.

"I'm looking forward to today." She peered out of the window. "I just hope the weather's decent enough to be outside."

"Weren't you totally against the idea of a

christening?"

"Yes." She chuckled. "But it's nice to get the family together."

He hovered in the doorway, an intense look in his eyes. "It's good to see you so happy."

She bit her lip. When had she become so miserable that getting up and having a normal conversation became something of note? Maya pulling on her hair was a good reminder as to when things had changed.

"I'm actually really excited about talking to Emily about the book. I'd love to work with her again."

She was glad she'd invited Emily and Jack to the christening and had a feeling that having something other than the twins to focus on would make a huge difference to her life.

She hoped so, anyway.

Chapter 32

It was lunchtime when Emily and Jack arrived at Seaside Cottage. They could hear chatter coming from the back garden and bypassed the front door, instead wandering round the side of the house hand in hand.

Lizzie was heading into the kitchen with a couple of empty plates. Holding them to one side, she kissed their cheeks in greeting.

"Sorry we didn't make it to the church," Emily said. Jack had joked about her being rebellious and that was exactly how she felt. She'd never been a rebel in her life and it didn't sit well with her. Guilt had niggled at her all morning.

"Don't be silly." Lizzie smiled brightly, then flashed Jack a warning look. "Lots of people are talking about last night. You're probably going to get quizzed. So far I've heard a story that you're a hero for chasing off thieves and a story that you saw the ghost of a smuggler from a hundred years ago."

"Jack!" a voice called from further down the garden. It was Annette from the kennels waving at them. She was sitting amongst a group of people Emily didn't recognise and patted the space beside her on the bench.

"See," Lizzie said. "Your audience awaits!" She leaned in closer and lowered her voice. "Sorry about

Conor. Josie told us what happened. I'll have a word with him later. I'd just like to avoid a scene between him and his dad."

"Don't worry about it," Jack said.

"Thanks for looking out for him." Lizzie smiled ruefully. "He's a good guy deep down. Anyway, there's food and drink over there." She nodded to a buffet table. "Help yourselves."

Emily's fingers were loosely hooked around Jack's as they set off towards Annette, but she broke away when Josie smiled at her. She was sitting on a blanket with the babies.

A couple of older kids ran past as Emily joined Josie on the blanket. "I'm really sorry about this morning."

"You're forgiven," Josie said cheerily. "Everything okay?"

"Yes. Everything is great." Glancing down the garden, she smiled at the sight of Jack laughing with Annette and her little group. "Who is everyone?"

"You know Dotty, she lives next door." Emily nodded; she'd met Dotty before. "Then there's Tammy, the postwoman, and her husband and kids. And the old guy with the dog is Bill. Verity works in the cafe – she did the food. They're all locals. I think you know everyone else . . ." Max and Sam were deep in conversation with Josie's parents, and Conor and his parents stood nearby too.

"How was the church?"

"Boring," Josie said under her breath. "You didn't miss much."

"We were on the beach all morning, but I feel a bit guilty."

"Don't." Josie waved a hand. "No one cares. The beach sounds much more fun."

"It's so lovely here," Emily said. "I wish we were staying longer. Back to Oxford tomorrow and then I really need to get on and get the next book finished."

"How's the first one selling?"

"Really well," Emily said. "Better than I expected."

"Why do you look so worried?"

"It's stressful." Emily returned a toy to the baby nearest her. They were wearing matching dresses and she had no clue which baby was which. "I cut down on my hours at the castle so I can focus on getting these books out, but doing it without a publisher means a lot more work and all the costs. I feel like I have much more to lose if they don't do well."

"But more to gain too," Josie pointed out. "If you're not sharing your profits with the publisher . . ."

"True," Emily said, taking a deep breath.

Lizzie joined them on the blanket. "Are we talking books?" she asked excitedly.

"Emily's stressed," Josie said. "So we were just about to change the subject."

"No! I want to hear," Lizzie said. "Is the next book almost finished?"

"I'm about halfway. I've set the release date for October. I could probably make it earlier but I'm worried about putting too much pressure on myself."

"That's sensible," Lizzie said. "What about editing?"

Emily felt suddenly awkward. Lizzie had edited her first books, but for the last book she'd found someone else – the twins had been tiny and Lizzie didn't have the time.

"I booked the woman I used last time," Emily said sheepishly. It somehow felt like a betrayal, but she'd assumed Lizzie wouldn't have time again. "I'll send it over to her in September."

"I could probably do it if you want . . ." Lizzie's mouth twitched at the corners. She glanced at the girls playing happily on the blanket. "It might take me a little longer than normal but I'd really love to do it . . . and I'm more than happy to do it as a favour again. You've brought so much work my way it's the least I can do."

Emily picked nervously at the blades of grass beside her. She'd always been grateful to Lizzie for editing her projects for free – in return she'd recommended Lizzie in her online writing circles. However, this time she was working to a deadline and couldn't afford any hold-ups.

She grimaced slightly. "I already paid a deposit to the other editor," she said. "And to be honest I would need a fairly quick turnaround."

Lizzie's smile didn't budge but she occupied herself adjusting a sock on one of the girls. The sock looked perfectly fine to start with.

"Sorry," Emily said quietly.

"No." Lizzie shook her head too fiercely. "I understand. It's fine. Of course. You're right – I definitely couldn't guarantee to get it done quickly. And I'd hate to mess up your schedule."

"But when you're back working properly and

the girls are in nursery or whatever I would definitely want to work with you again. It's not that I don't want you to do it . . ." She felt terrible and was having trouble stopping talking.

"You're absolutely right," Lizzie said. "You need to do what's best for you." The smile looked painful.

Jack walked past, heading to the buffet table. "Anyone need a drink?"

Emily nodded furiously. "I'd love a wine."

"Me too," Josie said.

"I'll get them." Lizzie stood abruptly and laid a hand on Jack's shoulder as though she might just force him to the ground. "You sit down. Beer, Jack?"

"Please . . ." He looked confused but took a seat and picked up a baby, holding her up and pulling faces at her so she giggled.

"That was awkward," Emily said, looking to Josie for reassurance.

"Uh oh," Jack said mockingly. "Have you offended Lizzie again? What did you say this time, that her house is a mess, or her children are ugly, food's not up to scratch . . .?"

She glared at him until he cowered away and focused on the baby again. "Lizzie offered to edit my next book and I politely declined . . . I was polite, wasn't I?" she asked Josie.

"Yes. Don't worry about it. You're running a business now, it's not a hobby."

"I thought Lizzie wasn't working again yet," Jack said.

"She's not," Emily said. "She thought she could

fit it in around the kids. But it's a lot of work so I think she's being unrealistic."

"She misses working, that's all," Josie said. "She won't be offended. It was completely reasonable the way you explained it." She trailed off as Lizzie came towards them with her hands full of drinks. Emily jumped up to relieve her.

"Thanks a lot for letting us stay at the house," Jack said as Lizzie hovered over them. Emily was sure she'd been about to walk away again. She'd definitely offended her, and the atmosphere was tense.

"You're welcome." Lizzie glanced around as though looking for an excuse to move away. Hesitantly, she sat down. "Sorry it's such a mess."

"It's such a gorgeous house," Emily said.

"I think I'm going to have trouble getting her out tomorrow," Jack said with a playful smile. "She's a little bit in love with all the old books."

"They're amazing," Emily said wistfully.

"I thought you'd like them." Lizzie's smile became more natural again.

Emily took a sip of wine. "What will you do with them?"

"I'm not sure. Max was supposed to box things up for the charity shop, but he's not had much time."

Emily tried not to react but she felt her eyes widening in shock as she realised Lizzie was being serious. They were actually going to cart them off to a charity shop as though they were junk.

"Hey, Em!" Jack said. "Don't forget to breathe!"

"Sorry." She looked apologetically at Lizzie

when she realised she'd completely failed to hide her disgust. "It seems like such a waste. And you should check that none of them are valuable." Of course, they were all valuable in Emily's eyes, but she wouldn't be surprised if there were some collectors' items among the books with monetary worth too.

"Do you want them?" Lizzie said flippantly. "You're welcome to them if you do. I'd be happy to see them go to a good home."

Emily's jaw dropped. Was she serious? Emily began trying to mentally fit all those books into their apartment in Oxford. It was actually a sad thought. The books seemed to fit the house on Lavender Lane so perfectly.

"Hey, Jack!" Josie said lightly. "Don't forget to breathe!"

He was looking slightly flustered. "I'm just not sure where we'd put them all. It's a lot of books."

"We really don't have space for them," Emily agreed sadly. "But maybe I'll take a few, if that's okay?"

"Help yourself," Lizzie said. "And who knows – by the time Max gets round to sorting out the house you might be filthy rich and living in a mansion with its own library."

"I can dream! You know what you could do?" Emily said hopefully. "Do the house up and turn it into a writing retreat. It's perfect. You could keep the bookshelves. They'd be a great feature."

"It's actually not a bad idea," Lizzie mused. "I could offer discounted editing for anyone who stays!"

"Yes!" Emily said excitedly. "I would love to come back and spend a week writing there. It's the perfect spot."

"You're welcome to come back whenever you want while it's still sitting empty. It's nice that it's being used."

"Don't tempt her," Jack said. "She'll move in!"

Emily laughed. "Unfortunately we really need to get back to Oxford tomorrow." It was a lovely thought, though – spending more time in Hope Cove and hiding away in the wonderful house and getting lost in her writing.

"I really want you to write a book set in Hope Cove," Lizzie said. "You could come and stay while you research it."

"It's like you're trying to steal my girlfriend," Jack said jokily. He put the baby gently back on the blanket and stood up. "I think I'll grab some food. Anyone want anything?"

"I'll come too," Emily said, standing. "I'm really hungry."

They were filling up their plates when Conor sidled over to them. He slapped Jack on the back. "I'm really sorry about last night."

"Don't worry about it," Jack said.

Emily bristled, still annoyed with Conor. "You're lucky Jack went after you," she said. "You could've drowned."

"I know," he said. "I was stupid. I don't know what I was thinking. I feel like a prat."

"You definitely acted like one," Emily said.

Jack shot her a look telling her to drop it.

"Sorry," Conor muttered before wandering

away.

"He feels bad enough as it is." Jack took a bite of a sandwich. "Now you're terrifying the poor guy."

"He's not terrified of me."

"I'm fairly sure he is . . ." When they looked over at Conor he shifted his gaze quickly away from them. If she'd managed to scare him, Emily decided it was probably a good thing. It was also probably the first time in her life that anyone had found her intimidating, and she quite enjoyed the idea. He stayed well away from them after that and the afternoon passed quickly and pleasantly.

Before she knew it, the guests began to disperse and Josie came over to say goodbye. She and Sam were leaving with Annette.

There were lots of hugs and goodbyes but eventually Emily and Jack were walking back up to the house. They'd offered to help Lizzie clean up, but she waved them away, saying they should go and enjoy their last evening in Hope Cove.

"That was a nice afternoon," Emily mused as they ambled up the road.

"Yep." Jack slipped his hand into hers. "The food was great."

She gave him a playful nudge. "I even saw you chatting to Josie's parents."

"I get the impression they like me a lot more now I'm not with Josie."

He glanced at her as though he'd said the wrong thing and was expecting a reaction. In fairness, any mention of his and Josie's relationship tended to send her into a spin, but she was feeling more relaxed about it since their chat on the beach – or maybe it was the wine.

She was also feeling content generally after how easy the afternoon had been. Her worries about what everyone would think about Jack and his run-in with the police were completely unnecessary. No one was talking about the previous evening with anything other than amusement. She was also glad that Josie had told Lizzie and Max the truth.

"It's great to have the place to ourselves again," Emily said when they arrived back to the empty house. She kicked her shoes off and shivered. It was a draughty house and it seemed much warmer outside than in. "It's a shame the fireplace is out of action. It'd be lovely to get in my pyjamas and spend the evening cuddled up in front of a roaring fire with a good book."

"Thanks a lot!" Jack said. "You're not interested in cuddling up with your boyfriend – just a good book."

"I'd cuddle up with you *and* a book." She smiled sweetly and gently kissed his lips. "And a nice cup of tea! I'm going to get my pyjamas on, anyway. It's that kind of house, isn't it? Makes you want to wear your pyjamas all day long."

"I'll put the kettle on," Jack said.

When she arrived back downstairs five minutes later, Jack was sitting on the floor by the hearth. The only lights were a couple of dim table lamps and a glow from Jack's phone which was propped in the fireplace.

"What's that?" she asked, chuckling.

"A fireplace app," he said with a boyish smile.

"Wow." Emily sat next to him and stared at the phone. There was a video of a log fire complete with sounds effects. "That's actually quite soothing. There's an app for everything. You can't exactly toast marshmallows on it, though."

He passed her a cup of tea and flashed a wide grin. "I'd pay money to see you try!"

Chuckling, she leaned into him and watched the fire crackling on the phone with great amusement.

"You realise the next time we see Josie, she'll be getting married."

"Sam invited me to the stag night," Jack said. "I'm not sure if he just invited me because it's in the Bluebell Inn on the night before the wedding, and we're staying there that night . . . but I like to think he'd have invited me anyway."

"I think he would," Emily said. "You two get on well. I'm really glad they're not having crazy stag and hen nights. I always imagined Josie being the sort of hen who'd get drunk before she left the house and do a pub crawl with a pink sash and a tiara – all that tacky stuff. A chilled-out evening at Annette's place sounds perfect."

"It is quite surprising," Jack agreed. "She seems so much calmer and settled now."

"I'm just a bit worried how determined she is to play matchmaker," Emily mused.

"What?"

"She's got this idea about getting Tara together with her boss at the bookshop." Josie had mentioned it to Emily again, convinced it was a great idea. "She wants to invite him to the wedding. She thinks that will get them together. But I know for a fact that

Tara won't appreciate it."

"It sounds like the sort of thing Tara would do, so I'm sure she'll take it in the spirit it's intended."

Emily blew gently on her tea. "I hope so."

Chapter 33

Lizzie was exhausted by the time the last guests left. Her parents took the girls for a walk so she and Max could get the place cleaned up. She was lost in a daydream, staring at the leftover food on the table outside.

"Are you okay?" Max broke her thoughts, and she swung around to find he'd put all the extra chairs back into the shed.

"Fine." She knew she didn't sound at all convincing. In fact, she sounded like she was about to burst into tears. When Max wrapped her in a hug she did just that.

"Sorry." Her words were muffled as she snuggled into him. "I'm being pathetic. I just feel worn out all the time."

"Why don't you go to bed. I can finish tidying up."

"No. I don't want to leave it all to you." She sat heavily on a patio chair. "It was a really lovely day. But I spoke to Emily about editing her book . . ." She trailed off as tears filled her eyes again.

"And?" Max pulled up a chair beside her.

"She already booked an editor. And she's working to a deadline so needs someone who can guarantee they can get it done quickly."

"But I could take the girls on the weekends

and—"

"No." She cut him off. "Emily's right. She needs someone who can focus on it. I don't even know if I could manage it at all. I'm so tired all the time. I probably couldn't concentrate on it."

Max reached for her hand but didn't manage to find any words of reassurance. She was glad – there wasn't anything he could say to make her feel better. "It's just really hard. I see Emily so focused on her career, and it makes me miss having a career. I feel like I'll never get it back."

"You will," he said softly. "This is all temporary. The girls will be in nursery before you know it."

"I know that." She pulled her hand from his. He didn't understand. From now on her career would always come second to the girls. And what made it worse was the guilt she felt for being annoyed by that. Especially when she thought of Josie and what she was going through.

The time with her girls was precious and she knew she should be enjoying it. And that they wouldn't be little for long. She heard that gem so often. She also felt guilty because they knew they were in a nice position to be able to have one parent staying at home with the kids. Increasingly, she just wished it wasn't her who was the stay-at-home parent.

"Why don't we leave the tidying up?" Max suggested. "We can do it later. Let's go for a walk. We can cuddle up on the beach and watch the waves for a while." Tilly trotted over as soon as she heard him mention a walk, and he stroked her face as she waited eagerly in front of him.

"I want to get the place straightened up and try and go to bed early." She stood and started stacking empty plates on the buffet table. When she turned back, Max was looking at her sadly and she felt another pang of guilt. Part of her would love to go and sit on the beach with him. But there was so much to do around the house. There was always so much to do.

"Sorry." She went back and stroked his cheek, then kissed him softly. "I don't mean to be in a bad mood all the time."

"I know." Standing, he snaked his arms around her waist.

"I love you." She didn't say it often enough any more.

Max looked tired too. "Good." He gave her a quick peck on the lips. "Let's get tidied up then."

Chapter 34

June and July went by in a blur for Emily. The first book in her Oxford Castle series was selling far better than she'd expected. It was also getting great reviews, which made her even more determined to get the rest of the series written as quickly as possible.

Taking tours around the castle became something of a nuisance, interrupting her writing time. But a nuisance that paid, which was more than could be said for the writing. The money she made from her books was all going into publishing the next one. Gradually, her finances were getting her down.

"What's wrong?" Jack asked when he came home from work one Friday at the end of July.

Emily was sitting on the floor with her back against the couch, staring at her laptop on the coffee table. When he squeezed her shoulder, she leaned her head on his hand.

Living with Jack was lovely, but she had the feeling that she didn't see him much more than when she was living at her mum's. He worked his regular job all week and then spent his weekends working for his uncle at the Boathouse. He'd never complain, but she knew part of the reason he worked so hard was to offset Emily's lack of income.

"I still can't afford to pay you any rent."

He kissed the top of her head. "I told you it doesn't matter."

"It matters to me," she said sadly.

"You gonna move out then?"

She swatted at his leg but couldn't help but laugh.

"There's no point worrying," he said. "One day you'll be a successful author with loads of money. Until then, just keep writing your books. Worrying won't help."

"No," she said gravely. "But getting a proper job will."

"Your writing is a proper job."

"I mean a job that pays."

"I thought the new book was selling well."

"It is." She turned the laptop to him with all the sales data. "But with all the costs involved it's going to take me a while to break even."

He squinted at the screen and joined her on the floor for a better look. "This is what you've made so far?" he asked, pointing.

"That's what I made this month," she said. "The previous month is there . . ." She prodded the screen. "But I get paid two months in arrears, and most of this will go towards the cover and editing for the next book."

He looked at her and then back at the numbers. "This is decent money."

"Yeah." She was quite amused by the surprise in his voice. "I still can't afford to pay you rent yet."

He shook his head. "I don't care about that. If you make this much from one book, then it's only going to increase with more books."

"Except it costs money to publish them," she said wearily.

"I know, but . . ." He paused and shot her a quizzical look. "Have you made a proper business plan? Figured out the projected income over time?"

"No. Because I'm not a numbers person. I stick to words."

"Pass me your pen and paper . . ."

For the next half hour, he asked her questions and scribbled down numbers, talked about profit margins and return on investment and a load of terms she had no idea what they meant. Jack patiently explained it all to her.

"How do you know so much about business?" she asked when he finally put the pen and paper aside.

"Clive taught me. He wanted me to learn about the business side of things in the cafe as well as serving customers. Sometimes I do some bookkeeping for him."

"Wow." She was still learning things about him. "That's useful."

"Yep. So do you feel better now?"

"I suppose." Since he'd gone to so much effort she didn't want to sound too negative. "It doesn't really change much, though. Saying that I'll break even in year one and start making profit in year two doesn't help my financial situation now."

"But look at year five," he said excitedly, jabbing the pen at the notepad. "Of course, this is all presuming you keep writing books at a steady rate but theoretically you will be doing *really* well in a couple of years' time. And I've been conservative with the numbers, by the way. *And* you've not mentioned the money from your first two books."

"Because it's not worth mentioning." She forced a smile. Jack's enthusiasm was sweet, but in reality she thought he was being overly optimistic. It was a fickle business, and she knew that just because her books were selling well now didn't mean they would be in a month or in a year. How had she ever thought she could make a living from writing her stories down?

"I'll get a job with a steady income for now and do the writing on the side, and then if at some point the books are doing well, I can write full time then."

Jack shook his head. "No." Picking up the notepad, he dropped it in her lap. "You have a great business plan doing something you love. You have to do that."

Tears filled her eyes. He'd always believed in her far more than she did herself.

"Just worry about finishing the next book," he said. "Don't worry about the rent."

"I can't let you keep paying the rent," she said.

"Yes, you can. I'll even feed you too."

"I don't want that. I really don't. It's not fair on you and it's just going to put pressure on our relationship. I definitely don't want that." Tears spilled down her face. "Remember how angry I was when I found out Josie didn't pay you rent? It's completely hypocritical of me to do the same. Getting a regular job and putting the writing career off a little longer isn't the end of the world."

His eyes were full of sympathy. "It's nothing

like how it was with Josie. Call it me investing in your business if you want."

"It feels like I'm taking advantage of you."

His brow furrowed. "It doesn't feel like that to me. As far as I'm concerned, what's mine is yours and what's yours is mine, and on that basis I think we're better off if you stick with the writing. It's going to pay off in the end."

"You're much more confident than me."

"Because you doubt yourself too much. At least give your writing career a proper chance before you give up."

"Okay." She leaned into him and buried her head in his neck as more tears flooded her eyes.

"What now?" he said with a weary chuckle.

"If I'm barely making any money, how are you going to do the paramedic training?"

He rubbed her back. "I wasn't that bothered about that anyway."

She sat up quickly and gave him a gentle shove to the chest.

"What's that for?" he asked, clutching his chest and pretending to be pained.

"For lying!"

"I wasn't lying."

"You were. And I don't want to be in a relationship where you act like some sort of saint who does and says anything just to make me happy."

"Okay." He draped his arm along the couch behind her. "You should probably leave then."

She sat staring at him until he pulled her to him, laughing. "That was a joke! Please don't leave me."

"But everything doesn't revolve around me.

What do you want?"

"I want you to become a really successful author so we can buy a big house and I can retire at thirty and spend my days hanging around the mansion annoying you!"

She slapped his leg. "I'm serious."

"I'm honestly quite content already," he said. "I enjoy my job. I like helping Clive out on the weekends. I'm already happy."

"That makes it sound like I'm not!"

"Well I like to think it's just your career that you're still trying to figure out . . ."

"It is." She put a hand on his cheek as she kissed him tenderly. "I love you."

"I love you too," he mumbled into her lips. "I'm also starving."

"Oh." She grimaced. "I'm really quite useless round here, aren't I?"

"Completely." A dimple appeared as he smirked and he kissed her again before going in search of food.

She followed him into the kitchen and watched him go through the fridge. "You know what I'm kicking myself about?"

"What?" He abandoned the fridge and raided the freezer instead.

"Refusing Lizzie's offer to edit the book. Editing's my biggest cost. She might have taken longer but getting it done for free would have made a huge difference."

"Tell her you changed your mind."

"I can't. It's awkward. I offended her when I turned her down. She might never speak to me again."

"Would you like my expert advice?" Jack asked with a smirk.

She nodded.

"Get her drunk at the wedding and ask her then!"

HANNAH ELLIS

Chapter 35

Emily wasn't convinced of the wisdom of having the hen and stag parties the night before the wedding. It seemed like a tradition that had died out for a good reason. Someone was bound to get roaring drunk and be in a state the next day. Although, she supposed as long as it wasn't Sam or Josie it didn't really matter – and that seemed unlikely.

Her bet would be on Conor or Tara. Although, it turned out Conor wasn't even going. Emily lost track of people but apparently he was Max's side of the family and didn't know Sam well. There was also a rumour that he'd calmed down and spent the summer working for his dad, but Emily couldn't imagine him anything other than wild and partying.

She and Jack were staying at the Bluebell Inn again, and she gave Jack a strict warning not to drink too much before she walked over to Annette's place for the hen party. Lizzie and Amber were there, sitting in the living room with Annette and Josie. They chatted amiably for ten minutes, at which point Tara burst in with her hands full of bags. Her energy seemed to infect the whole house and the evening felt much livelier.

"What are we drinking?" she asked from the edge of the living room. She set one bag down and held up another. "I've got a few bottles of champagne. I was going to do cocktails but I'm concerned about hangovers tomorrow if we start mixing spirits . . ."

"Champagne sounds good," Josie said.

A couple of minutes later they were clinking their glasses together.

"I brought some more fun stuff," Tara said, fetching the bag she'd dumped in the doorway and sitting on the floor in front of the fireplace with it. She emptied it in front of her, and they laughed at the array of swag that fell out.

Everyone dived in to examine the goods.

"What's this?" Josie giggled as she pulled out a poster of a life-sized naked man.

"That's pin the junk on the hunk! Here's a tiara for you." Tara passed the sparkly piece of plastic to Josie. "And there's a sash somewhere . . ." She found it and draped it over Josie. "I've got a mother of the bride sash too. Where's your mum?"

"Putting the girls to bed," Lizzie said. "I think she probably fell asleep too. Which might be a good thing, looking at all this!"

Annette reached down and pulled at a piece of paper that was half hidden under the pile. "I love . . ." she read aloud. "Oh, my! That's graphic."

They choked on laughter at the picture Annette was holding up.

"More junk!" Tara said. "I know you're not familiar with this part of the male anatomy, Annette. I presume it doesn't offend you." She took it from her. "It's actually a sticker. Who wants it?"

"That's vulgar," Emily announced.

Tara threw it back in the pile of stuff and a

smirk twitched at her lips. "I'm surprised you're such a prude, Emily. All things considered."

"What's that supposed to mean?"

Josie snorted a laugh and Amber also looked thoroughly amused.

"Have I missed a joke?" Emily asked.

"No," Tara said. "It's nothing. Just something I heard . . . a few whispers at the Bluebell Inn. You know what that place is like for gossip!"

Emily's eyes bulged. What on earth had people been saying about her?

"Tell me!" she demanded through the chuckles of the others.

"Something about you writing naughty books," Tara said with a wicked grin.

"What?"

Josie spluttered out a laugh. "Tara started a rumour that you write porn."

"Are you serious?" Emily said, glaring at Tara.

"Erotic romance were my exact words. I said you write those books under a pen name."

"You're such a bunch of idiots," Emily said lightly. "It's not even that funny. And I'm sure whoever it was didn't believe you anyway."

"Except it was big mouth Belinda, who's one of the most gullible people I know. And I told her it was a huge secret."

Amber grinned. "Which just means she whispers when she tells everyone in a three-mile radius."

"People actually believe it." Tara wiped tears of laughter from her eyes. "Last week Graham came into the bookshop . . ."

"That's my neighbour," Annette said. "The dirty old sod."

"He came in asking for one of your *alternative* books."

Emily sighed. "Why do I get the feeling you didn't tell him no such thing exists?"

"Probably because you know me so well," Tara said. "I sold him one of your saucy romances under your pseudonym, Jessica Velvet."

Emily rolled her eyes and pushed her hair off her face. "That's wrong on so many levels."

"It's not!" Tara insisted. "It's good for everyone: it's good for our sales and it's good for the author. And old Graham is getting his kicks. Everybody wins."

"Not me!" Emily protested. "I don't want people thinking I write dirty books."

"Why not? There's nothing wrong with it. Some of it's really well written and the storylines are great."

"Are they?" Annette asked seriously.

Tara nodded. "You want me to get you some?"

"Yes. Lesbian romance if you can."

"No problem."

"Oh my God!" Josie buried her head in her hands, giggling. "I think you've had too much champagne, Annette."

"Ignore them," Tara said. "Bunch of prudes!"

"I can't believe you're spreading rumours about me," Emily said. She couldn't help but laugh, though.

"It was just a bit of fun." Tara chuckled as she stood. "Who wants to pin the junk on the hunk?"

They groaned their protests, but it turned out to be a lot of fun. After that, Tara coaxed them into a few more silly games while they consumed a steady amount of champagne. Emily had far too much to drink, but it was going down so easily, and Tara kept topping up her glass.

When she eventually complained she needed to get to bed, Tara and Amber said they were getting a taxi home and would drop her at the pub on the way.

She wobbled slightly when she stepped out of the car in front of the pub.

"Wait," Tara said, stumbling out after her. "I need to give you a hug." She wrapped her arms around Emily and patted her affectionately on the back.

"You're so drunk." Emily wriggled out of the embrace and shouted goodnight to Amber as Tara climbed ungracefully back into the car.

The pub was busy and she scanned the room for Jack. When there was no sign of him she headed for Sam and Max, loitering near the pool table. There was a crowd of guys there – presumably all part of the stag party.

"Have you seen Jack?" she asked, speaking louder than she'd intended.

"He went up to bed," Sam said. "Only about five minutes ago."

She was distracted by snorts of laughter and glanced over her shoulder. A couple of older guys at a nearby table quickly averted their gaze.

"I'll go and find him," Emily said, turning her attention back to Sam. When low voices and more laughter drifted over her shoulder, she swung around to face the men at the table. "It's rude to whisper!" she snapped. Did people really believe Tara's silly rumour about her?

Behind her, Max and Sam snorted and she turned back. "So you think it's funny too?"

Max erupted with laughter, doubling over and clutching the edge of the pool table for support.

"You're so immature!" She glared at Sam, who was trying his best to stifle his laughter but his shoulders were shaking and his cheeks were getting redder. Everyone around was chuckling. "Even if I did write erotic romance, it's really not that funny." More laughter. "It's actually a very popular genre so if I did write it, *I'd* be the one laughing . . . about how much money I make!"

She'd drawn a lot of attention to herself, and as she turned to leave, everyone behind her guffawed. Bunch of immature idiots.

"Emily!" Sam took her arm to stop her.

"What?" she hissed.

He took a breath to compose himself. "There's a sticker on your back."

She grabbed over her shoulder to no avail and then twisted her arm up behind her back, turning in a circle like a dog chasing its tail.

"Here . . ." Sam stopped her and peeled it off, handing her the vulgar picture which announced that she loved a certain part of the male anatomy.

"I'm going to kill Tara," she growled.

The laughter from the pub could still be heard as she walked up the staircase at the back of the pub that led to the guest rooms.

Jack was face down on the bed, fully dressed.

"Everyone's being mean," she said, pouting as she sat heavily beside him.

He grunted. "Who's being mean? I'll beat them up."

"Max and Sam . . . and everyone in the pub." She shook his shoulder to try and rouse him further. He hadn't managed to open his eyes. "Look what Tara put on my back . . . everyone was laughing at me."

Jack opened an eye and choked on a laugh.

"It's not funny!"

"It's funny. Especially because everyone in the pub thinks you write dirty books. Now you've got a sign on your back that says you love—" He couldn't finish the sentence for laughing. "It is a bit funny, Em."

"You weren't supposed to get drunk," she said.

"You're drunk too!"

"No, I'm not."

But that probably wasn't true judging by the way the room spun when she lay down beside Jack.

Chapter 36

When Emily arrived at Annette's place the next morning, Josie was in the front bedroom. The hairdresser was just leaving, and Josie sat in her dressing gown, staring into the mirror.

"What do you think?" she asked. Her hair was tied up in a neat French twist and loose tendrils framed her face.

"I love it," Emily said. "I thought you were having your hair down though."

"I changed my mind at the last minute. You really think it looks okay?"

"It looks amazing. Don't you like it?"

"I think so." She turned her head to look from a different angle. "I always thought I'd have a slightly quirky wedding, but I've ended up being quite traditional."

"Nothing wrong with that," Emily said.

"I knew you'd approve! I always thought it was a bit cliché . . . the white dress and looking like a princess. But when it came to it, that's all very appealing. How often will I get to dress up like a princess?" She took the dress from the back of the door. "Will you help me put it on? Since I'll only be wearing it today, I want to make the most of it."

It took a couple of minutes to get it on and zipped up.

"Wow." Emily stood beside her at the mirror. "You look beautiful. Traditional and beautiful."

"You've not seen my shoes yet," she said with a grin. "I stayed well away from traditional with my shoes."

"Converse, I presume?"

"Of course! That's how Sam and I met – talking about my love of Converse. I'll show you them." She picked the shoebox from the bed. It was tied with a blue ribbon. "I need to get Lizzie first." At the bedroom door, she called out for her sister.

"Yeah?" the voice shouted back from downstairs.

"Come up for a minute . . ."

Lizzie looked flustered when she trudged up the stairs, but the moment she saw Josie, her features crumpled and she bit her lip.

"You're already in your dress."

"I only get to wear it once," Josie said, beaming. "I want to wear it for as long as possible."

"You look stunning." Her eyes filled with tears. "I'm sorry. I'm so tired and emotional."

Josie put the shoebox aside and gave her a big hug.

"I'll mess up your dress," Lizzie said but hugged her back anyway, then wiped tears from her cheeks as she stepped back. "Are you nervous?"

Josie shook her head. "Just excited."

"Good."

"I got you a present." Josie handed over the shoebox. It confused Emily, who'd previously thought they were Josie's shoes. Oh God. Was she going to make them all wear Converse? Emily had picked out a lovely pair of strappy sandals. She really didn't want to wear trainers.

Lizzie took the box with trepidation. She glanced at Emily, apparently having the same thoughts. "You're making us wear Converse?"

"Just open it!" Josie clapped her hands together.

The ribbon fell to the floor when Lizzie untied it. "Blue Converse." Lizzie took a breath and held one up to show Emily. "Are you serious?"

"They'll look great with your dress. And how much fun will it be if we all wear Converse?"

No fun at all, Emily thought.

"A pink dress and baby-blue shoes?" Lizzie said. Apparently she wasn't even going to try and be tactful. "We're going to look like idiots!"

Josie snorted a laugh. "You're so easy to wind up. Of course I'm not making you wear trainers!"

"Then why have you given them to me?"

"Because they're blue and brand new, and I'm going to swap the laces for some old ribbon that Annette gave me. I just need you to lend them to me . . ."

Lizzie chuckled. "Something old, something new, something borrowed and something blue. All in a pair of shoes?"

"Yes! So can I borrow them?"

"As long as you make it like all the other times you borrow my stuff and don't return them."

"Thank you!" She smiled sweetly as she took the box back. "And stop looking at me like that!"

"Like what?"

"Like you can't believe I'm actually going to wear them."

"I can definitely believe you're going to wear them." Lizzie's eyes darted downwards. "At least your dress is floor length. Maybe no one will see them."

"Apart from when I show everyone! I love them." Josie sat on the bed and began pulling the laces out of the shoes. "The first conversation I ever had with Sam was at your wedding. He thought I must have forgotten my shoes because he couldn't believe I actually intended to wear trainers with my bridesmaid's dress."

"I was so annoyed with you about those shoes." Lizzie leaned on the doorframe and smiled at the memory.

"No, you weren't." Josie picked up the beautiful cream ribbons and began carefully threading them through the eyelets. "You were annoyed when you were going to marry Phil. When you married Max, you didn't care. Which proved one of my original arguments: if you marry the right person you don't care what shoes people wear. That's also why you got to choose your own shoes today – it's a sign of true love!"

There were chuckles all round.

"See." Josie held up a shoe, laced with Annette's ribbon. "They look great."

Lizzie nodded. "Much better with the ribbons." She went and kissed Josie's cheek. "I'm going to get dressed and head over to the Town Hall soon. I want to walk the girls round the block a few times and see if I can get them to sleep for the ceremony."

"Good luck!" Josie said.

"Same to you," Lizzie said with a sly smile. She

looked emotional when they exchanged a quick hug, then she followed the babbling and banging noises from the twins back downstairs.

Josie began lacing the ribbon into the second shoe. "Lizzie cracks me up. Did you see the look on her face? She really thought I was going to ask her to wear Converse."

"I'll be honest," Emily said. "I was a bit concerned too for a minute."

"It's actually a great idea . . . all of us wearing Converse. Shame I only just thought of it."

"Such a shame," Emily said mockingly.

Josie chuckled. "How was Jack this morning? Did you get any gossip from him about the stag party?"

"He wasn't awake when I left. I'll call him in a bit and make sure he's up. All I know about the stag party is the glimpse I got when I went back to the pub last night."

"And?" Josie reached down to put her shoes on. "Was it a wild night in the Bluebell Inn?"

"It seemed like they were having a lot of fun . . . most of it at my expense!"

"Why? What happened?"

"Tara put a sticker on my back. Everyone thought it was very funny."

Josie pursed her lips to stop herself from laughing. "*That* sticker. I saw Tara put it in her pocket before she left. I wondered what she was up to."

"It was very embarrassing." Emily shook her head and then smiled. She was starting to see the funny side.

Sunshine streamed in the window as Josie walked around the room testing out her new shoes. She stopped by the window and Emily joined her to watch everything being set up outside. The marquee had been erected the previous afternoon, and now all the finishing touches were being made – tables were being set and flowers arranged. They laughed at the same time as Annette stood over a waiter, obviously giving him advice on how to set the table. Charlie, the docile golden retriever, wandered around, watching what was going on and getting lots of attention.

"It's going to be such a wonderful day," Emily said. "I already feel like it's going to go too fast."

"Me too," Josie said. "I want to savour every minute."

Emily put an arm around her and gave her shoulders a squeeze. "I'm so happy for you."

"Me too." She took a seat by the dressing table. "And I'm happy for you as well. I know I was a bit of a cow about you and Jack to start with." She raised an eyebrow and her eyes sparkled with amusement as they exchanged a knowing look. "But I really am glad things worked out for you two. It'll be your wedding next."

"Yes." Emily smiled lazily as she watched everything going on outside. "I can't wait to marry him. I love him so much." Their relationship had settled into something wonderfully stable. The chat on the beach at Hope Cove had changed things. Emily had stopped worrying about losing Jack and instead focused on appreciating everything she had. She felt incredibly lucky every day.

Josie was grinning at her. "How's it looking out there?"

"It's looking perfect." The sky was bright blue with only a couple of clouds, the sun was shining, everything really did seem perfect. "Tara and Amber are here now. I'm glad I got here in time to have you to myself for a while."

"Me too," Josie said. "It's hard to get a word in around Tara!"

"I never thought you'd find someone to make you look quiet," Emily said with a mischievous grin. "I still can't believe she put that sticker on my back."

***

Lizzie was an emotional wreck. She had no idea how she'd make it through the day. The girls had woken a couple of times in the night and Phoebe had decided 6 a.m. was a good time to get up. The combination of a late night, too much champagne and almost no sleep had left Lizzie exhausted. Max had stayed at Sam's place. She'd been fine with the idea when it was originally suggested, but after a horrendous night's sleep, she was somewhat begrudging. It was going to be a long day.

She'd have loved to help Josie get ready and sat and chatted with her like Emily did, but the twins were so demanding, it was a struggle to juggle getting them ready as well as herself. Her mum's efforts to help seemed only to hinder. Maya had developed an aversion to her grandmother and screamed any time she came near.

When she saw Josie in her dress, her emotions

had taken over, although the tears soon dried up when she thought her little sister was going to make her wear trainers with her beautiful dress. Thankfully, she'd only been joking.

The wedding ceremony was conveniently taking place right around the girls' nap time, and Lizzie was desperately hoping the girls would sleep through the whole thing. She drove over to the cute little market town early and felt a ridiculous sense of achievement when both the girls nodded off as she walked them round the streets in their buggy.

It was such a relief when they were settled in the Town Hall waiting for Josie to arrive. The buggy was parked beside her at the edge of the room and she rocked it gently, confident they'd sleep for a while.

Max and Sam were standing at the front of the room, chatting easily as the guests took their seats. It was a lovely big airy room with huge windows and high ceilings. When the music started up, Lizzie stood and looked to the back doors as they opened. Tears filled her eyes again at the sight of Josie on their dad's arm. She looked absolutely radiant and her smile lit up the room.

Glancing into the buggy, Lizzie saw Phoebe's eyes pop open. She tried her best to soothe her back to sleep with the movement of the buggy, and then frantically picked her up when she realised it wasn't going to work. It was too late – her shrill cry woke Maya. As the music died down and the room fell silent, Lizzie panicked.

Maya screamed at being rudely awakened. When Lizzie passed Phoebe to her mum beside her,

Phoebe wailed too and thrust herself back in Lizzie's direction. It was carnage. Two babies clinging to her and Maya sounding like she was on a mission to scream the place down. She needed Max to help her but he was at the front with Sam and only shot her a sympathetic glance.

"Sorry," she mumbled as everyone looked at her. She'd have to take them out.

"Do you want me to take one of them?" a low voice asked.

She turned to find Jack crouched beside her.

"Can you take Phoebe?" she said, trying not to cry herself. "I'll have to take Maya out . . ."

"I'll take Maya." He looked so calm as he gently reached for the screaming child. "You watch your sister get married."

She felt awful that he'd miss the ceremony and wanted to protest, but he was heading outside with Maya before she knew it. At the front, the officiant had been waiting for the noise to die down before he started the ceremony.

"Sorry," she muttered again.

Chapter 37

Emily was filled with pride as she stood beside Josie while she made her wedding vows. Her best friend looked absolutely stunning and radiated happiness. She and Sam made the perfect couple. The ceremony was short and sweet. She'd felt sorry for Lizzie, who looked flustered trying to manage the babies alone. Luckily Jack had swooped in and taken the screaming child outside for her. He'd slipped back in just in time for the vows. The baby was asleep and he walked up and down the back of the room as he gently rocked her in his arms.

Emily caught his eye, and when he winked at her she felt herself blush.

As soon as the ceremony was over, she went and found him. She was feeling overwhelmingly emotional. "It was so lovely," she said. "I kept crying. I couldn't help it. Josie looked so happy."

"She did," he said, leaning in to kiss her.

"Oh my goodness." Lizzie came rushing over and gave Jack a big kiss on the cheek. "You are a lifesaver."

"Any time," he said, handing the peaceful baby over.

"Thank you." Lizzie beamed at him and moved away.

"What happened to your suit jacket?" Emily

asked.

He grinned. "Maya puked all down me."

"You seem devastated!"

"You know me and suits. She did me a favour."

A middle-aged woman smiled as she walked past. "You're the writer, aren't you?" she said, touching Emily's elbow.

"Yes," Emily said politely.

The woman nodded and carried on.

Jack leaned in to Emily. "Do you think she's read *your* books or Jessica Velvet's?!"

"I can't believe Tara said that." Emily rolled her eyes and they followed the crowd outside.

The wedding guests stayed around the Town Hall for a little while, throwing confetti over the newlyweds and taking photos. Then they all set off back to Annette's place for the reception.

It was a wonderful setup. The marquee was a modest size and thanks to the lovely weather, all the sides had been tied up. Inside the marquee, tables were set for the wedding breakfast, and there was a small dance floor at one end.

Out on the grass, hay bales made for rustic seating and big wooden beer barrels provided casual tables. An acoustic band played modern tunes softly in the background. The atmosphere was wonderful, the meal was delicious and the speeches were a wonderful mix of charming, emotional and funny.

Over the course of the day, several people approached Emily asking if she was the writer, often with a funny look which made her wonder what genre they thought she wrote.

When daylight began to fade to twilight, the

people who'd been milling on the grass moved into the marquee. It was strung up with fairy lights and looked absolutely magical. Emily had been chatting to Josie's mum and was walking towards Jack when an elderly gentleman stepped in front of her.

"You're Emily, aren't you?" he said with a silly grin. She braced herself for the inevitable writer comment with a forced smile.

"I'm Graham." He extended his hand. When she took it, he leaned in and lowered his voice. "You're the porn star, aren't you?"

She opened and closed her mouth and was vaguely aware of Jack, who stopped dead behind Graham. His mouth was clamped shut but she saw his shoulders begin to shake.

Emily blinked her eyes rapidly. "No," she spluttered. "I'm sorry, what?"

"Don't worry." He tapped his finger to his nose. "I won't tell anyone. There's no shame in writing dirty books though."

"But I'm not a porn star . . ."

"Don't be so modest. I think you're great. The writing is top quality, the storylines are original. You're definitely a star."

"That doesn't make me a porn star," she whispered. "You're mixed up . . ."

"Don't worry, I understand." He tapped his nose again. "It's Jessica Velvet who's the star. Your secret's safe with me."

Her jaw went into overdrive again as he walked away, though she didn't manage to produce any words.

Jack was staring at her with wide eyes. "Does

he think . . .?"

"Don't even say anything!" she warned.

"But did he just say . . .?" He put his knuckle to his mouth and looked as though he might explode from excitement. "This might be the best day ever."

"I think so," Josie said cheerily as she and Tara joined them. "What are you looking so happy about?"

He pointed behind him. "The old guy thinks Emily's a porn star!"

Josie and Tara snorted laughter.

"He got his words mixed up," Emily said. "He thinks people who write erotica are called porn stars."

"He's drunk," Tara said. "He'll have told everyone you're a porn star by the end of the night."

"It's not funny," Emily insisted as the three of them cracked up around her.

"My girlfriend the porn star," Jack said proudly as he slung an arm around her shoulders.

Sam joined them and casually high-fived Jack. "I just heard from Graham!"

Emily elbowed Jack in the ribs. "Why would that be a good thing? Why on earth would anyone want their girlfriend to be a porn star?"

"For all the porn star sex!"

"But I'd be having porn star sex with lots of other people and wouldn't have time for sex with you." She glanced behind her as everyone fell silent. "Oh, hi, Annette!"

"Don't let me interrupt. This sounds like an interesting conversation."

"It's a ridiculous conversation. Tara, you need

to go and tell Graham I'm not a porn star!"

"No way," Tara said. "It's too funny."

"Maybe I should tell him," Annette said. "It was me who told him the wrong word in the first place. He's very easily confused when he's drunk."

"Annette!" Emily gasped.

"It's just a bit of fun," Annette said, chuckling as she walked away.

"Don't look now," Josie said, directing her attention at Tara. "Your date just arrived."

"My what?" her smile faded as she followed Josie's gaze to the gate. James was walking casually up the path.

"What's he doing here?" Tara asked.

"I invited him. I didn't say anything because he wasn't sure he could make it. I knew he'd turn up though. Just get together with him, will you? You're not fooling me. I know you like him. It doesn't matter that he's your boss—"

"Josie!" Tara snapped, close to tears. "You don't know what you're talking about." Quickly, she walked down the path towards James. "I can't believe you invited him," she mumbled.

"I told you not to play matchmaker," Sam said.

Josie seemed taken aback. "I really thought she'd be happy about it."

Emily watched as Tara walked up to James. Even from a distance you could tell it wasn't a warm greeting. She had a hand on his arm as she walked him back the way he'd come. They stopped at the gate, deep in conversation. Emily couldn't bear to look.

"I don't understand Tara sometimes," Josie said.

Thankfully she was distracted as the musicians launched into a new song. "I love this song. I want to dance." She grabbed at Jack's hand. "You haven't danced with me yet. Come on."

"I hate dancing," he grumbled.

"But it's my wedding day. You have to do what I want." She pulled on his arm, and he followed with an awkward backward glance at Emily.

"Do you want to dance?" Sam asked.

"No, thanks." Emily took a seat on the hay bale behind her. "I don't like to dance."

Jack and Josie were laughing as he waltzed her around the dance floor. For someone who claimed to hate dancing he was very good at it. She directed her attention to her drink instead.

Sam sat close beside her. "Does it bother you, seeing them together?"

She thought for a moment. "Not any more." She squinted, not sure how honest she was being. "Maybe a bit. It used to bother me a lot so I'm getting somewhere."

"Me too." He leaned forward with his elbows on his knees as he watched them dance.

"Really?"

"When I first met Jack I wanted to punch him. And then when Josie started insisting we were all going to be friends . . ." He looked at Emily and rolled his eyes. "I went along with it hoping it was just another of her crazy ideas that would eventually fizzle out."

"Josie's always been one for crazy ideas," she said lightly.

"It's actually slightly annoying how well I get

on with Jack," Sam said. "I'm getting a lot of 'I told you so' vibes from Josie."

"She usually knows best."

"That's true. I think she was right about us all being friends. I get the feeling we'll all be hanging out together a long time from now."

She beamed at him. "I hope so."

"Me too." He took her drink and set it on the floor. "Time to dance I'm afraid."

"No!" She laughed as he pulled her up. "I don't dance."

His eyes were full of mischief. "But it's my wedding day. You have to do what I want . . ."

"I'm fairly sure that rule only applies to the bride!" She smiled anyway as he led her to the dance floor.

"What's going on?" Josie asked. "Emily doesn't dance."

"It's my wedding day," Sam said, twirling Emily around. "If I want to dance with a porn star, I will!"

Emily gave him a playful shove. She had a feeling that joke would be around for a while.

"Swap?" Jack asked.

As the music slowed, Emily moved to Jack and relaxed in his arms. "We don't have to dance," she said. "We can go and get a drink if you want?"

"No," he whispered, swaying gently.

"But you hate dancing."

"I like dancing with you," he said. "I might make you dance with me all evening."

Emily stopped and looked up at him.

"What?" he asked.

She pushed her hands into his hair as she kissed him. "I love you."

"I love you too," he said happily.

Chapter 38

Lizzie was mesmerised by the dancing as she gently rocked Phoebe in the buggy. There was something magical about the dance floor at a wedding. It was so full of joy. All those couples happily twirling and swaying and gazing lovingly into each other's eyes. Max was beside her, trying to settle Maya with a bottle. It wasn't long since their wedding day.

"What?" Max asked when he caught her looking at him.

"Seems like forever since our wedding, doesn't it?"

He smiled. "Quite a lot has happened since then."

She peered in the buggy at her sleeping baby and then went back to watching the dancing. It was a couple of minutes later when Emily and Jack left the dance floor. Emily smiled and they'd almost walked past them when Max shouted her back.

"Could you take Maya for a few minutes?"

Panic flashed in Emily's eyes. "Yes."

Hesitantly, she took Maya and sat down. She stared at Max when he gave her the bottle of milk. "I've never fed a baby before."

"Just stick it in her mouth," he said, then turned to Lizzie. "Time for a dance, Mrs Anderson."

Jack automatically took over rocking the buggy.

"Are you sure you're okay with her?" Lizzie asked Emily.

"I can take her if you want," Jack said.

"No," Emily said. "I'm fine." She looked at the bottle. "I can't get this wrong, can I?"

"Not really," Max said lightly. "Unless you drop her, of course."

He and Jack chuckled and Lizzie felt sorry for Emily.

"Don't tease me." She carefully put the bottle in Maya's mouth. "I just don't have any experience with babies."

"You look like a natural," Lizzie reassured her before taking Max's hand and following him to the dance floor. She felt quite emotional as they danced cheek to cheek, swaying in time with the gentle music.

"Are you okay?" Max asked.

"Yes."

He pulled back, scrutinising her. "Really?"

A lump formed in her throat and she buried her face in his neck. She was such an emotional wreck, and the truth was she didn't feel okay at all, but it seemed like the wrong time to discuss it.

"I had an idea," Max said gently. "But I'm scared to suggest it in case you bite my head off . . ."

"Well if you think I'll be annoyed the chances are I will be." When he fell quiet the suspense got to her. "Tell me anyway," she prompted.

His shoulders tensed. "I was thinking we could put the girls into the nursery sooner than we planned . . ."

"What?" Her heart rate increased and tears filled

her eyes.

Max sighed heavily. "I knew I shouldn't say anything."

"Why did you think I'd be annoyed?"

"I don't know. Because maybe you'd think I was saying you can't look after them or something. And I absolutely don't think that. I only thought you might like the break. They're pretty full on."

She lost control at that point and started to cry in earnest.

"I'm sorry," he said quickly. "Ignore me."

She took his hand and moved quickly from the dance floor, hoping no one noticed what a blubbering mess she was. At a quiet table she sat and dabbed at her eyes with a stray napkin.

Max pulled up a chair in front of her and took her hand. "It was only a suggestion. We don't have to."

"I really want to." She laughed through tears and leaned forward to kiss him.

"I'm confused. Why are you crying?"

"Because I really want them to go to nursery. As soon as possible! But I feel like a terrible mother for thinking that."

"You're not a terrible mother." He gently wiped the tears from her cheeks with his thumbs. "You're amazing."

"I hate being a full-time mum." Her face crumpled as she finally admitted it. "I love them so much, but I hate spending every moment of every day with them and having nothing else to think about. And then I feel so guilty for feeling like that."

He moved until his forehead touched hers. "I'll

let you in on a secret," he said. "I've never enjoyed going to work as much as I do now."

She laughed. "I'm always so jealous when you go to work."

"So they can go to nursery and you can start working again. Or just have the time for yourself, whatever you want."

"But the nursery can't take them until January."

"They can't take them full-time until January but they said they could take them part-time until then."

Her lip quivered. "You already spoke to them?"

"There didn't seem much point suggesting it if it wasn't possible."

She took a deep breath. "When could they start?"

"Week after next?" he said with a raised eyebrow.

"Oh my God." She threw her head back and happily wiped the remaining tears from her cheeks. It felt like someone had lifted a concrete block from her chest and she could breathe again. "I shouldn't be this excited!"

"You can be as excited as you want." He pulled her gently onto his lap. "I just want you to be happy. And I know I said I love going to work, but I love coming home too."

"Even though I'm always shouting at you?"

"Yes! Even when you're shouting." He paused for a moment. "Why don't you talk to Emily again about editing her book? You'll have time now."

"I can't," she said. "It was awkward enough last time she turned me down. She's got a plan and she wants to stick to it. I don't blame her. Hopefully once I'm working again, she'll want me to work on future projects. I like working with her."

"I'm sure your old clients will be glad to hear you're taking on work again."

"Yes," she agreed, excited by the thought. She snuggled into him for a moment, then sighed. "We should get back to the girls."

"Or we can find some champagne and a quiet corner to drink in . . ." He glanced over his shoulder. "Looks like Jack and Emily have got things under control."

"He's very good with the girls," Lizzie remarked.

"What's the deal with Emily?" Max asked. "She looked like I was trying to pass her a ticking bomb when I wanted her to take Maya."

"She's just not used to babies." Lizzie stood and took Max's hand. "Let's go and find that champagne."

* * *

Emily could feel Jack's eyes on her as she glanced down at the sleeping baby in her arms. Maya was very cute.

"Don't look at me like that," Emily said, without looking at Jack.

"Like what?"

"You know!"

He moved closer and his words tickled her cheek. "I can't wait until you're holding our baby."

She felt herself blush. "You've got a few years to wait."

"I know you said five years but I was thinking two years."

Her eyes darted to his. "You said three before."

"Okay, fine. Three it is!"

"That was sneaky." She smiled and kissed him before turning her attention back to the dance floor. Secretly, she loved how keen he was to have a family.

Emily had mixed emotions as she watched people dancing. On the one hand, so many people were having a wonderful time, laughing and grinning as they danced. But in amongst it all, she caught Lizzie crying on Max's shoulder before dashing off across the room. And then there was Tara.

She was dancing to one side with James. If you didn't know the situation, you'd swear they were madly in love. They were, Emily supposed sadly. But she knew there was a lot more to the intensity of Tara's gaze than just love.

It was hard not to watch as they slipped away from the dance floor. Emily kept glancing over her shoulder as they walked down the drive and hugged beside the gate. A moment later, headlights lit up the dark country road and then faded again. Tara stayed by the gate, an eerie silhouette.

"I need to go and check on Tara," Emily said to Jack. "Can you take the baby?" Thankfully Maya didn't wake when she handed her to Jack.

Hurrying down the drive, Emily found Tara in floods of tears.

"What happened?" She rubbed Tara's arms while she waited for her to calm down enough to answer.

"He wanted to explain about his girlfriend." She sucked in a huge breath and wiped frantically at tears which wouldn't stop pouring down her cheeks. "He said he was angry with me. That's why he went back to her. The pregnancy wasn't planned. But he wants to stick by her . . ." She paced in front of the gate. "And I don't know why I'm so angry with him. I told him I didn't want to be with him. I couldn't be with him anyway so what does it matter if he's getting married and having a baby."

Emily felt utterly useless. She never knew what to say, and it was heartbreaking seeing Tara so upset.

"I won't even get to see him any more." She stopped her pacing and gripped the gate. "I'm quitting my job. And he said I don't need to work out my notice. So that's it. I'm done. I have nothing." Her features morphed from anger to complete anguish.

"I'm so sorry." Emily leaned on the gate beside her and they stayed in silence for a few minutes.

"I have no idea what I'm going to do with my life," Tara said.

"You'll figure it out. It seems really bad now, but things will get better."

Tara stood up straight, shaking her head. If only Emily had something meaningful to say. All she had were clichés and empty words.

"I can't go back to the party," Tara said. "Can you make up an excuse if anyone asks about me?"

"Yes." Emily smiled sadly. "I wish I could do something."

"Just go and have a good time. Make sure Josie has fun. She deserves some fun."

"I will." Emily hugged her and was almost in tears herself as she left her to rejoin the party.

When anyone asked where Tara was, Emily claimed she'd had too much to drink and had to go home to bed. No one questioned it. Except for Josie, who joked that she thought Tara had sneaked away with James. Emily opened her mouth to correct her but decided it wasn't the time. It wasn't her secret to tell, and it wasn't fair on Josie to make her worry about Tara on her wedding day. It was the first time she'd seemed truly happy in a while and Emily wasn't going to ruin that.

***

The evening was a great success. Apart from poor Tara, everyone seemed to have a fantastic time. Jack ended up being left with the babies for most of the evening but he seemed quite happy with the situation. Eventually, Max and Lizzie took them into Annette's house to put them to bed. As the band packed away, the guests gradually dispersed until it was only Josie and Sam and Jack and Emily left. They were all a bit tipsy.

"We shouldn't really be sitting in the marquee," Josie said, wandering out onto the grass barefoot.

"No." Emily followed her out with Jack by her side. "We should be in bed."

"No." Josie laughed. Her arms splayed out to the sides and she turned in a circle, looking up to the sky. "We should be out under the stars. It's so magical out here."

"It is pretty spectacular." Emily wobbled when she stared overhead and bumped heavily into Jack. "I'm drunk. I need to go to bed."

"No!" Josie sat on a hay bale, staring overhead. "Stay and look at the stars with me. In fact . . ." She leaned back and fell off the hay bale, laughing loudly as she landed on her back. Sam sat down and reached out a hand to her but she only pulled him down too. "It's the best view from here."

When she instructed Jack and Emily to lie down, they did as they were told. Josie was right about it being magical; the sky was perfectly clear and the stars twinkled as though someone had thrown a handful of glitter overhead.

"How long are we going to lie here for?" Sam asked. "You realise you married an old man and I need to go to bed sometime soon."

"Just until we see a shooting star," she said. "Then we can go."

"What are you doing?" Lizzie appeared, looming over them. Max stepped into view too.

"We're waiting for a shooting star," Emily said, moving closer to Jack.

"You're all drunk, aren't you?"

"Yes!" they chimed at once, then laughed loudly.

"I *was*," Lizzie said, joining them in lying down. "But I think I sobered up again."

Max lay beside Lizzie. "What are you going to wish for, when you see your shooting star?"

Josie giggled. "I just want to see a shooting star. That's my wish. That's quite ironic, isn't it?"

Jack snorted and the rest of them joined in

laughing.

"You know the chances of seeing a shooting star are pretty slim?" Lizzie said.

"It's my wedding day," Josie said. "I get whatever I want."

Lizzie's voice was light and teasing. "I think we all know you're good at controlling people . . . I'm not convinced you can control the universe."

"Don't be mean. Just keep watching. Any minute now . . ." They all looked up mesmerised.

"See," Lizzie said. "Nothing."

"Wait!" Josie laughed. "Just wait."

It was perfectly silent for a minute. Then Josie let out a squeal of delight as a streak of silver sailed gracefully across the sky.

"I can control the universe!" she declared elated.

Lizzie groaned. "I'm never going to hear the end of this."

"What did everyone wish for?" Josie asked.

"Sleep," Max said. "An eight-hour block of sleep."

"That would be nice," Lizzie said. "But it's probably best to wish for things within the realms of possibility."

"I didn't even make a wish," Sam said. "I already have everything I want."

"That's really soppy," Josie said, as the rest of them faked vomit noises.

"It's true," he said. "Jack, what did you wish for?"

Josie snorted a laugh. "He's got a porn star for a girlfriend. What would he wish for?! Emily, what do you want?"

"I wish . . ." She paused. "I wish I hadn't turned down Lizzie's offer to edit my book."

Out of the corner of her eye she saw Lizzie sitting up quickly. "Really? You still want me to edit it?"

"Yes," she said weakly. "And I don't mind if it takes you longer than usual."

"The girls are starting nursery so I'll have time," Lizzie said excitedly.

Emily sat up to look at her. "Really? You'll do it for me?"

"I'd love to."

"I'm not just asking because you do it for free," Emily said quickly. "I love working with you."

"Me too," Lizzie said beaming.

"Just to be clear," Jack said. "She's got no money so take that last comment with a pinch of salt."

"Shut up!" Emily punched him playfully when she lay down again.

"Yay!" Josie cheered. "Your wish came true."

"I couldn't decide whether to wish for that," Emily said, "or for everyone to stop referring to me as a porn star."

"That seems about as likely as us getting eight hours of sleep," Max said. He stood and pulled Lizzie up. "But maybe if we go to bed now, we might manage three hours."

Everyone called goodnight as they headed back to the house.

"We're going too." Sam stood, then reached for Josie's hand. "Now you're my wife you have to do what I say." He gave Jack a gentle kick when he laughed too hard. It was an amusing idea, though – that anyone could control Josie.

"See you tomorrow," they called as they left.

"That was a lovely day," Emily remarked with a sigh. She was nestled into Jack's chest and was in no rush to move.

"It was good fun," he agreed.

"So you're feeling happier about spending more time with Josie's family?"

"Why?" he asked sceptically.

"I've had this idea that's been niggling me . . . a series of books set in Hope Cove."

His chest vibrated as he laughed. "What about the Oxford Castle books?"

"I'll finish them first," she said. "But after that …"

"After that you want to keep dragging me down to Hope Cove while you write more books?" Jack stood and pulled Emily up with him.

"Yeah," she said hesitantly, realising she had her head in the clouds and life wasn't as simple as that. "That was what I was thinking. It suddenly sounds a bit silly. I think I live in a dream sometimes."

"I like your dreams." He draped an arm around her shoulders as they set off towards the village. "And I'll follow you anywhere."

THE END

**Don't miss the next book in
the Hope Cove series...**

The House on Lavender Lane
(Hope Cove book 5)

One shocking incident forces six friends to re-evaluate everything

Emily only meant to spend a week in Hope Cove. But when the quirky locals involve her in various events, she's more than happy to extend her stay. She just wishes Jack were with her and not stuck working back in Oxford.

For **Lizzie**, Emily's visit is well timed. She's struggling to balance work and family life, and having her friend nearby is exactly the breath of fresh air she needs.

Josie has everyone worried. She's trying her best to stay upbeat but after two failed pregnancies she's definitely lost some of her sparkle.

When disaster strikes, the three couples reunite round a hospital bed. As their lives are thrown into perspective, they're forced to take stock. And look to the future.

Sometimes, it takes a twist of fate to make you appreciate what you've got and fight for your dreams…

Other books by Hannah Ellis

The Cottage at Hope Cove (Hope Cove book 1)
Escape to Oakbrook Farm (Hope Cove book 2)
Summer at the Old Boathouse (Hope Cove book 3)
The House on Lavender Lane (Hope Cove book 5)

Always With You

Friends Like These
Christmas with Friends (Friends Like These book 2)
My Kind of Perfect (Friends Like These book 3)

Beyond the Lens (Lucy Mitchell Book 1)
Beneath These Stars (Lucy Mitchell Book 2)

Printed in Poland
by Amazon Fulfillment
Poland Sp. z o.o., Wrocław

59447318R00193